NEW YORK TI
CATHERINE BY
MACCOI

BINDING VOWS

"Binding Vows whisked me into an adventure I was sorry to see end."
~Romance Studio

"...full of all the things I love, action, romance, history, and a knight in shining armor."
~Night Owl Reviews

"...you cannot help but feel completely mesmerized."
~Coffee Time Romance

"Catherine Bybee does an exceptional job of making her time travels come to life."
~Romance Junkies

SILENT VOWS

"For being the stuff of folklore, the storyline is surprisingly convincing..."
~ Romantic Times

"...absolutely brilliant and hilarious."
~Affair de Coeur

"Silent Vows" earns an unequivocal five stars because it is just that much fun to read!... a light, fun, absorbing read that disappoints only because it ends."
~TJ Mackay~Goodreads

REDEEMING VOWS

"Redeeming Vows takes readers on a journey that's steeped in dangerous magic and breath-taking suspense."
~Nights and Weekend

"...filled with suspense, action, magic and of course romance."
~Nocturne Romance Reads

"Catherine Bybee knocked this series out of the park."
~Forever Booklover

HIGHLAND SHIFTER

"It's wonderful; merging druids, magic, time travel, action, and romance. It will hold you captive until the end."
~Booked Up Reviews

"Ms. Bybee does such a fantastic job of world building in HIGHLAND SHIFTER, it would actually serve as a standalone title if not for the captivating final scene."
~Author Sarah Ballance

Discover other titles by Catherine Bybee

Contemporary Romance
Weekday Bride Series:
Wife by Wednesday
Married By Monday

Not Quite Series:
Not Quite Dating

Paranormal Romance
MacCoinnich Time Travel Series:
Binding Vows
Silent Vows
Redeeming Vows
Highland Shifter

Ritter Werewolves Series:
Before the Moon Rises
Embracing the Wolf

Novellas:
Possessive
Soul Mate

Erotic Titles:
Kiltworthy
Kilt-A-Licious

BINDING VOWS

BOOK ONE

BY

CATHERINE BYBEE

Binding Vows
Catherine Bybee

Cover Art by Crystal Posey

Publishing History
First Edition, Faery Rose Edition, 2009
Second Edition, Catherine Bybee, 2013

Published in the United States of America

Dedication

For David, my Knight in Shining Armor.

For Sharon, who read this book first and encouraged me to pursue my dreams.

For Aithne, whose advice and enthusiasm helped me on the road to publication.

Chapter 1

They weren't even at the county line and Tara McAllister already regretted getting in the car. She entertained a beautiful yet brief fantasy of turning the late model Honda Accord around and heading back home.

The pounding behind her eyes began about ten miles ago when Cassy, her best friend, started reading the information she had downloaded from the Internet.

Traveling down a dirty highway, in the heat of summer with a broken air conditioner, Tara repeated the words Cassy lived and breathed by, 'You're only young once.' *YOYO* Cassy would say anytime Tara started balking, as if the words were the secret code to life itself. Tara scolded herself for falling headlong into her oldest friend's world of piss-poor planning and lousy accommodations.

"Remember, this was your idea," Cassy said, glancing up from the papers she was reading.

"No. I suggested going to Medieval Times for dinner and a show. *You* came up with The Renaissance Faire. You'd think after last time, I would have learned," Tara muttered.

"Who could have known Wyoming would be so cold in February?"

"It *was* winter! And *cold* doesn't describe what twenty below zero feels like. "I never even got on the back of a horse. Who goes to a Dude Ranch in the winter?"

They did, and Tara would never forget how sick she'd been. She hadn't left her bed the entire time they were there.

"This will be better, just wait and see."

"Right." Tara couldn't believe she'd gotten herself roped into another one of Cassy's adventures. This time, she'd agreed to a Medieval Renaissance Faire and an extended weekend in some Podunk town with what she imagined was a compound filled with circus freaks.

They weren't even going to have a bed for God's sake. They were going to sleep in tents, in the middle of some grimy field, with strangers and only thin strips of fabric separating them. Tara imagined the sounds and smells she'd be forced to endure over the next few days.

As if the rugged sleeping accommodations weren't enough, from the minute they arrived until they left, dresses were the required attire for all women—dresses with entirely too many undergarments. Aside from the dress code, they could eat only food available during the fourteenth and fifteenth centuries.

"Ah ha!" Cassy screamed, waving the papers in front of Tara's eyes, all but causing her to swerve into traffic.

"Would you mind? I'm trying to drive here."

"Listen to this!" Cassy ignored her and read the pamphlet aloud. "When ye arrive, all ladies are asked to wear the costume they think is most befitting their station in life. If ye are a vendor or entertainer, it is understood your garments and color choices lean toward the drab, while honored guests and people of wealth are encouraged to bring their most colorful, fetching gowns. Ladies' hairstyles should represent their station in relevance to the time."

"Remember, only young unmarried maids are allowed to wear their hair down and uncovered. If ye are married, divorced, or are no longer virtuous, your hair should be bound or covered the entire time ye are at the Faire. In an effort to maintain propriety and honesty, everyone must pass the scrutiny of the town's Gypsy Queen. She will decide if the costume and appearance is appropriate to each guest. Don't think ye can befuddle our Queen!"

Cassy just loved this shit, her voiced hitched higher, adding drama. "She is most accurate in her visions. In fact, parents of young maidens often bring them for the sole purpose of determining if their offspring has experienced carnal knowledge." She took a breath and ignored Tara's eyes as they rolled in the back of her head. "This is going to be so great. I can't wait until we get there."

"Do you really believe that crap? How can anyone know if you've slept with someone just by looking at you?"

"I'm not sure. But it says here, she can."

"I'll bet there's more to it than that." Tara switched lanes to merge into the traffic on the connecting freeway.

"More to it than what?"

"More to it than looking at you. Maybe she has naked men standing beside her." Tara pictured how a virgin might react to seeing a naked man for the first time. Some would giggle and hide their eyes, while others might stare open-mouthed and dumbstruck. She laughed at the thought.

"I like the sound of that."

"You would!" Tara said. "Or maybe the Gypsy has some good looking guy hitting on the women as they come in and watches from some remote camera for their reactions."

"You're such a cynic, Tara. I thought you liked this type of thing, or at least believed there's more to magic than what you read in books?"

Tara did in fact think there was more to magic than fiction put on paper. On the other hand, she was a realist. The Gypsy Queen would have to prove herself before Tara forked over any of her hard earned tips acquired by working countless hours waiting tables. "That doesn't mean I believe everything I hear."

"I don't believe *everything* I hear, just some of it. I wonder if the Gypsy reads palms. I would love to hear what my future holds," Cassy said.

The sign on the highway indicated the off-ramp they needed was coming up. "Oh, I'm sure. For money! And since she won't be around after the weekend, it's not like you can get a refund if she's full of shit."

"Cynic!" Undaunted by her friend's attitude, Cassy reached into her purse and removed a tube of lip gloss.

"*I* can tell you your future."

Making popping noises with her lips, Cassy asked, "Oh yeah, what is it?"

"You'll begin your brilliant nursing career, along with me, after we graduate in December. Then you'll find Mr. Wonderful or, even better, Dr. Wonderful, and settle down to a fabulous life in the suburbs in two or three years. See, I didn't need to look at your hand, and it didn't cost you a dime."

"Ha!" Cassy tossed her bag aside. "A lot you know. I'll have a passionate affair with Dr. Wonderful, but I won't marry him. Who wants to be married to a doctor who's on call all the time?"

"Good point." The stop sign at the end of the off-ramp forked in both directions. "Which way now?"

Cassy picked up the map. "Go right. The brochure says we should fuel up at the next town. Apparently, there aren't any services for the next forty miles."

"This place really is in the middle of nowhere." Tara started toward the one stop town in search of a gas station. "I hope it's not going to be too hot. It's enough to have to sleep next to strangers, but sweaty smelly strangers? Yuck!"

"The picture shows the Faire set in the woods by a stream. It looks very shady."

The pictures could have been taken after a rare California rain. They were probably headed into a dust bowl. Tara grabbed her purse and fumbled around in the bottom to find the aspirin she knew was there.

~~~~

They drove away from the gas station with a couple of ice-cold sodas and a bag of barbequed potato chips.

The whole non-twenty-first century food thing was a drawback for both of them. As tempting as it was to stock up with snacks and chips, Cassy thought it would be best to make the most of the authentic experience. Besides, Tara had already stashed an emergency supply of chocolate in her purse.

"So, do you think the Gypsy will peg you?" Cassy asked.

"Peg me for what?"

"A virgin?"

Tara let out a manic laugh and almost choked on the soda. "Twenty-five year old virgins are hard to come by. No pun intended. So no, I don't think she'll peg me."

"What if she does? Will you let her read your palm?"

"She won't. I'm not the poster child for virginity. I'm not Amish-looking. I'm in no way shy, or fat, and I don't think I'm ugly."

The only physical flaw Tara saw when she looked in the mirror were her breasts. By California standards, they were considered too small.

"...and besides," Tara continued, "I've seen my share of naked men...more than most...for a virgin, anyway."

"That's true. But if the Gypsy singles you out
~~~~

as a virgin, you need to promise me you'll let her read your palm and...no more cynicism for the rest of the weekend!"

It was a sucker's bet. There's no way some self-proclaimed Gypsy Queen would suspect she was a virgin. "You got yourself a deal."

~~~~

It couldn't get any worse, it just couldn't! The parking lot was two miles from the actual encampment where the Faire was taking place. Cassy and Tara were told to leave the car, secured and guarded by what looked like executioners, then walk the final couple of miles. If they were lucky, they could catch a ride on a passing cart or carriage. They, of course, were not lucky.

The information packet failed to tell them everyone would ostracize them if they arrived out of costume. They were looked down upon like lepers, as if they sported oozing wounds and all. People stopped, put their noses in the air, and rode along their merry friggin' way.

The bitchy blonde at the reception tent took one look at their modern shorts and t-shirts and blurted out, "Well, I see the two of you are unable to read the Queen's English. Your welcome pamphlet specifically said to arrive in costume." She tossed Tara a map. "Here, return when you are properly attired and not a moment sooner. I'll give you the schedule of events at that time."

Tara bit her lip to keep from telling the witch to bite her.

The tent was tall enough to stand in, but that was the only good thing Tara could say about it. The straw mats on the floor contained two blankets tossed on them. A water basin with a tin bowl sat in the corner rounding out their luxurious amenities. Once the flap of the tent came down to give them some privacy, the interior became stifling.
~~~~

Cassy, anxious to join in the chaos outside, started stripping the minute the flap dropped. "They weren't kidding when they said primitive. Isn't this cool?"

"Hmmmm... Cool," Tara muttered, biting back the insult off her tongue.

"Did you see those guys on the horses? I wonder if there'll be a joust, or whatever it's called."

"I'm sure." *Not that I care.*

"The brochure said at tonight's feast, the Gypsy Queen will assign the court. Some unsuspecting guests will be given upgraded accommodations and regal costumes to wear for the duration of the Faire."

"I wouldn't count on that being us, especially after the reception Blondie just gave us. It feels like we crashed a party and got caught putting soap in the fountain. I'll bet most of these people come to these things all the time. Kind of like a cult."

Tara slipped a cotton camisole over her head then followed it with one of the two gowns she had. The laces up the back did a marvelous job of acting as a corset. The cut of the dress was low enough to give her minimal bosom the image of cleavage, something Tara secretly longed for.

Cassy had found the gowns in a second hand store in Hollywood where old costumes were sold after plays struck their sets. Tara had to admit the dresses were perfect. The bimbo at the reception desk might have a problem with the colors and style they chose, Tara mused. Tara's gown was a beautiful maroon with an empire waist and long flowing sleeves. Cassy's dress was black with red fringe and pushed her breasts so far up, they damn near flowed over. There was nothing drab about either of them. Tara smiled and made a mental note to walk by the bimbo and strut.

"It's not a cult! But I'll bet you're right about these people doing this all the time. What's wrong with that?" Cassy turned around when her dress was secure, and she laced up Tara's.

"Nothing I guess." *If you like being a freak.*

"People need to escape from reality sometimes. I wonder how many lawyers are out there, or policemen."

"I'll bet most of these people are art students or drama majors. Not much chance of meeting Mr. Right in this venue."

"'Mr. Right-now' would do for me." Cassy patted Tara's hip indicating the lacing-up was complete. "Oh here." Cassy reached for a small linen bag held together by a long rope.

"What's this?" Tara asked.

"It's a purse. You tie it around the waist and hide it in the folds of your dress, like this." Cassy demonstrated its use. "That way we don't leave anything of value behind. It's not like there's a lock on the canvas."

~~~~

Tara had to hand it to the Faire patrons, or whatever you called them. Stepping outside the tent in full costume was like walking onto a stage and into character. Everyone was dressed for his or her part. Their roles didn't stop with their costumes, but continued with their accents and gestures. Lady this and Lord that. It was hard not to get caught up in the spirit of the event.

After all, what woman didn't like dressing in a full-length gown? Tara enjoyed the feel of material brushing against her thighs and the wisp of air that sometimes touched her skin. Every woman walked differently in a dress. These costumes really played a part in the whole Renaissance Faire experience.

Tara tucked long strands of hair back into a ponytail because of the heat. Secretly however, she
~~~~

thought if the Gypsy Queen was everything the brochure said perhaps there were scouts watching the crowd. If so, Tara wanted to throw them off. A small tingle of excitement started to build at the thought of duping some hokey palm reader. This weekend, the thrills would have to come from wherever she could find them.

Vendors were everywhere selling wares. Most items had no modern day use to Tara. There were amulets to wear, crystals for luck and ornate gothic crosses for warding off evil spirits.

Tara realized she lacked many medieval day essentials, such as a tin cup and a knife. These would be vital, if she wanted something to drink. The beverage department offered only three choices, water, beer, and wine. Vendors were happy to pour you what you wanted, but you had to have your own cup. A paper cup was nowhere to be found.

With a tin cup dangling from her fingertips, Tara glanced down at the knives for sale. The salesman smiled. “If you desire to cut your food, you'll need one of these.”

Her gaze landed on a slender blade with a jeweled handle.

“That is one of the finest daggers I have, my lady.” Gaston stood six foot one, his fake English accent made Tara laugh and Cassy flirt.

“I'll bet it's one of the most expensive, too.”

“You do have a keen eye and exceptional taste. Here you see an ornate Celtic design. These are not only beautiful, but are also very rare pieces of amber.”He lifted the knife and handed it to her.

“It's stunning,” Tara whispered while turning the knife over to examine the carvings.

“That it is, my lady. That it is.”

Knowing she would never return to a Renaissance Faire again, she haggled over the man's price, agreeing to spend twice what she suspected her purchase was worth, before walking away.

Once Cassy and Tara heard the official announcement that the Gypsy Queen was seeing all women, the two made their way to the massive tent to join the others as they all paraded through. The line rivaled any you'd find in a California amusement park at the height of tourist season. It seemed as if they'd been there for over an hour when Tara felt her first sting of sexual discrimination. "Did you notice there are only girls in this line?"

"The brochure said only the women were mandated to go through."

"Medieval women held a low station in life, but this was ridiculous."

After asking around, Tara determined that some men chose to go into Gypsy's tent out of curiosity, wondering what happened behind the drawn curtains of the largest, most elaborate tent in the Faire. At least, the men had a choice. Tara, Cassy, and the rest of the women didn't.

As they inched their way closer to the entrance, an icy chill surrounded Tara's body. Someone once told her the sensation was caused by a person in the future stepping on your grave. Today she passed it off to hunger and fatigue. Still her body shuddered.

"Hey, are you okay?" Cassy asked when Tara shivered.

"Fine. I'm just cold."

"Cold? It's hot out! How can you be cold? You're not getting sick again are you?"

"No. I'm not getting sick."

"Good!" Cassy rubbed her hands together as they waited their turn. "Damn, this is so exciting. I wonder what she looks like."

There were only two groups left in front of them. "You won't have to wonder for long."

"Are you going to say anything," Cassy lowered her voice and whispered in Tara's ear, "About being the big 'V'?"

"If the Gypsy is a real psychic, she should be able to sense something without me saying a word." Making small talk with the Gypsy wasn't high on Tara's priority list. The sooner they were done, the sooner they could eat.

A tank of a man, hidden behind a dark brown cloak, stood guard at the entrance to the coveted tent. Every so often, he pulled the cloth back and allowed the next party to enter.

Tara couldn't hear any sounds coming from inside. The thick velvety drapes prevented her from seeing in as well. She couldn't tell how they summoned the next group. There weren't any visible wireless remotes or radio devices signaling the Hulk to open the drapes. Somehow, he simply knew when it was time for the next group to go in.

When their turn came and they crossed over the threshold, Tara shivered. If someone from the future stepped on her grave a few minutes ago, he was definitely dancing on it now. Walking inside felt as if they'd stepped into an abyss. She didn't want to inhale the stale air and couldn't see in the blinding darkness. Her eyes slowly adjusted to the flicker of candlelight. Yet still she could see very little. Tara's eyes skirted around to find clues divulging the gypsy's secrets. However, no tempting Adonis stood next to the lone woman in the room.

A voice, frail in tone but firm and demanding, asked them to step forward.

"Let me see you," the voice commanded from the shadows.

Bold and without hesitation, Tara stood up making sure her frame was within the path of the light. Directly behind her Cassy bumped her side trying to get a better view of the person behind the voice.

Violent shivers ran up and down Tara's arms.

The gleaming eyes behind the voice raked her, digging deep, seeing all. Tara felt naked, exposed. The need to flee overwhelmed her hard and fast.

Frozen, Tara heard her friend speaking as if from another realm.

"We are so excited about being here, Madame Gypsy Queen... Ahh geeze, I'm not sure that's right. Is that what we should call you? Or do you have a name?"

The Gypsy's laugh stiffened Tara's spine more, if that was possible. The crackling sound grated down deep inside, like nails on a chalkboard. "My name is Gwen. You may call me Madame Gwen."

She's lying! The thought came so quickly it took her by surprise. *Her name isn't Gwen, but something similar.*

Tara needed to get a better look at this woman. She couldn't really see well in the dimly lit room. She forced her feet to move to get a better look at *Gwen*.

Madame Gwen leaned forward, her face caught in a flicker of light for a brief moment. Her hair, gray as a winter sky, hung long, past her shoulders. Eyes black as midnight pierced through the dark, watchful as an owl. The crater deep lines carved into her face told Tara she must be in her late eighties.

And she's obviously never heard of Botox.

The Gypsy laughed, almost as if she heard Tara's thoughts. Pointing at her, she challenged, "You, what brings you to our fine Faire? You don't seem to be enjoying yourself."

"I'm having a fabulous time, thank you," Tara stated with just the right amount of sarcasm. She didn't like how Madame Gwen's eyes dilated as she leaned toward her. It didn't look natural.

"Your tongue speaks false, much like your

dress. Tell me, why do you try to deceive me?" Gwen sat back so only her leathered old hands could be seen. She folded them in her lap.

Tara held her head high. "I don't know what you're talking about." The cold crept in despite the outside heat.

"Yes, I think you do." She dismissed them with the flick of her wrist.

Tara and Cassy headed toward the door, more than a little confused.

At the doorway, Madame Gwen followed them with her demand. "Wear your hair down, fair maiden. That would be your place while you are with us."

Tara turned around, astonished.

"Come back tomorrow," she said, her eyes never leaving Tara's. "I very much want to read that palm of yours."

A smile crept across Tara's lips. She'll be asking for money next, she mused.

"Keep your coin. Who knows? Maybe the stars will deem you both in favor and elevate your station while you're here."

Tara's mouth dropped open. Cassy nearly dragged her from the tent.

Gwen's laughter followed them out.

They didn't get two feet outside before Cassy clasped both her hands over Tara's. "I told you she was legit. Wow! That was un-flippin' believable."

The warmth of the night found its way back into Tara's blood stream. "She was a bit surreal."

"You can say that again."

Another burly, hooded guy stopped them. He said nothing, but held out his hand.

"What?" Tara asked. "You want money don't you? I knew it!" she said to Cassy. "It's all a ploy to extract money."

Disappointed, Cassy reached in her purse.

"Your binding, young maiden." he pointed to

Tara's hair.

Tara's jaw dropped again. "How do you...? How does he know?" She reached to the leather strap holding her hair and pulled it free. "Here! But I want it back before I leave."

Tara stormed off, unable to shake the chill settling in the pit of her stomach, or the uneasy feeling of being watched.

~~~~

Gwen removed a strand of Tara's hair from the binding and placed it in the cauldron. The Gypsy Queen pulled back her lips, exposing yellowed teeth. Her piercing cackle erupted as she tossed her head back and gave in to the exhilaration of her discovery.
~~~~

Chapter 2

The darkness closed in, slowing down Duncan and Finlay MacCoinnich's speed. Riding horses hard after night fell was never wise, especially if the rider didn't know the landscape.

Sounds and voices drifted on the night wind blowing past them. Light flickered from torches surrounding the encampment.

They rode through with barely a glance from the people. At home, they would stand out against all others. The people of the village would know them by sight and greet them with smiles and blessings. They were brothers with less than two years between them, and were often mistaken as twins.

Duncan tugged on the reins at what stood as a stable. A young lad, dressed in a worn tunic and brown leggings, came out to help.

The first thing Duncan noticed were the boy's shoes. He stared at them, baffled. Fin cleared his throat before Duncan managed to bring his attention back to the present, remembering why they were there.

Both brothers dismounted with the grace of seasoned riders. Duncan tossed the boy the reins assuming the lad knew what needed to be done. "Give him an extra measure of oats, lad. He has come far this day."

The horse was black as tar and stood over twenty-two hands, dwarfing the child. Once in the child's grip, it whinnied and pulled.

The lad stumbled.

Duncan steadied his horse with a few words and a firm hand. "Easy, boy."

The boy's father came out when Duncan spoke. "Oh, let me help you." He rushed forward, dislodged the straps from his son's hands.

"But Dad! You said I could get the next one." The boy kicked the dust off his Nikes.

"Yes, well... I'll let you get the next."

"But you said..."

"They're too big for you, Travis. Now run along." The father turned his attention to Duncan and Fin.

"This is boring!" the boy shouted. He stomped into the temporary stable. "I don't see why I couldn't bring my Gameboy."

"Sorry. He just isn't in the spirit of things I'm afraid." The man ran his hand down the stallion's neck, and regarded the animal with awe. "Wow! These are fine horses. I don't think I've seen them here before. Is this your first time?"

Duncan had a hard time understanding the accent. It was Fin who finally spoke up. "Yes. Perhaps you could point us in the direction where we might find some food."

"Great accent! It's Scottish, right?"

"Aye."

The man nodded his approval and went back to the horses. "Food is past the Gypsy's tent, and then hang a left. You can't miss it."

"Hang a left?" Duncan tested the words out.

"Yeah. Wow, this bridle is authentic. It must have cost a fortune."

Duncan exchanged a look with his brother. "Ye know what you're about, sir?"

"Yeah. I can handle it."

"Good." Fin seized his brother by the arm, forcing him to leave behind his most prized possession. "He'll be fine. Come, we're late."

"We wouldn't be if ye hadn't stopped to stare at the iron horse. Had ye forgotten from the last time we were here?" They marched forward with a purpose and continued their conversation.

"Forgotten? Nay. But you have to admit, they are fascinating. I'd like to ride in one just once while we're here."

"We've no time and ye know it." They slowed when passing the Gypsy's tent. Both of them gave it a wide berth and a long stare. "The parade of women is already done. Our work will be harder this time."

Duncan clicked his tongue. "I don't believe I'll hear ye complain. What was it last time? Three or four?"

"Two actually, the others were false." Fin's wicked grin had Duncan patting him on the back when they entered the arena set up with food.

~~~~

Who would have thought a dinner could last so long? Once the final course was finished, the tables vanished and the musicians started to play.

The music was lively, and most of the patrons were drunk. The effect created an unlikely combination, considering few people knew the steps to the dances popular during the Renaissance era.

Cassy, a few sheets beyond tipsy, did her best to be the life of the party. She went from one lap to another, asking men to dance. Many were all too eager to please. When a few of them pulled Tara into the mix, she shrugged them off to find solitude away from Cassy's new friends.

Nursing the warm wine helped dull some of the strain as Tara wandered around and studied the people. She avoided conversations. The mix of accents made it difficult to understand what people were saying. Add to that the alcohol factor and the burrs became thicker and more butchered.

She attracted a fair amount of attention, even without Cassy at her side. Some of the stares had her looking down at the dress to make sure she
~~~~

hadn't spilled something or to make sure her bra strap wasn't showing. It wasn't until the fifth man approached her Tara realized why.

"What do we have here?" He slurred then reached out to touch her hair. "So...the Gypsy let your hair loose."

Drunken eyes took in the length of her body and rested on her chest. It was then it dawned on Tara, she might as well have worn a t-shirt saying, "I'm a virgin, come and get it."

Disgusted, she stormed away from the sneering man, found a forgotten pencil, and quickly put the telling tresses in a knot on top of her head.

A quiet corner called out her name. It was almost midnight, the hour she told Cassy she'd turn in. With only a little longer to wait, the night would soon be over. *One down, three more to endure.*

Replacing the wine with water, Tara sat, closed her eyes, and counted down the minutes until she could leave.

~~~~

Fin approached his brother with a smile that could only mean one thing.

"Found one did ye?"

"Aye and she is a beauty, too." Fin finished his ale. "Don't wait up for me, old man."

"Ye know where I'll be. Make sure she's of age, Fin. We don't want trouble while we're here."

"Ah. You worry too much. Best of luck to you, brother. It looks like there aren't many this time around. Maybe tomorrow will prove more fruitful."

Duncan watched his brother retreat outside the festival with a giggling lass on his arm.

Tired and wanting some quiet, Duncan noticed a dark corner where he might observe the people without the assault of another's voice for a short time.
~~~~

The sky had grown dark, the shadows long. Fabric draped bales of straw made for the seating around the room. Years of training kept him from turning his back to the crowd. He backed into the seat, completely unaware someone already occupied it.

Brushing his cloak aside, Duncan dropped his weight onto the bale. Expecting the feel of course straw and wool, he was shocked when the bale moved from under him.

Then the straw spoke.

"Son of a bitch."

Duncan jumped aside, thinking the seat possessed. He swirled toward the offending chair and reached for his sword.

Heaving a sigh at the sight of a woman and not a foe, Duncan almost laughed at his reaction. She, on the other hand, was not quite as amused.

Her eyes captured his in fury. They changed colors in a split second. He realized his mistake when her gaze went to his hand on his weapon.

"Haven't you done enough damage?" She muttered another oath under her breath.

Duncan straightened up to his full height, and let his sword arm fall to the side. Just a lass, he thought. *Fiery red hair and a temper to match. Too bad she isn't a maiden. I would have enjoyed her for a time.*

"Damn it." She found the hole in her dress and brought her hand up. It was covered with blood. "Ouch!"

"You're harmed." He took her hand, but couldn't get a good look at what was bleeding, so he tugged her toward the light of a torch.

The lass limped alongside him, cursing a streak all the way to the fire. Once there she raised her skirt well above her knee.

Duncan wasn't sure why she was lifting her skirts in a room full of people, until he realized it wasn't her hand that was cut, but her thigh.

Her skin was marred, but not dangerously so. His ease was instant. He would never willingly take a knife to a woman, and still wasn't sure how it happened.

"What are you smiling about?" the woman scolded. "Can't you see I'm hurt here?"

"'Tis a scratch, nothing more."

"Can you drop the accent? You cut me and you still put on a show." She brushed away at the blood until it slowed, and then let her skirt fall back into place. "This place is full of freaks!"

"I did not cut ye. I sat on ye."

"You sat on me, I sat on this." She held out her knife, showing him the blood on its blade.

He glanced at the blade, noticed the blood, and then noticed the markings. "Celtic," he whispered.

"Yeah, that's what the con-artist told me." Her eyes caught his and for one brief moment, held. As her gaze slipped over his form, the corners of her mouth tilted up to such a small degree, Duncan would have missed it had he blinked. Standing a little taller, he pulled back his shoulders and brought his hand up the edges of his cape. Her eyes slowly roamed up his form and settled on his hair, hanging between his shoulder blades. The lass pulled her bottom lip between her teeth before her eyes returned to his. Her softened expression quickly returned to annoyed.

A woman's voice called out over the crowd, demanding the attention of the lass in front of him. "Damn, McAllister, have you gone deaf?"

"What?" She pulled her attention away from him and glared at her companion.

"I asked, 'Why is your hair up?'"

"Because I was tired of all the leering looks, Cassy."

"But the Gypsy told you to let it hang loose." Cassy unceremoniously tugged the pencil out of the lass's hair, sending a cascade of red down her back. Duncan's attention strained to find the meaning behind the words being said. At the same time, his mouth went dry.

"I don't care what she said." The wee lass grabbed the pencil and quickly tied her hair back. Once again disguising her virtue. "I'm tired of all the drunks drooling on me. It's disgusting!"

Cassy wobbled on her feet. The red haired maiden steadied her with a bloody hand.

"What happened?" Cassy asked.

Duncan felt the weight of the lass's stare as her eyes traveled back to him. He stepped closer to help. It was then the lady Cassy took notice of him. "Who's this?"

"This..." The maiden pushed against his chest, attempting to put some space between them. "...is some wise guy, who sat on me, causing me *great pain.*"

"I'm sure he didn't mean to cause you *great pain.*" Cassy batted her eyes and licked her lips. Duncan lifted a brow, enjoying the attention despite himself. "Would you like to sit on me?"

"Oh, puleeease... I think you've had enough for one night." The lady draped an arm around Cassy's waist. "I know I certainly have."

"Ahh... come on. The party's just gotten started." Cassy's drunken weight nearly knocked them both over.

"You can catch up with it tomorrow."

Duncan waited two steps before offering assistance. His mind wrapped around the facts quickly. This was a maiden Grainna took notice of. "You could use a little help, lass. Here, let me." He pulled Cassy away from her.

She pulled back. "I don't think so."

"You're injured," he said, tugging again. "Remember?"

"I'm fine, 'tis just a scratch!'" She tossed his

words, and his accent back. “Remember?”

“Aye, I do,” he said with a twinkle in his eye. “Let me assist ye. We wouldn’t want ye to start bleeding again.”

Cassy started looking a little green. Her role of a human rope in a game of tug of war wasn’t mixing well with her intoxicated state.

“Listen, buster. I’m done.” The girl glared at him. “I’ve had a lousy flippin’ day and an even more memorable night. All I want is to be left alone. So if you don’t mind, we can manage just fine without you!”

Defeated and at a loss as to what to say, he let go after one final tug. Cassy almost fell, but somehow managed to stay on her feet.

With one hand around Cassy’s shoulders and the other trying to hold up her skirt to avoid falling, the woman he searched for walked away.

All Duncan could do was watch.

~~~~

Fin strolled to the camp he and Duncan had made well past two in the morning. Whistling a tune and wearing a smirk.

“Still awake?” Fin asked.

“Aye.” Duncan watched the stars.

Fin stretched out on his bedroll, still whistling.

“Enough, Fin, you’ll bring attention to us.”

“No one cares if we’re out here.” He drew out his sack, took a piece of bread, and ate. “It’s not like at home, Duncan. There are no thieves in the trees looking for a fight or handout. Why do you think the men in this time are so large and slow?”

Duncan agreed. Still he was tired of the tune Fin was singing through pursed lips. He said nothing and continued to brood over the stars. Those at least appeared the same.

After a few silent moments Fin, knowing something was bothering his brother, spoke out.
~~~~

"So, are you going to tell me what has a burr up your arse? Or are you going to sulk all night long?"

"I found her." Duncan's voice was grave. His meaning didn't have to be explained.

"And?" Fin waited for his brother to elaborate. But when he didn't Fin came to his own conclusions. Laughter boomed over the treetops, stopping the crickets in their song. "Turned you down, did she?" Fin held his sides without any effort to hold in his mirth.

"Nay! She didn't turn me down. I didn't even try," Duncan said soberly.

"Why the hell not?" Fin asked. "Was she ugly?"

"Nay."

"Then what?" Fin picked off more bread, tossed it in his mouth.

"I don't think it would have done any good." Duncan suffered his brother's laughter when he relayed the story of how he met the woman.

When the laughter stopped, Fin wiped a tear from his eye and said, "I don't think you could have mucked it up more. I'll have to come to the rescue, again."

The thought of his brother setting eyes on the lass stiffened Duncan's spine. He would think on why later, for now he simply told Fin no.

"Then you have a plan on how to handle her?"

"I'm working on a plan."

"I'll keep my eye out for others."

"I don't think that will be necessary." Duncan brushed off a leaf that had fallen on his arm. "Her friend called her McAllister. The blade she carried was ornate with Celtic carvings." He saved the best for last. "There were specks of amber in its hilt."

Sober now, Fin put the bread aside and asked, "Do you think Grainna knows of her?"

He nodded. "It was her friend who confirmed that and the truth behind her virtue."

"Then she'll be watched."

"Aye, she'll be watched."

"Damn Duncan, I wish we had our powers of sight. How are we to know if Grainna is on to us?"

"We have to trust what Da told us. If we came here, as anything but mortals, we wouldn't have stepped one foot inside Grainna's village without her knowing it. We have three days until the solstice. This gives us plenty of time to woo a maiden and keep Grainna here in this time and place."

"I hope you're right." Fin leaned back, closed his eyes to get some sleep.

Duncan looked at the stars and pondered words the maiden had said during their brief meeting. "Fin?"

"What?" he asked, half asleep.

"What is the word *freak*?" Duncan regretted asking when his brother had another fit of laughter.

~~~~

Bells rang in her ears, waking Tara up like an alarm clock. No. Not bells, horns, and not in her ears, but outside their tent.

Cassy rolled over, dragging the blanket over her head at the interruption of sleep. She would undoubtedly be hung-over, Tara thought, before stumbling out of bed and going to see who was making all the noise.

A man, dressed in a bright yellow and orange oversized shirt and brown pants, stopped blowing his horn when Tara popped her head out of the tent.

His voice boomed out, demanding the attention of all who stood by and watched. "Hear ye! Hear ye!" He removed a scroll from under his arm and started to read.

"Madame Gwen has declared the fair maiden Tara and her chaperone Cassandra, to be the royal
~~~~

guests for the duration of the Faire. Hereby granting them the privileges bestowed upon royalty. From this time forward, all are to bow and pay respect to our Lady of the court."

The man stopped bellowing, rolled the parchment, and handed it to Tara. The spectators started clapping, drawing even more attention.

"Oh great," Tara grumbled.

The man started to leave. Tara yelled, "Wait! Just wait a minute." She ducked back in the tent, kicked Cassy's side, and hissed, "Get up."

Cassy muttered, and rolled over.

Tara snatched the blanket off of her. "Get up!"

Tara poked her head outside the tent again to find the man still standing there. The size of the crowd grew by each passing moment. "Just one more minute."

She hurriedly yanked on her dress and stared into the bloodshot eyes of her friend. "You got me into this," Tara snarled between clenched teeth.

"Got you into what?" Cassy rubbed her eyes.

"There's some guy standing out there saying we're royalty or something. Get up and fix it."

"What? Royalty?" Cassy's eyes focused. She scrambled out of her blankets and poked her head outside. "No shit," she said with glee. Cassy tossed her dress haphazardly over her head. "This is great. This is going to be so awesome!"

"Great my..." Tara left off the insult and stepped outside the tent. At her appearance, the men bowed, and the ladies curtsied. "Oh, great."

Cassy stumbled into her, noticed the people, and clapped her hands together like a six year old on their birthday.

"Listen, mister," Tara addressed the ridiculously dressed man.

"Your Highness."

"Yeah, about that…" Tara batted Cassy's hand away when she pulled her back. "We don't…"

"Yes, we do."

"No. We, don't!"

Cassy turned Tara around. "Yes, we do. Come on, Tara, this is a once in a lifetime. What's it going to hurt?"

"Excuse us," Tara said and yanked Cassy back inside the tent.

~~~~

Outside the crowd waited. Muffled voices from inside the tent could be heard as the women argued. Heated shouts and the occasional head popping out kept the onlookers entertained.

After several minutes, Cassy emerged smiling and triumphant. "We accept."

"Very well. Gather your belongings and return to Madame Gwen's tent before breakfast. You will be told what is expected of you then."

Elated, Cassy went back inside.

The crowd erupted in laughter.
~~~~

Chapter 3

"Do you see her anywhere?" Fin asked after their third trip around the camp.

"Nay."

"Say 'no' Duncan. We need act as they do." Fin smiled at a brunette who openly swept his body with suggestive eyes. "You don't want the lass to think you are a *freak*, do you?"

"Nay...No. I don't."

"Try and smile as well." The infamous MacCoinnich scowl was one of his brother's most favored expressions. Also the most annoying. "What good is all the work we've been doing to learn the speech of this time if you come here and keep saying nay and ye? 'Tisn't right!"

"I'm not hearing many people saying *'tisn't*!"

"Ah, but the bonny lasses do like a bit of our Scottish flair. Try and remember where we are supposed to be from."

Fin continued his verbal tips while searching for the red-haired lass. He rattled on and on until he noticed he talked to himself.

Duncan stopped. A smile tugged at his mouth, with a hint reaching his eyes.

Fin followed his gaze and saw the object of his expression. "God's teeth, is that her?"

Gazing at her beauty, Duncan's mouth had gone dry. "Aye!" *Dear God, was she really so fetching last night?* Heart pounding, he trembled. He remembered her puzzling look and the blood on her hands.

Now she stood as regal as a queen surrounded by her court. Her flamed hair flowed to her hips. Flowers woven into soft tresses made it even lovelier than he remembered. A deep emerald gown with specks of gold and black enhanced her beauty. Even from the distance, Duncan saw the green of her eyes matched the elegant dress.

Although stunning beyond words, the smile she wore was forced, her movements stiff and unnatural. She was flanked by two men standing as guardians at arms, her protectors or more to the point, keepers.

Cassy, on the other hand, smiled, laughed, and carried on with one of her many admirers. Her grin was genuine and not at all alarming.

Duncan watched the maiden move along with her entourage. He wished he knew her name and made a mental note to find out soon.

Making their way toward the dining area, Duncan saw her eyes roll back in disgust when strangers bowed as she passed. *Freaks,* Duncan heard in his head, almost like she whispered it.

One of the protectors caught her arm when walking over a step. The lass flinched, obviously uncomfortable, and pulled away.

Seeing her shy away in distaste, Duncan was instantly on alert. He moved a hand to the hilt of his sword.

Fin's voice broke the spell. "Easy, brother." Fin's arm shot out. "Those are Grainna's men. We don't need them knowing we're about. Come, let's eat and watch. We'll have our chance."

Fin led Duncan to a table occupied by others. Soon, a serving woman brought them a plate of food and filled their cups with ale.

Duncan surveyed the room and became aware of the many men watching her. Their lustful looks made Duncan's hair stand on end. The reaction was natural to want to guard a virgin from the sneers of men, or so he told himself. They only wanted to dishonor her. But somehow, he knew his protective instincts meant more.

Hell, if one of the men here had made good on their promising look, she wouldn't be in such danger now.

Fin made conversation with the others. It didn't take long for the talk to go to what was happening with the women at the head table.

"I haven't seen them before," a stout man of middle age told them. "Most of the time Gwen picks patrons who have been with us previously."

"What have they been picked for?" Fin inquired.

"You're looking at much of it. They are treated as Faire royalty, complete with costumes, service, food and accommodations."

"Don't forget the tournament," his wife reminded him.

"Oh yeah, the tournament."

"What happens then?" Duncan spoke up.

"The knights fight for the right to take the arm of the chosen one." The older man nodded toward the head table. "Since her hair is down and she's posing as a marriageable virgin, Gwen will ask for a mock handfasting ceremony at the end. It's all very entertaining. When was the last time we saw that, Marge?"

"Goodness, John. I don't really remember. It must be at least two years." Marge waved a hand in front of her face, shooing away a fly.

"Handfasting adds another layer to the games. She'll be a beautiful prize for the winner," John said between bites.

"Who are the knights?" Fin asked while glancing around the room.

"Anyone can join in the games, as long as they have a horse. But Gwen's men always prevail. Not too many of these weekend players know a knight's game."

Duncan and Fin exchanged a knowing look and a quick nod.

~~~~

"I'd like to talk to my friend in private," Tara told the Neanderthal.

He didn't budge.

"If I am going to go along with all this, you need to give me some space."

He didn't even smile.

"Listen, as your queen, princess or whatever, I demand you leave." She pointed to the entrance of the tent.

Knowing she was losing Tara by the second, Cassy spoke out. "Hey Bruno?" She took his arm and tugged. "Have you ever heard of PMS?" That got him moving, but only outside the doorway.

"There." Cassy brushed her hands together. "You just need to know what to say."

"I thought he'd never leave."

"It's not so bad." Cassy picked up a brush and ran it through her hair.

"For *you*, you can walk out of here without being chased. Bruno won't leave me for a minute." They came up with Bruno on their own. He never volunteered a name, and only spoke when he had to, which wasn't often.

"You have to admit the room is awesome and the clothes are fantastic."

Tara regarded their spacious tent. The thing was so large, it could have held seven others. The beds were feather soft and draped in gold silk. She stared into a floor length mirror, and marveled at her reflection.

"We have been transported to the middle ages as much as we can be." Tara picked up her skirt and let it fall to the floor.

"Gwen has seen to our every need." Cassy popped a grape in her mouth. "I wonder where she's been."

"Sleeping, most likely. She'll show up soon enough." Not that Tara looked forward to seeing
~~~~

her again. Something about the woman made her uncomfortable. Which was stupid, she thought. The lady had only been nice to them.

I really should try and get into the spirit of things.

Cassy certainly had. In fact, Cassy hadn't stopped singing the praises of Madame Gwen since they met the old bat.

No matter how uncomfortable Tara was, this vacation would go down as one of Cassy's better ideas in the end.

They were busy taking pictures of the room when Madame Gwen finally showed up with two more generic *Brunos* at her side.

Gwen dominated the space with her presence. Her robes were less like a Gypsy's and more like a queen. Her arms were filled with bracelets. Every finger held a ring. In the light of day, the woman appeared even older. *Her smile is puzzling and doesn't suit her.*

"I see you're settled in," Gwen said to Cassy.

"Yes, we are. Thank you so much for everything. These clothes are marvelous, and this tent is so much nicer than the one we were in before. I'm not sure why you picked us, but we're glad you did."

"And you?" Gwen turned to Tara. "All of this suits you?"

"The dresses feel like they were made for me," Tara admitted. "The room is lovely."

"But...?"

"I'm not used to all the attention." Tara put a little distance from Gwen who had inched too close for her personal comfort.

"Ah, *that*...well, that can't be helped." Gwen played with one of the many sparkling gems hanging around her neck. The glitter caught Tara's eye and held her attention.

"No. I suppose it can't." Tara's knees went

weak. She had a sudden need to sit.

"The patrons look forward to the coming games and celebrations, you wouldn't want to disappoint them?"

"No. I don't want to disappoint them. I just..." Tara closed her eyes for a moment as she lost her train of thought. What were they talking about? She shook her head to clear it and sat down.

"It sounds like fun. The tournament I mean." Cassy walked to Tara's side and attempted to get her to smile by sending a silent glare.

But Cassy's face turned fuzzy and all Tara could do was close her eyes.

Nervous, Cassy did what she always did in such a state, she rambled. "Will there be knights in armor? What will you want us to do? Will we have lines to practice?"

Gwen stared at Tara. Her smile dropped but only for a fraction of a second.

A chill shot up Tara's spine. That grave dancing thing was happening all over again. She snapped her eyes back to Gwen, whose face softened.

Tara got up and stood next to Cassy. "We have plenty of time before the jousts to worry about our role. Isn't that right, Madame Gwen?" Tara wanted to get out of the tent. She needed some fresh air. And she needed it now.

"Plenty of time, my dear. Plenty of time," Gwen said. "Why don't you both get some air? It's too nice of a day to stay in here. Your minions await." Gwen spoke directly to Tara. "If you need anything, you only have to ask."

~~~~

Duncan stayed in the back of the crowd, waiting and watching. He searched for a vulnerability in the guard, any weakness he might skirt, to get her alone.

"Tara." He rolled the name off his tongue,
~~~~

enjoying its sound. He had learned it from others who asked who she was.

Tara caused quite a stir amongst the people of this time. She wasn't one of them. Some considered her an outsider and unworthy of the post she was given. Others, mostly unattached men, found her fetching and looked forward to the coming games, games in which they would compete for the opportunity to stand next to her and be handfasted.

It was expected that Tara would let the winner kiss her. But, judging by what Duncan had seen, she didn't know that part of the bargain.

None of these people believed in handfasting. They'd think it was only entertainment. Duncan knew it was more than a sport. Grainna was much more cunning than even he gave her credit for. She had managed to sequester the virgin without raising an eyebrow from anyone.

Grainna knew these people and knew what motivated them. That was one of her advantages. He and his brother had only journeyed to this time on two other occasions. Both were in the camp which Grainna had procured, but neither time before had Grainna gone through the effort to isolate a virgin.

Then again, Duncan and Fin saw to it there were none. Grainna hadn't known they were there. Or that they sabotaged her plans.

His father's words rang in Duncan's head. *"Don't underestimate Grainna. She lived for five hundred years before she went into exile. She will crave youth like a lover craves release. And stop at nothing to get it. With her power restored by the virgin, she would crush you with a thought. With power gained by your death, Grainna will return here and destroy us all."* This time Duncan knew they played Grainna's game of chess, and unlike before, she already held the Bishop.

While Fin rode deep in the forest to bring their armor, Duncan purposely spent time talking to the people of the Faire. The women melted at his accent. His smile had them stepping on their tongues.

Once he learned where Tara's tent was, he spent much of his time finding its weak points. He set up an entry, or more important, her escape. Then set out to find the maiden once again.

He found Tara in the dining area pushing food around on her plate. She hadn't eaten anything. Every so often she would glance up, as if knowing another set of eyes were on her.

She saw him from across the yard. A flash of recognition went over her before she darted her eyes away.

She appeared tired and annoyed at all the attention. The men who approached her were met with dismissive eyes. Duncan didn't need any special gifts to realize her temper was starting to boil.

The wait wasn't long before Tara abandoned her friend for the serenity of her tent. She stormed away, practically running to her quarters.

Once inside Duncan heard her shouting at Grainna's man. "Get out!"

Duncan waited.

"I didn't sign on for this, Bruno. If you don't leave, I am, and to hell with your court, your fancy dresses, tent and everything!"

The man retreated and stood guard outside the entrance of the tent.

Duncan slowly backed around behind the canvas, careful to keep his movements natural. He ran his fingers along the tent and found the straps he had loosened earlier. Within seconds, he slipped inside, completely unnoticed by anyone.

~~~~

Tara sat at a vanity with her head lowered in
~~~~

the fold of her arms. Long strands of hair fell to the sides cocooning her face. Her fists clenching several times did nothing to ease her frustration.

"What the hell am I still doing here?" Tara asked herself out loud. "Cassy's off playing lady of the court, or whatever the hell else. What would she care if I left right now?"

A movement and rustling of fabric caught her attention. Her eyes flung open, her breath caught at the sight of a massive form in a dark cloak standing inside the room. She opened her mouth to scream and found a large hand covering it up.

He moved so fast, she didn't get out the smallest shriek. "Quiet, lass, I'm not going to hurt you."

The voice was familiar, but Tara couldn't see his face. She opened her eyes wide and started to struggle in his grip.

"Stop, or else you'll call her man in here." The man removed the hood off his head with his free hand. She relaxed slightly once she recognized him, but kept her eyes alert. "You won't scream if I let go?"

She shook her head. With his grip loosened she turned away from him and gave herself a few feet of distance. She calculated how fast she could make it to the opening of the tent. "What are you doing here?" she hissed out, careful to keep her voice low.

The man opened his mouth to give an explanation, shut it, then opened it again. "I never had the opportunity to apologize for last night for your injuries. Today I can't get near ye, ah, you without one of those men blocking my way."

Suspicious, she creased her brows. Her eyes peered deep inside him to see if he spoke the truth. "In that case, apology accepted."

He gave a timid smile. "I'm sorry to sneak in on you. I hope I didn't startle you too much."

"You scared the hell out of me."

"Then I must apologize again." He bowed. "I'm very sorry."

"Don't do it again."

"As you wish."

Slowly the hair on Tara's arms started to return to normal. The massive man standing before her felt less like a threat than the guard at her door. "What I wish doesn't seem to be what anyone around here is thinking of."

"Perhaps I should leave the same way I came. No one will know I was here." He turned away.

"Wait." Tara scanned the tent. "How did you get in here?"

"There's a hole in the canvas." He moved to the opening and lifted the folds, showing her the daylight. "Look for yourself."

Hope springs eternal. I have an out! I can breathe a bit of summer air, without Bruno breathing down my shoulders. Peace, tranquility.

She shuffled for a few seconds, almost giddy with the possibility of getting away. "Hey, you wouldn't mind helping me get out of here for a while would you? This whole royalty thing is making me nuts."

He sent her a puzzling look and a slightly wicked grin. "Aye, I'll help you escape."

Her words came on a thankful sigh. "Great. Let me just leave Cassy a note." She scribbled a message and placed it on the mirror where it would be noticed.

"Here, you'll need this." He took off the cape he wore and draped it around her shoulders. It was dreadfully hot, but Tara knew she would be spotted the minute she showed her face. She tucked her hair down her back and pulled the hood over her head.

"How's this?" she asked.

"Good, follow me." He took her hand and led

her to freedom.

No one saw them leave. They moved quickly, skirting the parameter of the campground. Tara wasn't sure where they were headed, and frankly didn't care. She was just happy to get away from all the people.

His horse was settled and grazing beyond the makeshift village. He mounted in one fluid motion, like a dancer. Hesitating when she noticed the size of the horse, Tara stood with her feet firmly on the ground.

"Are ye coming, lass?" He held out a hand.

She stared at his hand and then the horse. "This is crazy!" She grabbed her gallant stranger's hand and felt her weight being tossed on the back of the horse.

He didn't give her time to get comfortable before yelling a command. "Hold on."

The horse took off in a full gallop. She clenched his waist to keep from being thrown off.

Once the camp was no longer in sight, Tara tossed the hood of the cape back, and let her hair flow through the wind. "Yee Haw!" she yelled at the top of her lungs. "Freedom... at last!"

~~~~

They stopped when they found a stream. Enough water flowed to make a soft gentle whisper. Trees held back the afternoon sun and wild flowers bloomed on the stream banks.

He dismounted before lightly plucking her off his horse.

"Hot damn, we ditched them." Tara did a little dance. "That was great."

"I'm glad to be of service, my lady." After removing a pack from his horse, he led him to a patch of grass to graze.

"You can drop the act. My name is Tara. Not, *my lady*." Tara took off the cape and handed it back.
~~~~

"Aye. I mean yes. I know your name."

"Then why say, my lady?" She watched as he draped the cape on the ground so they had a place to sit.

"It's hard to address you as anything else, dressed as you are."

"Your accent... It isn't fake is it?"

"Nay, it isn't."

"You're originally from Scotland?" Tara sat down and crossed her legs.

"Aye."

"I suppose all the women in Scotland dressed like this. And you call them all, 'my lady'?"

"Not all the women. But, those who are, I give them their due respect and title."

He's kind of strange. Drop dead gorgeous, but strange. Who comes to a different country to visit a Renaissance Faire?

His accent liquefied more than her knees. She was having a hard time concentrating on his words instead of the twinge that tickled her thighs when he talked. If she didn't know better she would think he was chivalrous.

"Huh. So what? You go around the world checking out Renaissance Faires?"

He shook his head and then laughed a deep rich baritone, starting that tingling sensation again. "Nay. My brother and I came on a..."

"A vacation?" Tara asked.

"Aye, we came on a vacation."

"Well you certainly dress the part."

She stretched out on the cloak. *What is he thinking about?* Her eyes drifted to his, making her suddenly aware of the seductive picture she presented laying there. Tara squirmed under his pointed stare.

He shook his head, sat beside her, and removed a flask of wine.

Tara closed her eyes and relaxed, enjoying the

sun on her face.

"Would you like some?" He held out a cup.

She opened one eye and fixed her gaze at him. "It just occurred to me. I don't even know your name."

"You haven't asked."

Turning to her side, she took the glass. "Okay. What's your name?"

"Duncan."

She nodded in approval. "You look like a Duncan. Tell me, Duncan. You don't happen to have any cheese or fruit to go with this, do you?"

She was really starting to enjoy herself. When he turned to pull a sack to his lap, and his hair fell in his eyes, Tara longed to push it away. Her fingers actually itched to touch him. It took physical restraint on her part to keep her hands at her side.

"As it so happens..." Duncan produced exactly what she asked for.

"Now this is perfect. What is wine without cheese and fruit?" Glad to have something to do with her hands, other than succumbing to the pictures in her mind of running them through his hair. Tara picked off a few grapes and popped them in her mouth. "So, why did you come to my rescue today?"

"I told you. I needed to apologize." He watched her nibble. "How is your leg?"

"Fine..." She picked up her skirt. "...see, just a scratch. Bled like heck for a while though."

He tilted his cup back for a long pull of the wine, and an even longer glance at the view of her perfectly shaped thigh. "I hope it didn't pain you much."

"No, just my pride."

"Your pride?"

"I don't usually fall asleep in a crowded room."

He smirked. "And I don't usually sit on

someone's lap... uninvited."

"We're even then. To a fresh start." She held her wine to his for a toast.

"A fresh start." Their eyes caught and held.

His stare was so intense Tara lowered her eyes. "Did you bring me out here to seduce me?" Now why had she asked that? She regretted the question almost immediately.

When Duncan's answer didn't come quickly, she glanced up again. He was measuring her question and deciding on an answer.

"I believe 'twas part of my intent."

"Well, I have to give you points for honesty." Tara busied her hands to cover up her nerves. Hands shaking, she attempted to cut off some of the cheese.

Duncan placed a hand over hers and removed the dagger from her fingers. He sliced the cheese and handed her a bite.

Tara felt a spark when their fingers touched.

"I have made you uncomfortable. I am sorry." His voice was as polished as his moves.

"It's okay. I really do applaud your honesty. It's refreshing in this day and age. So many people lie to get what they want."

"Truth is important to you?" Duncan looked away.

"Yes. I'll be honest with you." Tara took a long-suffering breath and slowly explained what she needed to say. "Having sex with someone I barely know isn't on my list of things to do today." The air thickened while she awaited his reply. Her shoulders tensed.

With a straight face he asked, "What about tomorrow?"

Laughter bubbled over. Tears of happiness stung her eyes.

He laughed along with her. The tension ebbed for the moment.

"Thanks, I really needed that."

"You didn't answer the question."

"Maybe you haven't noticed." Tara raked her fingers through her hair emphasizing her point. "But I've been deemed the quintessential virgin for this dog and pony show."

"Are you?"

"Yes." She couldn't find the question insulting, and wondered why. "Are you?"

"Nay, but I think you know that."

"Ah, but I wanted to see how you would answer."

"Points for you, then."

"So why else did you rescue me, other than the sex part and the apology?" Tara sat back again and allowed herself to unwind for the first time in days. She watched the water flow down the stream.

"You looked miserable."

"I was," she grumbled.

"But you're not miserable now?" Duncan put the forgotten food to the side and stretched out alongside her.

"No."

"Why don't you leave? Why stay if you're unhappy?"

"You remember my friend, the drunken one from last night? This was all her idea. Cassy's having a ball. I couldn't ask her to leave."

"Loyalty. 'Tis a rare quality in a person."

"Maybe, but Cassy would do the same for me if the situation were reversed. So I'll stay and deal with all the stares and pointing for a few days. The tournament sounds interesting—should be fun. Have you been to one before?"

"Aye, I've been to them once or twice."

"What about after, *the ceremony*? Have you seen that?" She picked a flower and started plucking the petals, one by one.

"Aye, but not quite the way they have this one planned."

"Gwen told us all about it. Handfasting is like an engagement ceremony right?"

He nodded. "Engagement to most, but 'binding' when the right words are employed by the right people. Does the ceremony worry you?"

She shrugged her shoulders. "How bad could it be? It's not like I'm selling my soul or anything. I'll pretend I'm acting in a play."

Duncan's smile faded.

"Gwen gives me the creeps." Tara finished her wine and sat the glass down.

"Why?"

"First, is her name. Gwen. She doesn't look like a Gwen. I'll bet it's some kind of stage name. Second, her smiles always look so fake. It's as if she wants everyone to think she's this great person, when under it all she's doing all of this for some perverse reason. I mean, why single out virgins? I think if I could read people like her, I would use the gift for something good. Not to announce something as personal as one's virginity to the world."

"Do you think she has a gift?"

"Oh yeah, she has one! When Gwen looks at you, it's like she is looking through you." Just talking about Gwen turned Tara's hands to ice. "You don't believe in those kinds of things, do you?"

When he didn't answer, Tara looked and found him staring. His eyes told her he felt the same way.

"I guess maybe you do. Which makes us both a little crazy."

"It isn't crazy to see beyond your own thoughts. You called it a gift a moment ago, why change your view now?" Duncan watched her lips as she spoke.

"It sounds crazy, believing in a psychic ability to read someone else's mind."

"Do you think 'tis mind reading?" The wind blew Tara's hair across her face. He reached out and pushed it back. Duncan let his fingers linger on the side of her cheek. Heat rose to her face with his gentle caress.

Duncan's touch distracted her train of thought. She had to force herself to answer his question. "It might be." Her tongue moistened her drying lips.

He moved in closer, focused on her lips. His gaze drifted back to hers.

She should back away, but like two magnets, Tara sensed the pull and the unavoidable joining she knew would happen.

Duncan was going to kiss her. She was powerless to stop him and, in fact, didn't even want to stop him.

"What am I thinking, Tara?" He hovered inches away. His eyes shifted between her lips and her smoky eyes.

Tara caught her trembling lip in her teeth. "You want to kiss me." Her words were only a whisper, as unsteady as her pulse.

He moved closer, only a breath away. "Will you let me?"

Her breath came in short gasps. *Please,* her mind screamed, when her heart and lips said, "Yes."

Chapter 4

Duncan's lips swallowed her answer. His gentle tasting liquefied her insides more than his words could. Shock registered in her brain, not because he was kissing her. That, Tara expected. But, the completeness of their connection staggered her.

He changed his angle, probed her lips with his tongue, requesting entry. She returned his kiss with a timid caress of her tongue. Her arms slid around his neck, drawing him closer with a moan of compliance.

Slowly he lowered her off her elbows until she felt the grass on her back. His glorious weight held her in place. Not that she was planning to go anywhere. His lips held her hostage in a wicked kind of way.

This weekend vacation was heading in a completely new direction.

His fingers traveled the length of her waist and burned a path of fire to the pit of her stomach. Little flutters of desire peeled away at her resolve.

Her world spun out of control. She had been kissed before, but never like this, leaving her desperately wanting to find what came next.

She should stop him. Tara was well practiced in the art of refusal. Any twenty-five year old virgin would have to be. But instead of halting his actions, she followed his lead. Her head tilted back when his mouth left hers and moved to her neck. Her body quaked, a new sensation, and she expected more if she let him continue.

God help her. She wanted him to continue.

"You're so beautiful."

Duncan's lips sent tremors over the lobes of her ear. An ache deep in her stomach started to grow.

She dug her nails in to his back and arched toward him. Wanting. Needing. "Oh God," she gasped, giving in to each new sensation. "This isn't happening."

"Aye, love. It is." His mouth fused again with hers, giving no time to think and only time to feel. His movements grew bolder.

She encouraged him with eager cries.

Smoke whirled around in her head with each new touch and taste. His hand captured her breast...

Instinctively she pushed it away.

"Let me, Tara. Let me show you how it can be."

His words were so tender and tempting.

Her brain engaged. "Wait." What was she doing? Duncan told her he brought her here for seduction and here she was letting him. "No."

Although he stopped with her first request, Duncan left his body where it was, glued to hers. He dropped his forehead to her shoulder and gasped for breath.

Embarrassed, Tara felt like a tease. She had always prided herself on keeping a man at arm's length. Men weren't switches who could be turned off and on at a woman's whim. "I'm sorry."

"No, lass, I'm sorry. You told me you weren't ready for this. Here, I am pushing you." Duncan looked at her and brushed the hair from her eyes. "I couldn't seem to stop myself."

"I suppose that's a compliment." She attempted a laugh to change the mood, but it came out as a soft moan.

"The best kind of compliment." He brushed a brief kiss over her lips before he moved away. "We should head back. We don't want Gra...Gwen's men to send a search party to look for you."

Nerves rapidly replaced passion. Duncan stood up and gave her a hand, bringing her to her feet. "It's getting late." Tara fidgeted with her dress, smoothing invisible lines in an effort to act natural.

Tara admired his muscular body from lowered lashes while he packed their things. His broad shoulders narrowed to great hips and an even nicer ass. She rolled her eyes and looked away. She shouldn't be thinking about his ass.

Duncan's horse snorted when Tara approached him. She spoke calmly and stroked his cheek. "He's a beautiful animal. Is he yours?"

Duncan secured his bag before rounding the animal to catch the bridle. "Aye, I've owned Durk for many years now."

"So, you live close by?" She hoped.

"I wouldn't say close."

He was being evasive. Why? "Where is your home?" Best way to get a direct answer was to ask a direct question.

He paused. "I told you I was from Scotland."

"Oh, right. You brought your horse on vacation?" Her heart sank in her chest. Scotland. Too far for any chance of a relationship. But he hadn't asked for a relationship, had he?

He said nothing.

Disappointed, Tara looked up to see him watching her. "So, you and I..." She waved a finger between the two of them. "...would have ended up being a weekend affair, if we didn't stop?"

Duncan hesitated. Before he could answer, she held up a hand. "No, please don't lie. I'd like to believe there is honor amongst *some* men." She swallowed hard trying to remove the dryness, which crept into her throat. "When are you planning to go home?"

He searched her eyes, then said, "My brother

and I will leave after the Faire ends."

"I thought so. Since you've been so honest to me, I'll be perfectly honest with you." She took a calming breath and looked away. "If I were into casual sex, I wouldn't have remained a virgin for twenty-five years. I'm not sure if the man I marry will be my first. But, it needs to mean more, to me and the man I'm with, than just a fling. I hope you can respect that."

Tara scratched Durk's nose to look more confident than she felt. She had said similar words to other men in the past. Some would outright lie in an attempt to get her in bed. Others would say they understood, but never called again. Either way, Tara was glad she didn't sleep with any of them, even if it meant she spent her Saturday nights alone.

Duncan took her trembling hand, the one stroking the horse, and brought her fingers to his lips. "Tara, you are more a *Lady* than any I have met."

She sighed. "We should get back."

Tara rode in front of him, but kept her body stiff, fearful of getting too close after refusing him. This proved impossible. Duncan pulled her frame to rest against his and told her quietly, "I didn't take you back there. I won't do so while riding a horse."

Tara relaxed and enjoyed the strength of his body holding hers. The burnt orange and gold of the sun was low on the horizon. Tara couldn't stop from thinking they were riding off in the sunset.

Get a grip, she scolded herself. *He's going back to Scotland in a few days. Romantic imagery won't change that.*

~~~~

Now what was he going to do? He failed at seducing her, and didn't imagine he would have another chance before the solstice. He considered
~~~~

deceit in an effort for making her angry enough to leave the Faire. Yet there was no guarantee Grainna wouldn't follow her and take her against her will.

Nay, he thought. I'll stay close to her side, for her safety. To keep Grainna from breaking her spell.

Maybe if Grainna could be fooled into believing Tara was no longer chaste, she would look elsewhere. He didn't think it was possible, but what choice did he have? He couldn't come right out and tell Tara the danger she was in.

She wouldn't believe him.

Duncan's thoughts turned to Grainna's curse and the purpose for his visit to this time.

She had been born, like he and his family, from Druid descent. Magic permeated their blood. With magic however, came responsibility, honor and respect for the gifts they had been given.

Grainna followed the sacred ways until she met a man whose beauty mystified her, and she fell in love. She thought Elic a perfect match for her as a husband. His blood was also Druid, not as untainted as hers. Nor as powerful.

But Elic's intentions were anything but pure. He looked at her as a conquest, an innocent no man had taken before. During the course of one summer, she gave him her virginity. He fell in lust and took it. As the summer wore on and his attention waned, Elic set up a meeting where Grainna would find him in the arms of another woman.

Grainna heard their cries of passion. All she could do was stand by and watch. Trembling with tears of pain streaming down her face, she pleaded with him to stop. On bended knee, she begged him to go away with her.

Elic laughed and scorned her for thinking she was the only woman in his life.

Bitterness and pain fueled the revenge she took on the man she loved and the woman he flaunted.

Grainna used her gift, the one she used to speak to animals. She cast the bats and rodents from every corner of the barn to feast upon Elic and his lover.

With wicked delight, she watched their slow and painful death. Their cries for mercy went unheeded. Her heart, the one he had so carelessly shattered, had completely closed off.

With Elic's death, Grainna felt a Druid's power sliding into her for the first time. It was a drug more powerful than seduction.

Using her gifts for revenge was forbidden by the Ancients. To avoid persecution from her own people, she fled the country of her birth.

For years, she practiced the dark arts and searched the land for people with powers. Druid or witches she didn't care. Those souls she could turn to her evil ways she let live. Those who refused, met with untimely deaths.

Her quest for blood and revenge on anyone who loved was insatiable. Her power grew as the years went on. In a final act of defiance, Grainna used the blood of her dead in a potion of immortality.

The Ancients who had watched and waited, gathered to stop her evil. They cursed Grainna to an eternity in an aging and powerless body. They bound her Druid powers and those she had gathered, making it almost impossible for her to return to her former self.

They pushed her five centuries into the future. Into a time and land she had little knowledge of.

Now, in order to break the curse, she had to find a woman of Druid descent, a virgin. Only the virgin's blood would set her free.

For seventy years, Grainna had lived in the

new world with all its technology and ways. Even without her Druid gifts, she practiced the dark arts and perfected the ability of sight and mind control.

Grainna's plan for luring a virgin into her web was brilliant. Posing as a palm reading Gypsy, running a Renaissance Faire, and exploiting virgins, was a perfect way to draw in her prey.

Duncan and Fin were sent by their parents to prevent Grainna from finding all the requirements in a woman she needed. Up until now, Duncan found his missions pleasurable.

If there are no virgins, there is no threat. It was that simple.

Duncan watched the makeshift village come into view. His arm circled Tara's tiny waist. Her sweet scent permeated his senses.

His mission wasn't as simple, however, when the virgin in question was Tara McAllister.

~~~~

The people of the village watched them ride past. Duncan led Durk to the doorway of her tent. The man standing guard watched in astonishment, eyes darting between Tara and Duncan.

Tara untied Duncan's cape with a shaking hand and gave it back. Ignoring the stares of those who passed by. "Thank you so much for today."

Grainna's man took a step closer to them.

Duncan tilted Tara's chin and placed his lips to hers. He left them there long enough to feel her relax, then broke away. "Thank you, lass," he said against her parted lips. "I'll see you at supper tonight."

"Okay," she whispered.

Duncan laughed when her body swayed toward him instead of away. He turned her around and gave a gentle nudge.

She glided passed the guard. "Nice night, don't you think, Bruno?"
~~~~

~~~~

"She did what?" Grainna's voice could be heard well beyond her tent. Fury sparked from her eyes. She stormed past her guard, barely giving him the time to move out of the way.

Grainna stormed into their tent and found Tara sitting on her bed, wearing nothing but her underclothes, and talking to her friend.

She pushed her way into their minds.

Tara resisted her intrusion with a coveted power.

Don't you look cozy gossiping about your adventure with a stranger? Grainna could hardly contain herself at the sight of the laughing women. They didn't appear to have a care in the world.

Cassy's thoughts however, were wide open. They sizzled with excitement and sparks of love generated by Tara's romantic interlude.

Bile backed up in Grainna's throat as she read the thought.

Tara looked up. They locked gazes. The woman was attempting to look inside Grainna's mind. Tara didn't know she was doing it, but Grainna did.

She glared back in the face of Tara's defiance.

Tara addressed her. "Hello, Madame Gwen. We were just getting ready for dinner."

Grainna placed her practiced fake smile on her lips. "I understand you had a guest today, Miss McAllister. I trust you had a good time evading the men placed here for your safety?"

"My safety? From whom?" Tara moved behind the curtain, using the small amount of privacy to dress for the evening meal.

"From those men whose intentions aren't honorable of course, a virgin would be quite a prize to many." Grainna looked to Cassy. "I'm sure your friend would agree."

"I think Tara can handle herself."
~~~~

Grainna snapped her eyes to Cassy's, capturing them. She fingered the amulet worn around her neck. Instantly, Cassy's eyes glossed over.

"But you never know," Cassy said, airily under the spell's influence.

"I wouldn't put it past a man to force himself on someone who held your beauty, Tara. It's your safety which concerns me."

Cassy's eyes lost focus when she watched the stone shifting in Grainna's fingers.

"Convince her," Grainna whispered in her ear.

Cassy's lips curved on demand. "There are a lot of men who have been watching you since we arrived. I would hate it if something happened to you."

"Come on, Cassy, we live in the valley. Gang capital of California. I think I can handle myself by now." Tara came around the corner. "Listen, if it's my virtue you're worried about for your precious show, rest assured I didn't give it up. But the last time I looked, we live in a free country. I do what I want, when I want. If this doesn't work for you then we can just go back to our old tent and peasant status," Tara challenged.

Grainna forced an agreeable look on her face and pushed into Tara's mind. But the door was closed, which infuriated her even more. "We simply want all our guests to live a fantasy for a few days, in a better time," she lied. "You help with the image of royalty. If you want to visit with your new companion just say so. We'll have Samson go with you for the *image* of propriety. For the people."

"Please," Cassy pleaded. "It's only for two more days. What could it hurt?"

"Fine!" Tara relented. "I want two more places set for dinner at our table. Duncan and his brother will be joining us. I'm sure you won't have a problem with that?"

"Of course not, dear." Grainna's voice was syrup, laced with arsenic. *I'll look forward to snapping your neck like a twig.* "Of course not."

~~~~

Gwen hadn't booted them out. They still held the highest title at the Faire, outside of the Gypsy herself.

Tara took the time to make sure she looked her best before going to dinner. She applied a light amount of makeup and allowed one of Gwen's maid's to put her hair in a fashion fitting the times of the Renaissance.

Cassy's pointed hat with a veil flowing down her back, matched the pink silk of her dress. She spun in circles making the dress and veil float. "Get a load of this."

"'All the world's a stage, and we are all merely players.' I have to agree with Shakespeare, no one could have said it better," Tara said as she walked from the tent.

Unlike the night before, everyone in the entire village waited until Tara and Cassy arrived before beginning to eat.

Announced like royalty, Tara felt like the Queen she was treated like. It was hard not to be caught up in the moment. She walked ahead of Cassy and Gwen's guards by only a foot, yet it felt like a mile.

Men and women bowed, children snickered only to be reprimanded by their parents. Tara had to confess it was fun.

Someone pushed a glass of wine in her hand as soon as Tara made it to their table. "Good God. This is crazy. You would think we actually meant something to these people."

"You said we wouldn't have a good time." Cassy took a hefty pull from the glass in her hand. "Tell me more about this mystery guy. I don't
~~~~

remember much from last night."

"Really?" Tara asked sarcastically. "Maybe it had something to do with the amount of this..." She pointed to the glass Cassy held. "...you drank last night."

Unaffected by her friend's accusation regarding the sobriety of the previous night, Cassy asked again about Duncan and the time Tara spent with him. "Tell me what he looks like."

"Well, he is about yea high." Tara placed her hand a good six inches above her height. "His shoulders are out to here. He has dark hair that falls to his shoulders." She paused for a moment and closed her eyes. "I never thought I'd find long hair on a man attractive."

Cassy smiled as she continued.

"Once I realized his accent was real, I wanted to melt." Tara looked around to make sure no one else listened to her confession. "I've never been so tempted in all my life."

A man approached Tara from behind. Cassy saw him put a finger to his lips asking for her to be quiet. Playing along Cassy asked, "So what stopped you?"

"I honestly don't know. But man, does he make my blood boil." She sighed.

Cassy laughed and looked beyond Tara.

"Is that so, lass?" The voice was familiar, but not quite right.

Tara turned and looked at who must be Duncan's brother. He looked like him, so much in fact she wondered if they were born on the same day. "Nice try," she said. "You must be Duncan's brother."

"I'm gravely disappointed, Tara. All afternoon I've spent with you and you don't remember me?" He delivered his most charming smile in an effort to convince her she was mistaken.

"Ha! My guess is your mother tanned your

hide when you tried that on her. Your teachers may have been fooled, but I'm not."

They did look a lot alike, Tara thought. The height was off by a margin and this brother's nose was a little too straight, his expression much less serious than Duncan's.

Duncan's brother laughed and caught Tara's hand. Like Duncan, he brought her fingers to his lips and kissed their tips. "'Tis a pleasure to meet you, Tara. Our mother would appreciate your keen observation."

Yin and yang, she mused. Where Duncan was serious, this man was not. "I'm sorry, but in all our conversation Duncan never told me your name."

"My friends call me Fin." He snapped his legs together and gave her a quick bow. "At your service."

"It's a pleasure to meet you, Fin. This is my friend Cassy." Tara moved aside.

Fin kissed the back of Cassy's hand. She watched his every movement with a gaping mouth.

"Duncan will be along in a minute. I took advantage of the opportunity to see who it was he was talking my ear off about. It seems all he says is true."

"All good I hope."

"Of course." Fin took the wine that was offered him. "Ah, here comes my *much older* brother now."

Laughter peeled from Tara at the comment. "Much older my foot! What is it, twelve or thirteen months between you?"

Fin smiled but didn't answer her question.

~~~~

Watching the enemy from across the room, Grainna calculated her next move. Patience was never her strong point. With victory in sight it grew terribly short. It took every ounce of will to keep from snatching Tara up and hiding her until the solstice.
~~~~

No, it would not bode well to have the authorities alerted of a missing person. Besides, Tara was surrounded by Grainna's guard, and now that she knew of the threat, watching them would be easy. When all was said and done, no one would be able to touch her. Besides, by the time the authorities found Tara's body, Grainna would be long gone.

The anxious woman sitting beside her hung on every word Grainna muttered. *Fools, all of them are fools.*

If she told the woman what she really saw in her palm, or read in her mind, the woman would search out her unfaithful husband this minute. Telling these simpletons the truth only hurt the cause.

Grainna looked over at Tara and saw the man's hand take hers to his lips. The color flowing into Tara's flesh was telling.

Grainna smiled at her current customer, mumbled a cryptic, "You'll live long and love another." She then waved off the other patrons waiting for their turn.

Chapter 5

Duncan marveled at how easily Tara slipped into her regal role. She walked toward him with hands extended, her smile radiant. He kissed her in greeting, a chaste kiss, but powerful enough to put a blush in her cheeks. "You look lovely."

"Well you know what they say, if you can't beat them, join them."

Duncan didn't have a clue as to what she meant, but instead of pointing out his confusion, he nodded and stepped back when she announced dinner.

Duncan found her tales of school fascinating. Her effort to be a healer didn't come as a surprise, but without the knowledge of how it was done in this century he couldn't add anything to the conversation. He listened, and thought how much his mother would love to discuss how medicine would change in time.

Cassy and Tara did go on about their lives.

Duncan wanted to tell her tales of his own youth and the adventures he and Fin had had. However, it wasn't possible. How could he tell her of the time he learned the ability to light a fire without the aid of flint? How with his brother's encouragement, he almost burned down the west end of the Keep?

Nay. He could only listen. In an effort to feel closer to Tara, he took her hand. Heat surged to her face in the form of a blush, her pulse quickened under his thumb.

Not so unaffected by my charms.

Fin leaned forward and whispered so only Duncan could hear. "She comes."

Grainna walked toward them quickly, halting all conversation at their table. Duncan and Fin's inner thoughts turned to the music being played and the woman in their company. Both shielded their feelings so Grainna couldn't read them.

"Ladies." She gathered her skirts and stepped up on the platform. "I trust you are enjoying yourselves?"

"This really is amazing, Madame Gwen," Cassy answered.

Grainna's eyes pierced Duncan. Her smile painted on. "Aren't you going to introduce me to your friends?"

"Of course." Tara found her voice. "Duncan and Fin, this is Madame Gwen. The lady to whom we owe our elevated status."

Grainna extended her hand.

Duncan shook her hand briefly.

"You put on a lovely show. Have you been doing this for long?" Duncan asked.

"For several years now, Mr...?"

He wasn't about to tell her his surname. He had no way of knowing if she had encountered his ancestors before his birth.

Fin jumped in when Duncan stumbled on his reply. "Several years? Wow, it must be tiring for someone your age?" Grainna stared at him, displeased with his rude remark.

Duncan kicked Fin under the table. "I think what my brother is asking is if you plan on retiring soon? Although, I doubt any could do as good a job managing this event."

"If everything works out, gentlemen, I'll be retiring very soon." Her gaze drifted to Tara. The scowl on her face lifted. "Enjoy your evening." Grainna turned to walk away.

Duncan let out a silent sigh of relief.

~~~~

They called it roast duck, when they served
~~~~

what was really chicken. Not that it mattered, because Tara didn't taste a thing. Every once in a while, she would glance up when someone laughed a little too loudly or when a guest stumbled into their table. The party went on around her, but she didn't notice much except Duncan.

Tara didn't want to see the evening end. But as people started making their way to their tents, and the musicians stopped playing, she resigned herself to say good night.

Duncan walked her to her tent with Sampson close behind.

"Thank you for today." Tara felt the twinge of an awkward moment, the first she had felt since she had climbed back on his horse.

Duncan took her nervous hand in his and leaned in for the gentlest of kisses. "Sleep well, Lady Tara."

He turned on his heels, sailed past the guard, and disappeared into the night.

Tara watched him go. *Damn!*

~~~~

"Do you think he left?" Tara looked around the extra guard searching for Duncan in the crowd.

Cassy grinned through the haze of morning blur. "I'm sure he's here somewhere. Maybe he's sleeping like half the other people here." She protested their early hour viciously when Tara pulled her out of her bed. "Like we should still be doing," Cassy added.

Tara cocked her head to one side. "This was your brilliant idea. Don't go giving me lip because I'm starting to get into it."

"Yeah, yeah. Where's the coffee?"

~~~~

"What are you going to do?" Fin looked over the rim of his cup at the women who hadn't noticed them yet.

Duncan didn't acknowledge his brother's

question. He was too busy watching her.

Fin waved a hand in front of his brother's eyes to gain his attention. "God's teeth, Duncan, you have to focus. Our time is running out."

"Damn if I don't know that." He tore his eyes away. "She is undeserving of what we are doing."

Fin felt for his brother whose conscience was always getting in the way of the deed. "If we were home, I'd say pursue her as your wife. But since we are not, bed her and be done with it."

Duncan winced. "And if she doesn't go willingly, what then, Fin? Even you would not take when permission is not granted."

"You have all of today and tonight. If the time doesn't prove fruitful, then tomorrow's games will give her a taste of the man you are." Fin knocked his brother on his back and choked out a laugh. "Who knows, maybe I'll let you win the games so you can be handfasted with her."

"Let me win?"

"Aye, let you." Fin laughed at the rivalry, which had always been between them, but one they'd never taken to an extreme.

They both looked over at Tara. A tall well-dressed man stood in front of her. To Duncan's distaste, Tara smiled at him and laughed at something he said.

Duncan stiffened when he saw the man reach out to shake her hand and then hold it for a minute too long. Jealousy, green as moss on a tree, surged through him. What did the stranger say to make her smile in such a way? And why was he standing so close?

~~~~

"It's a pleasure to meet you, Mr. Steel." Tara smiled.

"Please call me Michael. After tomorrow's games, we might become better acquainted."

"I'm sorry?"
~~~~

"There are very few men here who can joust. I'm happy to say, I have the upper hand."

An image of a peacock popped in Tara's mind. This man strutted like an over-inflated bird.

She looked down, noticed he still held her hand and pulled back. "It's a compliment you would try so hard."

Feeling another set of eyes on her, Tara glanced up to see Duncan looking at them. In her delight at seeing him, his scowl went unnoticed. She said, "If you'll excuse me."

Duncan's eyes connected with Mr. Steel's, when she turned to walk toward him. His chin rose slightly. Tara glanced back at the man, then back at Duncan. *Is he jealous?*

Before Tara had a chance to say hello, Duncan swept down and captured her lips in a searing kiss.

The clearing of throats reminded her, they were in public. Not that she cared.

"Good morning to you, too." Tara staggered back. *Oh, yeah. He was jealous.*

His charming smile looked down at her while he placed her arm in his. "'Tis a lovely day. Let us see what we can do to entertain ourselves."

Maybe it was his old-fashioned words, or maybe the way his glance devoured her, but Tara would have followed him anywhere in that moment.

Even with Bruno trailing behind them, they managed to have some fun. Jugglers, jesters, a man who breathed fire and even a few really bad actors butchering Shakespeare entertained the crowd.

The children of the Faire grew bored. Tara noticed more than a few sneaking behind tents and heard the unmistakable sounds of handheld video games being played. She pointed the kids out to Duncan and rhetorically asked, "What did children in these times do for fun?"

"Most children of the villages work a large part of their day, helping their families in whatever trade they are in. Children of the wealthy have servants to do much of the work, so the males start practicing at an early age to become knights. The females learn early on the way to run their households."

"Well, aren't you an encyclopedia of medieval knowledge."

"'Tis what I've been told." He avoided her searching eyes. "Ah... It looks as if some of the men are anxious to win tomorrow." He lifted a hand, pointed to the men who were already in the arena practicing for the upcoming games.

Tara looked at the men on horseback with nervous anticipation.

"You are competing, right?"

Duncan's hand rested on the small of her back as they moved closer to get a better look at the men as they practiced. "Nay, Tara. I will not be competing."

She turned to him in shock. "But I thought... I mean since we've been..."

His face softened in a boyish, playful smile.

"You're joking," she said in relief.

"I'll not be competing. *I* will be winning," he declared with absolute conviction.

Her sigh came out in a rush, which was followed with her delicate hand hitting his chest. "Don't scare me like that."

"Are you worried I wouldn't fight for your hand?"

"You're the only guy here I've kissed! You damn well better fight for my hand!"

"I do enjoy your kisses."

"I'll give you another if you win," she promised.

He moved closer looking as if he would take

another kiss right then. Bruno grunted behind them, ruining the moment.

Damn, she thought, wishing they were alone.

~~~~

They were finishing their evening meal when Madame Gwen made her appearance in the dining hall. Tara noticed the look the brothers exchanged, but the plastic smile on Gwen's face made her forget what she was thinking and left her feeling chilled.

Polite greetings were made, and Fin started asking questions as soon as Madame Gwen walked up.

"What's next on tonight's festivities?" he asked.

Instead of answering, Gwen looked over at Tara. "Miss McAllister, you will be asked to dance with every man competing tomorrow. I hope you don't object."

"Well..." Tara straightened up to attention.

"We wouldn't want the men to think you've already picked the winner and there's no reason to play the games." Grainna directed her look at Duncan. "I'm sure your friend won't mind."

Tara noticed a slight twitch in Duncan's jaw. She hoped he would object.

Instead he smiled and said, "Of course not."

"Good." Gwen clapped her hands together, her bracelets jingled. Instantly, the music stopped and gave her the audience she demanded.

"Lords and Ladies," her voice rang out. "On the eve of the solstice, and the tournament commemorating the occasion, I want to thank you all for joining us tonight. As promised, tomorrow's games will fill the day and end with the joust."

Shouts went up from the crowd as drunken men raised their glasses.

"The winner will have the honor of partnering with Lady Tara in a handfasting ceremony."
~~~~

Whistles could be heard over the crowd. At least one man shouted something about a wedding night. “The celebration which will follow will rival any period wedding of the time of the Renaissance. One I hope you will enjoy.”

Clenching the goblet, Tara took a giant swig from her wine. Duncan’s hand found the other resting in her lap under the table. His gentle squeeze reassured and calmed her.

“Those competing for Lady Tara’s hand have the opportunity to meet with her tonight and are given one dance each.” Gwen signaled the musicians and sound filled the air. “Enjoy your evening.”

Gwen tilted her head and left the platform.

Men lined up, adding to Tara’s distress. The music was soft and resembled a waltz. Her knees trembled when the first man approached.

Tara smiled at Duncan and then glared at Cassy. She moved forward and let her first partner lead her to the dance floor.

He was short. His name was Jimmy or Timmy, Tara couldn’t remember. He counted while they danced which kept him from talking. It was awkward dancing with a stranger, but Jimmy or Timmy seemed as uncomfortable as her.

Outside of a sore toe, Tara was less scared than she thought she’d be when the next man came forward.

After the third dance partner, Tara’s earlier jitters started to subside. The men asked the same questions. ‘Are you having a good time?’ ‘How is it, being in the limelight?’ Harmless men, most of them married, or so they said.

Her fourth partner was familiar and handsome for a blond. It took her a few minutes of meticulous dancing to realize who the man was. He embodied the part of English knight, from accent to dress. He didn’t have to count to dance, which afforded him the opportunity to talk.

"You look ravishing, Lady Tara." His voice was smooth.

Her cheeks grew warm. "Thank you, Mr. Steel."

"Please, call me Michael. You wound me with your propriety."

"I'm more worried about wounding your feet." Almost on cue, her feet skipped a step, forcing her partner to hold her closer.

"Be careful, we wouldn't want you to injure yourself before tomorrow." He gazed down at her. "Unless you want out of the spotlight."

She chuckled. "Going to the dentist would be more fun for me."

Michael laughed, putting her at ease.

~~~~

The other man's laughter grated on Duncan's nerves. His hand rested on the hilt of his sword, the muscle in his jaw twitched. The man's hands rested far too comfortably around Tara's waist, and to his dismay, she was smiling at him.

"Easy brother," Fin warned, "'Tis only a dance, one she is obligated to have."

Duncan's eyes followed them around the room. When the dance ended, the man took for her hand, bringing it to his lips for a kiss. Duncan felt some satisfaction when she pulled away quickly after he released it.

"My turn." Fin jumped to his feet.

Fin cut off a clumsy, overweight man and whisked her around in a very large circle before pulling her into his arms, keeping a comfortable distance from his frame.

"How are you holding up?" Fin asked, with a loud enough voice for Duncan to hear.

"You don't happen to have a flask of whisky on you?" Tara teased.

She relaxed, and Fin swept her out of earshot.
~~~~

Duncan's eyes narrowed, wondering what secrets his brother whispered in his lady's ear.

"Tara tells me you're both leaving for home after this is over." Cassy moved to a seat closer to Duncan so he could hear her.

"Aye," he said, never letting his eyes wander from where his brother was making moves on Tara.

"That's too bad."

"What is bad?" He diverted his attention to Cassy.

"That you're leaving. Any chance you and your brother could spend a little more time in the States? I'm sure I could talk Tara into showing you both around L.A. for a week or so."

"That's not possible, I'm afraid."

"Bummer." His gaze slipped back to Tara and Cassy said, "I think you're good for her."

"Why do you say that?"

"I don't know, I just think you are. She would never have gone along with all this if she hadn't met you. Tara was ready to leave last night, and today she's more..." Cassy swirled wine in the glass she held. "That probably doesn't make a lot of sense."

He considered her choice of words. It was exactly how he felt since he had sat in her lap. "It makes plenty of sense." He smiled at Tara's friend, feeling a kinship with the woman who looked over his lady.

He thought for a moment about how his mind had drifted to those words, "his lady." Tara wasn't his. In no way could she be, yet it was how he felt.

"Oh... No!" Cassy interrupted his thoughts, and looked across the room. "Tara isn't going to put up with that."

The music had changed, and with it, so had Tara's dance partner.

She stood eye to eye with him. His girth

matched his obviously intoxicated state. His attempt to pull Tara close was met with resistance and brought Duncan to his feet, with murder in his eyes.

He looked every bit the medieval knight as he marched through the crowed with hardly a glance. He watched the man's hands slip below her waist. She struggled to put distance between them, only to be harshly tugged next to the ogre.

Duncan couldn't remember feeling as bloodthirsty for a man in all his warring days. The rogue would pay for touching her.

~~~~

"Get off!" Tara yelled at the slobbering drunk. She pulled her hand away only to have him place a vice grip on it.

"What's the matter lil' lady? I know you'll like what I got." His tongue darted out of his mouth to catch the drool beginning to fall from his lips.

Tara was about to knee the man's groin when she heard the sound of steel against steel. In a flash, she saw a three-foot long blade with a deadly point edging to the side of the drunk's neck. Frozen in place, all Tara could do was stare.

Everything went silent. Abruptly the voices and music stopped, a deafening quiet in a crowded room sent shivers down her spine.

Only the voice of one pissed off Scott could be heard. "Unhand her," Duncan ordered.

The drunk froze as the blade nicked his neck, drawing a tiny drop of blood. To the man's embarrassment, his bladder let loose, further adding to his humiliation. It was amazing how still he stood with his eyes so glossed over.

"I didn't mean any harm. Just havin' a little fun, mate."

Duncan pulled Tara to his side.

Stumbling back, the drunk tripped on a table, righted himself, and then ran from the room. Only
~~~~

then did Duncan put his sword back in its sheath.

Once the man was out of sight, Duncan shifted his eyes to Tara's. "Are you all right?"

Her jaw dropped.

"Would you like to take a walk?"

Not trusting herself to speak, she nodded.

Cassy stood and clinked a spoon against her half-empty glass. "All right folks! The show's over! Done. Go back to eating and whatever."

Fin directed Grainna's man to the drunk who needed to be put in his place. Duncan slipped away from the people with Tara on his arm. Alone.

~~~~

She was having a hard time processing what had happened. Never, not even in her wildest dreams, would she ever have imagined a man drawing a sword on another on her behalf. It was one of those defining moments, the kind that made her glad she was a girl. Her heart gave a flutter when she replayed the scene in her head.

It wasn't that she felt very threatened by the man. Annoyed was a better word. The fact that Duncan was ready to shed blood for her gave her a power she never thought possible.

They walked in silence for some time before Tara said, "Thank you."

"'Tis nothing."

"Are you kidding? That man was a jerk. Before I knew what was happening there you were, putting him in his place." She turned to him, smiled. "And all this time I thought this was a prop." She touched the edge of his sword.

"What is a prop?"

"A fake. You know, part of a costume," she explained.

"Oh." His hand rested over hers. "Nay, 'tis no prop."

"It looks heavy. Is it?" She grasped its hilt.

He drew it out for her, placed it in her hands.
~~~~

"You tell me."

Once he lifted his hand from the blade, the full weight pulled it down to the ground. "Wow." Tara strained to lift it back up with both hands. "I had no idea it was this heavy."

He had lifted it as if it weighed no more than a bag of marshmallows. Why did the thought send a tingle between her legs?

Embarrassed by her own thoughts, she handed him the sword. Her head turned toward the sky. She struggled with the sudden lack of conversation. "The stars are beautiful."

"*You* are beautiful. The stars are bright and many."

His eyes searched hers when they came to rest on his.

"What am I to do with you?" she whispered.

His arms circled her, pulling her close. "What do you want to do with me?"

"Well, what I want to do, and what I should do, are two entirely different things." Her breath quickened when he pulled her closer still.

He held his mouth only a fraction away from hers. "Tell me what you want, Tara."

His breath was warm and smelled faintly of wine. It was hard to think with him so close. She wanted desperately for his lips to join hers.

Just when she thought he would end her anguish, his lips sailed past hers and met with the beating pulse at the base of her neck. His hand grasped her long mane, pushed it aside, and exposed the long column for his pleasure.

Heat seared a trail where his lips traveled. "Tell me what you want," he repeated, never giving her time to think as his lips tormented her throat.

A burning, she could never call a mere spark, started to build. Her body molded itself to his of its own accord. His teeth found the sensitive lobe of her ear, sending shock waves down her spine.

"You," she gasped. "God help me, I want you."

Tara noticed his smile before his lips crushed to hers, devoured her.

The meeting of their lips was an act of spontaneous combustion. Unlike when he had kissed her before, this time, there was no slow mingling of tastes, or sensuous arousal. This was primal and needy with no room for thought, no question where it was leading.

Chapter 6

Grainna followed them out when they left the dance hall. She watched Duncan pull Tara into his arms. Grainna's eyes heated with fury and vengeance.

Patiently, she kept to the shadows and waited for both their minds to go blank. Her hands opened palm up, her eyes closed as she probed into their minds.

Duncan's was filled with visions of a more intimate mating with Tara. Grainna could feel his lust for the woman. She felt his triumph of being her first.

In Tara's mind, passion and trust drove her actions, along with a deeper attachment to the man. Her resolve to remain a virgin hung on by a thread.

Grainna looked deeper, into the part of Tara's memories, to where her thought process had kept her virginity intact until now.

Inside a fog, Grainna saw a woman, no—a girl, unwed and weeping over an infant in a broken down crib. The girl in her vision resembled Tara, a sister perhaps. Whoever she was, her life had a great impact on Tara. So much so, she had refused every man until now.

Grainna closed her eyes tighter and pushed the vision out of the corner of Tara's mind, sweeping it to the forefront.

The girl's desire was difficult to maneuver through and the effort to control Tara's mind came at a high cost. Even now, Grainna felt her body weakening with her effort. But she would suffer the deterioration of her body, because not taking the risk, could jeopardize her entire plan.

~~~~

Voices came from behind them. Duncan broke off their kiss, seeking privacy. He pulled her along with him until they were clear of any prying eyes from the camp. Alone, at the edge of the woods, he gathered her back into his arms.

He knew his goal and for the first time, he felt soiled by his intent. For her safety, he needed to complete this union, he told himself, justifying his actions. Her tantalizing mouth taunted and teased, God her mouth was sweet. Never had he wanted a woman more, goal or no.

Her hands moved over his back, tentative at first, and her nails dug into his clothes, growing bolder as his groans revealed the pleasure she brought him.

When Tara felt his hand reach for her breast, this time she let him. With her inhibitions pushed aside, she knew the minute he slipped his fingers under the material of her gown that this time she wouldn't turn him away. She felt her nipples harden and strain. Never had she thought someone's touch could be so pleasurable. His blazing kiss numbed her lips and made her body writhe with desire.

Her vision cleared slightly when he pulled her down to the soft ground. Tara felt his hands working the laces holding her dress together. Her hands pushed past his clothing to feel the warmth of his skin. "Tell me you have something." She was embarrassed to ask, but knew she needed to.

Duncan's breath caught at her words. "Have what, love?" His lips continued their descent as his hands pulled her gown off her shoulder exposing her flesh beneath.

"Protection?" The word came out breathy and sounded as if it came from someone else. *Birth control...Babies...* Tara's mind clouded over and a
~~~~

vision of her sister emerged. She pushed the image away. She didn't want to think about Lizzy now, not when she was on the verge of giving this man her virginity.

But Lizzy's image came back. Tara saw her holding her nephew, crying while Tara dressed for her senior prom. The memory was so vivid Tara could almost smell the powder Lizzy used on her nephew after his bath.

Shock stopped her. "Wait!" *What am I doing?* How could she have forgotten?

Duncan's feverish kisses slowed, but didn't stop.

"Wait." Tara shook her head. Both of her hands pushed him away. "Please, Duncan. Stop."

His ragged breathing sounded like a freight train. He stilled his advance, but he strained in his effort. "I have protection for you."

"Condoms break." Her sister's haunting words fell out of her mouth. *Don't sleep with anyone you don't want to be tied to.*

The man in her arms was leaving after tomorrow. He didn't deny their relationship would go no further.

Tara pushed him away. Pushed herself away. She couldn't think clearly with him so close. "I'm sorry. I should never have let things go this far." She scrambled away from him, putting her dress in order. "I'm so sorry."

He took to his feet and put some distance between them. Tara couldn't tell if it was disappointment or anger she saw on his face. He had a right to feel both. She was being a tease making him think they would make love and then stopping him. Tara put her hand on his arm only to have him pull it away. "You're leaving," she pleaded her case. "If I ended up pregnant, I'd be alone."

She watched him open his lips and bite back

his denial. "You can't deny it, can you?" She searched his angry eyes.

He paced and the air turned desperately cold. "I should go." Tara started to walk away.

Duncan stood his ground. "I'll see you tomorrow."

"No. I mean I should go home." Moisture gathered behind the lids of her eyes. She'd only known the man for two days, yet he had managed to sneak his way into her heart. A heart destined to break when he left. How could she be so stupid?

"Don't," he told her.

"Why not? This isn't going to happen." She moved her hand to point at him and then her. "It can't. Not with you leaving."

"Let's enjoy what we can for the small amount of time we have left. I'll not pressure you again. You have my word."

"Why do you have to leave?"

"This isn't my place, Tara. I wish I could offer you more, but it isn't possible." His stern look from before vanished, his anger drifted as he stepped closer.

With a cry, she moved into his open arms and pressed her face against his chest. He soothed her with words, while she shed her tears. "Hush, lass. All will be fine."

But his words were anything but convincing.

~~~~

Tara packed her bags twice, only to unpack them. Finally, she gave up and filled her glass to the top with the wine sitting on the table. Cassy was still out having a grand old time, while she paced the worn carpets thrown on the ground.

What was she doing? She had wanted Duncan, completely. She knew there was no future with him, yet that didn't stop her desire.

When he escorted her to the door of her tent, true to his word, he didn't press her for as much as
~~~~

a kiss goodnight. If he had, would she have offered him more?

She downed the wine, hoping it would put her quickly to sleep. At least in her dreams, she could enjoy the man. The wine did have the desired effect. Within minutes of putting out the candles and lying down, her brain filled with images of Duncan, and what life could be like with him.

~~~~

Grainna hovered over Tara's bed and watched her sleep. Slipping into her drugged mind was like putting a hot knife to butter. Grainna added force by lightly touching Tara's temples before she started her chant.

Visions and verses swirled in her head and remained behind the curtain of dreams in Tara's mind. Grainna slid in the image of the man she intended for Tara to desire. Tara struggled in her rest, her mind dark. She frowned in her sleep, and for a brief moment, Grainna worried Tara would wake.

To her horror, Tara replaced Duncan's form where Grainna's man once stood. Repeatedly, Grainna fought to erase the image of her would-be lover, only to come up against the sheer will of a first love.

After hours of fighting, she gave up and worked with the man Tara desired. The vows Grainna chanted into Tara's subconscious were easily placed once the vision of Duncan was secure.

Her task complete, Grainna left Tara's tent and made a slight alteration in her plans.

~~~~

The aspirin did nothing to resolve the headache plaguing her. To Tara's relief, Cassy looked as bad as she felt. "Where were you last night?" Tara forced the black coffee down even though it made her queasy.

Cassy picked her head off her folded arms.

Bloodshot eyes peered back. "Out."

"Yeah, I figured. But where and with who?"

"This is going to sound bad, but I don't remember. I remember Fin and I were talking after you and Duncan left. We both assumed you would end up here, so we stayed away. Once Fin saw Duncan return, he took off. I was on my way to see you, when the hunky blond you danced with last night stopped by. You know the one?"

With a nod from Tara she continued. "We danced a bit, drank too much, then nothing. Blank! I don't even remember how I got in here last night, or what time it was."

Tara's brow creased. "You and he didn't..."

"No. We didn't. I guess I drank too much. God, I hope I didn't make a fool of myself." Cassy cringed after sipping her coffee. "I'm giving up drinking."

Tara smiled and agreed.

Tara had already filled Cassy in on what had happened with Duncan. She agreed to leave first thing in the morning with the contingency that if things got crazy that night they would go after dinner.

Gwen arrived an hour before the games were scheduled to begin. "There you both are. I was worried when we didn't see you at breakfast this morning." She took one look at them both and gave them a sympathetic smile. "I see the festivities were too much last night, for both of you. Well, I can fix that." She opened the bag she kept at her side.

Gwen removed what looked to be a packet of herbs and mixed them with the water. She divided it between them both. "Drink. It's my own special blend to help clear the cobwebs."

Desperate, Cassy downed the brew in one quick swallow. Tara looked at it suspiciously.

"Drink it or not. It makes no difference to me."

Gwen swept across the room and pulled out the gowns they were both to wear for the day.

Tara's was a pale gold and white, virginal and perfect for a woman who would be handfasted at the end of the day.

Tara and Cassy had already signed releases, so their images could be plastered all over next year's brochures.

"Wow." Cassy stood up and looked into her empty cup. "What was in that stuff?" she asked Gwen. "It really worked."

"Only herbs," she smiled. "Healing was here long before modern medicine you know."

"You should try it, Tara. My headache is gone. You could market those herbs and be rich, Gwen."

Gwen smiled when Tara drank her portion of brew. "Maybe sometime I will, but not today. There are better things for this day." She turned to leave the room. "Take care in your appearance, ladies, and be sure and have a good time. Tomorrow you go back to your everyday life. Tonight is for fantasy and pleasure."

The ache in Tara's skull eased, although she hated to admit it.

"You know, the old lady kind of grows on you." Cassy murmured when Gwen left the room.

"Yeah, I guess so." The fuzziness and pain had completely cleared in a matter of minutes.

Tara looked at the gown she was going to put on and repeated Gwen's words to herself. *Tonight is for fantasy and pleasure.*

~~~~

Colorful flags and banners surrounded the arena. The wind caught their ends and the sound of flapping added to the scene. Poles, twenty feet in length, with massive rings stood at the entrance to where the games would be played.

All the Faire's guests were dressed in their finest attire. Even the horses were garbed in fancy
~~~~

blankets and ornate tack.

The day was meant for pomp and circumstance. Tara and Cassy were surrounded by guards dressed in intimidating black tunics. The platform, housing their special seating for the event, was placed center stage. On each side, large canvases created shade, keeping the area cool and comfortable.

Tara looked over the crowd in search of the man who held her captive in her dreams. Neither he nor Fin could be seen anywhere. A minor tremor went through her when she considered Duncan might have already left. She knew it was pointless to want to see him again, but she wanted to, nevertheless.

When Tara and Cassy approached their seats, trumpets sounded, drawing everyone's attention. The sound warned the crowd the games were about to begin.

Gwen had explained in detail what was expected of her. Tara imagined this event was simply another weekend for the old woman. It made sense she would pick new royalty at each Faire, to take the load off her. Besides, sitting in the sun for hours on end would be difficult for anyone her age.

A young boy dressed in finery fit for a squire bowed to Tara. "My Lady?"

Tara smiled at him and motioned for him to stand.

"My Lady, Madame Gwen said the games are to begin now." His teeth flashed once his role was done.

"Thanks," Tara whispered and winked at the nervous boy. She stood and motioned for the trumpets to sound.

The people settled down, and all eyes went to her. Tara's heart tripped over itself before she started to speak. She would never see any of these people again, and none of them would know if she said the wrong things. At least the thought kept her nerves calm.

Tara looked at Cassy with a wicked grin. "You owe me for this one," she said out of the corner of her mouth.

"Lords and Ladies, Warriors and Knights, Pages and Squires, welcome." She paused with their applause, her eyes searched for Duncan while she spoke. "For the brave men who will participate in our games and tournament we wish them good luck and good health." The crowd clapped their approval.

"Gentlemen." she presented the trumpeters who immediately called in the warriors.

They rode atop their horses, straight and tall. The horses pranced around the arena bringing many smiling faces and pointing fingers from the spectators in the crowd.

Tara recognized some of the faces from the previous evening dancing but some she did not. One by one, each rider came forward to Tara with helmet in hand. Each bowed, and then met with a nod and a smile from her. They went on, showing off their mounts and occasionally taking a ribbon or flower from a wife or sweetheart in the audience.

Fin and Duncan were the last two to make their entrance into the arena. Tara saw Fin first. His cocky smile lifted her spirits.

Duncan's expression intensified when her gaze rounded to him. The tense feeling eased from her neck when she saw him. Her shoulders fell with relief. As his smile reached his eyes, she realized his effect on her was no less powerful. The slight curve of his lips and the depth of his attention would live in her mind forever.

They stared at each other longer, and his bow was deeper than the previous riders had been.

When he turned away to circle the arena like the others, she called out.

"Wait." She leaned over the balcony and handed him the ribbon from her hair.

The crowd went silent when she picked her *favorite.* Duncan moved his horse closer to the stand and took her boon. He captured her fingers and leaned over them to brush his lips across their soft tips.

For a moment, there was no one else but them. She mouthed the words "good luck" before he let her fingers go.

She heard the click of Cassy's camera from behind her.

"That was romantic," Cassy told her once the procession was finished.

"For all the good it will do me."

"Lighten up. Remember... 'For pleasure and fun, or fantasy or whatever.'" Cassy who had sworn off alcohol only hours before, reached for the jeweled goblet, which held more wine.

An announcer bellowed over the crowd, telling them of the first event.

The men had replaced their armor with more comfortable clothing, designed to add agility to their feats of skill. The first of which was a challenge to see who could spear a target as close to the center as possible, while their horse was in full gallop.

The crowd had picked their favorite horsemen. Cheers and boos came and went with every passing of the lance.

The drunk from the night before was sloppy in his saddle and barely reached the target at all. Because many had seen his actions the night before, he was booed continually, except by those who were obviously his friends.

When it was Fin's turn, he grandstanded for the crowd by tossing his spear and catching it prior to lunging it at the target. He came close to its mark, drawing approval from the spectators.

Fin nodded to his brother in a challenge to beat him. Laughingly, Duncan pulled his mount forward and darted a glance at Tara who stood intently watching from the stands. His horse lunged forward with no outward sign from Duncan to do so. His aim was close, but Fin had beaten him by a hair.

So it went. There were similar games involving spearing rings from tall poles and other moving targets. A grand display was made of the mock battles. Swords clashed against swords, sparking cheers from the spectators.

A showman on horseback gave the audience a wonderful display of dancing his horse. He pranced, bowed and trotted to the tune played by the small band on the sidelines.

While the horse danced, Gwen made her way to Cassy and Tara's side. "How are you two holding up?" she asked as she made her approach.

In the light of day, Tara felt more comfortable around Gwen. She looked harmless in her soft blue gown and tinkling bracelets.

"I didn't think it would be this much fun," Tara admitted, embarrassed at her earlier behavior toward the woman. "I think I owe you an apology."

"For what?"

"I think I could have been more gracious this weekend."

"Nonsense." Gwen smiled.

The crowd roared signaling the end of the dancing horse and an intermission in the games.

Tara looked past Gwen to see if she could find Duncan. She hadn't caught a glimpse of him since he left the field. "Looking for your man?" Gwen asked, breaking Tara's train of thought.

"He isn't 'my man.'"

Gwen's laugh was unsettling. "How about you, Cassy, do you have a favorite?"

"So many men..." She smiled and waved at a brown-haired hunk as she spoke, "...only one of me."

"Are you ready for your part when the tournament is over, Tara? Do you have any questions?" Gwen circled in front of them both, cutting off their view of the stands.

"It's pretty straightforward," Tara said. "I don't have to kiss anyone do I?"

"Only if you want to, my dear. By the looks of some of the players, it might not be such a hardship."

"If Duncan wins, you'll kiss him," Cassy chimed in. "And if Fin wins, he'll kiss you to piss off his brother."

"It looks like you have the situation under control. I'll leave you to your food and drink." Gwen turned to leave, then stopped herself. "Oh, Tara, one more thing. When the handfasting is done, make sure you hold your partners hands like this." She took Tara's hands and placed them in hers. "Make sure you're looking at him, so the pictures look real."

Tara felt one of Gwen's rings scratch her palm when she let go. Tara pulled her hand away and saw a few drops of blood come to the surface of her skin.

"Oh, dear, I'm so sorry." Gwen pulled a handkerchief out of her bag. "Let me get that." She patted her palm with the cloth. "Let me see." Gwen turned her palm up and made a show of inspecting the damage.

"It's fine, really." Uncomfortable, Tara pulled at her hand firmly in Gwen's grasp. On the second tug Gwen released her and tucked the bloody cloth away. She muttered another apology then left.

~~~~
~~~~

"What is her game?" Duncan watched as Grainna left the platform. He and Fin had been making their way to Tara's side when they spotted the enemy talking with the women.

"I don't know, but I don't like it."

"A virgin's blood of Druid descent, only of age to give consent." Duncan repeated the curse out loud so they both could ponder its interpretation. "Virgin blood will set you free. This is your curse from us to thee." Duncan watched as Tara talked with Cassy. "If Tara has to give consent, then force isn't an option for Grainna. How can she force consent?"

"She can't. Not without mind control. Tara has a strong mind and is unlikely to fall under any spell Grainna can cast."

"Maybe," Duncan murmured. "Damn it to hell but she looks so confident. Like everything is going according to her plan."

"Agreed," Fin said in trepidation.

~~~~

Tara took the opportunity to walk through some of the vendors during the intermission. At least that was what she told Cassy. In reality, she wandered the crowd looking for Duncan.

"Searching for someone?" his voice came from behind.

She smiled but didn't turn. Instead, she got up on her tiptoes and looked over several heads in the crowd. "Just a tall, dark, and handsome man. You don't know where I might find one, do you?"

His laugh warmed her. She loved the musical sound of it.

Duncan turned her around and gave her hand a quick kiss. When she winced, he turned it over and saw the scratch. "How did this happen?"

"Gwen's rings caught. It's fine." Tara waved her free hand. "How is everything going out there? You look like a natural."
~~~~

Duncan rubbed her skin with his thumb.

"What is it?" Tara asked when he didn't respond to her question and comments.

He pulled her closer, his voice hurried. "What did Gwen tell you about today?"

"What do you mean?" His body had stiffened, alarming her.

"Did she ask anything else of you, any other task?" Duncan urged.

Tara shifted from foot to foot. "No, nothing, why?"

He forced a smile and brought her hands to his lips. His eyes closed, he brushed her knuckles to his cheek.

Something was bothering him.

Something was wrong.

"What is it?"

He looked through her. "If you fear anything, Tara, call on me."

"You're scaring me, Duncan."

The trumpets sounded, calling the warriors to the field.

The feeling he projected shook her to the core. Something was gravely wrong. "Trust me."

She searched his face, his eyes, trying in vain to see what was bothering him. An uncontrollable tremor went through her.

They both had places to be, both in opposite directions. His hand brushed her chin and left a blaze in its wake.

She watched him march away. His head held high, his stance and stride demanded people part in his path.

And…they did.

~~~~

"Her cure has begun," he told Fin when he met up with him.

"Tell me."

"Tara's hand was marred and crusted with
~~~~

blood. Grainna cut her with her rings."

"Is Tara suspicious?" Fin asked.

"A little, I think." Duncan put his armor on over his tunic. "I believe I know what Grainna has planned."

"What is it?" Fin fumbled with his own armor.

"She isn't stopping or changing the outcome of these games. Her salvation has something to do with the end result. Tara has to be consenting. The curse is clear on that account." He tugged his sleeve down under the armor.

"Aye, but how will she be consenting to a mere stranger? Even if Grainna could control her mind, Tara's heritage would keep her from making any grievous mistakes."

He spoke the truth, Duncan knew. "How are we to know she hasn't found a way around that?"

Fin's look said all he needed to know.

They didn't have any assurance Grainna would play fair. Truly, she would play dirty if her past was any guide to her character.

They placed their helmets on in unison. Both held a renewed interest in the outcome of the joust.

Chapter 7

Back in Tara's tent, Grainna prepared her altar. A platform of stone had been constructed with symbols of black magic—a pentagram carved in the center, her curse printed out in her native tongue surrounding it.

The cloth covered with Tara's blood soaked in her brew. When Grainna pulled it from the pot, the entire rag was thick with blood. Carefully, she carried it to the stone and dripped blood into the etchings of the circle surrounding the star.

Wisps of smoke emerged and sounds of sizzling and popping came with every drop hitting the sacred symbol.

Smiling in triumph, Grainna continued.

~~~~

The first two challengers faced each other on the jousting field. Tara sat in apprehension as she watched them prepare to do battle. It was all in fun, mind racking, but fun. She was certain the lances they held were made of some flimsy material, which fell apart easily. But still she worried about the outcome.

She couldn't help wondering if one of these men would be the victor.

When the horses took off in a run, Tara watched as the lances merely grazed the sides of their shields.

Only a game, she told herself. Breathing easier, she watched the first few matches and let her body relax.

It was when Fin had his turn, her interest in the game was renewed. He faced the better of the first few players. Tara wasn't surprised when Fin
~~~~

toppled the first rider with hardly a swipe and with only one pass.

Because Duncan was Tara's favored rider, his matches were held toward the end of the tournament. He took the arena much like his younger brother had, but with more accuracy and swiftness.

A powerhouse on the field, he took no chances and toppled his challengers one after another. Some saw him as a formidable foe and chose to dodge his blows, thus forfeiting their game.

Tara watched as the numbers of players for her hand dwindled to only three—Sir Duncan, Sir Finlay and Sir Michael.

Could she go through a mock ceremony with anyone other than Duncan? She would of course, but it was hard to imagine. She hated to think of pretending with anyone else but him.

"It won't be long now." Cassy handed Tara a glass filled with wine. "Here, I think you're going to need this."

"I can't. I'm too nervous."

"What's to worry about? Duncan will win. And if one of the others does at least they're cute."

Tara winced when she saw Fin take a hard blow to his arm holding his lance. "How can you be so sure Duncan will come out on top?"

"He has to. Besides, he likes you and wants it more than the others. Just look how he plucked them off earlier, like apples from a tree. Have some faith." Cassy took a large drink from the wine she had poured for Tara.

The crowd stood when the next pass ended with Fin off his horse. He brushed away the dirt and favored his sword arm. He bowed and shook hands with Michael then led his mount to the side.

Michael and his horse were given time to rest before the final match with Duncan.

Tara wanted desperately to find Duncan and

wish him luck and to issue a meaningless threat of great bodily harm if he didn't win. But getting away this close to the end wasn't possible.

Minutes ticked by which felt like hours. Faire patrons came and went during the intermission, taking pictures, asking questions. Nerves kept her from saying much to the people who stopped in. When her fingers started to tingle, she forced herself to sit down and slow her breathing. A lot of good she would do if she passed out before the match.

Tara's mind drifted from her body. The feeling of being on the outside looking in was overwhelming. She closed her eyes and thought of what Duncan had said earlier. *If you fear anything, call on me.*

What did she have to fear? Why did he say that? She closed her eyes and brought a picture of him to her mind. *Trust me.* His words echoed. A few deep breaths and concentrating on his final words helped slow her speeding pulse.

When the trumpets sounded for the final round Tara felt more relaxed.

More assured.

~~~~

Duncan sensed Tara's presence in his head.

From across the hordes of people he fixed her with a stare. Even from his distance, he could see her eyes were closed.

He knew she was troubled, felt her reaching out to him with her mind. He called on a power, which remained dormant until his return home. He closed his eyes and pushed words of trust toward her.

He couldn't tell if he was successful in his efforts, but when he opened his eyes he caught Tara's returning his stare.

Duncan led Durk to his place along the rope separating the riders His nostrils flared in
~~~~

anticipation of his flight. Skilled, it took only the slightest touch of Duncan's knees to command his horse to lunge.

The horse didn't flinch when Duncan's lance hit his opponent.

~~~~

Michael took the blow with rage. He wasn't happy with Gwen's orders to throw the match. He saw Tara's ribbon clenched in Duncan's hand and scowled. It was suppose to be him at the altar.

Him in her bed!

The next pass gave Michael the triumph he wanted. His lance caught and nearly toppled Duncan. He glanced up at the maiden who held her hand to her mouth, worry etched in her features.

His gaze went beyond her to Gwen's furious scowl. *Take the fall!* He heard her shout in his mind.

He played with fire for two more passes before he did as he was told and let Duncan toss him off his horse.

~~~~

Tara didn't realize she held her breath until it came out in a loud gasp. Her body nearly collapsed when she knew Duncan had in fact won the match.

She watched as he accepted the pats on his back from the other riders. She almost heard the heckling he received from his brother when he clenched his arm in a greeting more suitable for medieval times.

Tara wasn't given much time before Cassy fashioned a veil on her head and prepared her for the ceremony.

"This almost seems real, like you're really getting married or something." Cassy wiped her hand on her dress. "Are you nervous?"

Tara beheld Duncan's eyes as he walked forward to claim his prize. "No."

"Well I am." Cassy finished the last of her wine and stepped aside.

Tara had seen this before, in her dreams. The vows she was supposed to recite were etched in her mind. She no longer feared her role. Duncan would hold her hand and help her.

~~~~

Fin stood at Duncan's side, his Gaelic words hushed so only his brother could hear them. "Watch your step, brother, something is amiss. She is letting this happen for a reason."

Duncan knew his brother was right, but what choice did he have? Tara walked toward him with outstretched hands and a radiant smile, reaching out to his soul.

Once she stopped in front of him, his worries ebbed. She glowed under the veil trailing down her long red tresses. Her full lips curved into a smile. Her beauty was staggering.

She dropped into a deep and meaningful curtsey.

Duncan took her hand and led her to the middle of the field. A hush fell over the stands. Only the occasional sound of a baby crying could be heard.

He knew what was to happen next, not because Grainna's man had told him, but because he had seen many ceremonies like this in his life. The only difference was Tara reciting her part first, then he was to follow.

He saw Grainna watching from the platform Cassy and Tara had left, her glare victorious.

He shuffled briefly.

"It'll be over in a few minutes, Duncan. It isn't like this is real or anything." She took the cord Cassy handed to her and started. "Just repeat after me," she whispered.

Tara took his hand in hers and started weaving the cord around it. "From the North, to
~~~~

the South, In the East or in the West..." she began.

Duncan and Fin froze at the same time. Her words shook them both. "Stop her," Fin uttered in Gaelic.

"Where you go, I'll follow. Your light will shine my way."

The air around them changed. The force of her vow etched into them. They weren't handfasting pledges of love and devotion, but Druid wedding vows. Once spoken, they could never be taken back. Once spoken by one of Druid descent, they would bind you to the other person past this life and into the next.

He knew in an instant what Grainna intended.

Tara would say these vows to whoever stood before her and without the ability to stop. She would consent to that man and give Grainna the final piece of her curse.

If Tara continued saying these vows, a part of her soul would go with him when he left this century. With him gone, she would be nothing but an empty shell.

If he didn't pledge the same to her, she would live a short life of misery. The cruelty of such a life was beyond what even he could envision.

He felt Fin's anguish as Tara went on.

"It is my love I give you, past my dying day." She smiled up at him.

She was putting her soul in his hands. His heart leapt with the power of her vow. He searched her trusting eyes to see if she held any doubt. Seeing only love, something he didn't think possible, he made his choice and let her finish.

"Where two hearts beat, there is now but one. This tie that binds us together shall never be undone." Finished, Tara waited.

He took the dangling cord and bound his hand to hers. The air thinned. He placed her other hand in his and placed it over the other.

His look was direct, his eyes unquestioning.

Tara waited for him to speak. Her lips twitched slightly, anticipating.

When he did, it was as if they were the only two standing in the crowd of hundreds.

"From the North, to the South, in the East or in the West. Where you go I will follow, your light will shine my way. It is my love I give you, past my dying day." The air stirred. "Where two hearts beat, there is now but one. This tie that binds us together shall *never* be undone."

Lightning over a clear sky cracked, startling the crowd. The rope turned warm and glowed. His body shuddered as part of his very essence soared away from him and into her. If not for Duncan's hold, Tara would have fallen to the ground as the effect hit her.

It is okay, trust me. Everything will be fine, Duncan pushed his thoughts to her without moving his lips.

He lifted her veil and watched her eyes turn smoky as he bent down. Another burst of lightning pounded the sky when their lips met.

Their kiss was no mere meeting of lips, but one that charged the depths of their being. She sighed into his mouth as he pulled her into his arms. Knowing their lives were forever changed.

~~~~

The men took Duncan aside and helped him remove his armor. Fin questioned him in Gaelic.

In turn, Tara was surrounded by women who removed her veil and groomed her hair.

Cassy, caught up in it all, took pictures, and brushed away foolish tears.

Gwen came out of the crowd and approached them all with an extra gleam in her eyes. "Perfect," she boasted. "Everything was perfect. How do you feel, Lady Tara?" Gwen's amulet caught her
~~~~

attention and provoked her thoughts.

Tara envisioned Duncan again, this time they were deep in a passionate embrace. "I feel wonderful," she confessed.

"Magnificent, exactly what I want to hear. Remember, tonight is for fantasy, tomorrow your life returns to normal." Abruptly she turned and clapped her hands, gaining the notice of the crowd. "Let the celebrations commence."

~~~~

The dining area had been transformed with hundreds of candles flickering in the setting sun. Tables were lavishly set with flowers befitting the occasion.

A hand placed on her arm sparked. Tara knew it was him before she turned. They had only been apart for a short while. So why did it seemed so much longer?

No matter, she thought. They were together now.

Music started, Duncan took her to the dance floor. They said nothing at first.

"Come home with me, Tara."

His request would have shocked her had it come twenty-four hours earlier. Somehow, it didn't now.

"You would love my land and the people in it."

"I would love to visit Scotland," she told him. "Winter break will be here before you know it. I'll have to apply for a Visa, and I don't have a passport."

"If I could take you there tonight, without all those things, would you come with me?"

"Tonight?" She shook her head. "That isn't possible. Besides, classes start up next week."

Tara saw his rebuttal on his lips, but instead of talking, he kissed her.

Within seconds, her brain swam in a sea of Duncan. *Come with me tonight.*
~~~~

She broke off their kiss, thinking she heard him. "Stay in L.A. for a while. I'm sure you can change your flight home."

"We need to leave tonight."

"Would you leave without me?" She paused in her dance.

"I'll beg you to come."

His tone had changed, his body tensed.

Yes! I'll come with you. Tara visibly saw him relax, even though she hadn't said the words aloud. Her hair stood up, and a shiver went down her back. *Oh my God! You can hear me.*

"Aye, love, I can."

Blood rushed from her head, and breathing became an effort. She started seeing stars as the oxygen was sucked from the cells in her brain.

Nay, now none of that! Duncan held her with a firmer grip to keep her from falling as they danced.

I'm going crazy.

Then I am crazy, too.

How?

"'Tis difficult to explain," he said aloud for her to hear.

"Try," she demanded.

"You don't understand what I am asking, how could you? I needed to convince you to leave with me tonight. I used the means I knew would work."

"I don't understand."

He drew her head to his shoulder. On the outside for those who watched, they appeared like two lovers completely enthralled. Inside they spoke.

Remember when you thought Grainna could read people? he asked.

Grainna, you mean Gwen?

Her real name is Grainna, but I will tell you about that later. Remember, you said you believed she could read minds? he asked again.

Tara nodded. Unbelieving she was having a

full on conversation with Duncan in her head.

Sometimes when two people connect, they also have this ability. You and I have that connection.

Tara pulled back to look at him. *How? When? I don't understand.*

How is difficult to explain and unfortunately this is not the time, nor the place to do so. The when, was during the ceremony.

She stared him in the eye. "But all of it was make-believe, a play."

"For some, Tara, but not us!" He motioned behind him, sensed the weight of Grainna's stare. "Come." He led her to their table, putting much needed distance between them and their enemy. With only the shifting of his eyes, Tara knew Duncan thought of Gwen as an enemy.

Food was placed in front of them. Cassy sat on her right, and Fin on Duncan's left. Cassy started chatting to Tara the minute they sat.

"I can't believe this will all be over tomorrow. You had a good time, right?"

"I have." Tara tried smiling at her friend, but confusion and nerves kept her from really engaging in what Cassy was saying.

"So what are you going to do with Duncan?" Cassy whispered.

Her answer was immediate and required very little thought. "I'm going to Scotland."

"Get out! Really, when?"

"I don't... Soon, I think."

With so much noise and activity, it was difficult to hear Duncan's words. But when she did, they were stern.

Be careful how much you tell her.

Tara placed a forkful of food in her mouth to keep herself from saying more. *Why?*

Others listen.

She followed his eyes as they rested on Gwen. A chill came from the woman's stare. *She wants to hurt me, doesn't she?*

Aye.

But why? What did I do to her?

It isn't you, but what you are that she wants.

"I don't get it," Tara said aloud.

"Don't get what?" Cassy asked.

"Ahh... I don't get how I'm considering leaving with him." Tara recovered, "I haven't even known him very long."

"Well, I think it's awesome. When will you go, winter break?"

Tell her I have extended my stay, and you will be with me while I'm here.

Tara shot him a look.

Have her go home without you.

Tara wanted to question him further, yet Cassy's look demanded an answer now. Tara took a leap of faith. One she hoped she wouldn't regret. "Actually, he's decided to stay around for awhile. I want you to take the car and go back without me. Duncan and I are going to honeymoon for a few more days before he returns."

What's a honeymoon?

She laughed at his question. Cassy laughed at the implications.

"You go girl."

Chapter 8

The sun set during their meal. Light ocean breezes fanned the flames on the torches and candles. Everything about the evening was magical. What Tara didn't know was how magical it was going to get.

Duncan sent Fin out ahead of them to retrieve their horses and supplies. He was torn with how he was getting Tara to come with him. Time was running out.

He shut her out of his thoughts for a while to hide the truth from her until she was safe.

When they left the dining area, Tara gave Cassy a frantic hug. "Don't come back to the tent tonight. If I'm gone in the morning, know I am with him. I'll call you when I can."

"God, Tara it's just sex. Trust me, it kind of hurts the first time."

A single tear dropped. It was as if she was saying goodbye for more than a few days. "You've been the best friend I've ever had."

"Oh man, now you've got me crying. Knock it off." Cassy brushed at the tears on her cheeks. "Go, pop that cherry for God's sake."

When Tara turned to leave, Cassy said in a voice a bit too loud, "And use a condom."

Several people heard Cassy's comment. Laughter rose up and everyone watched as Duncan and Tara left together.

Because it was expected, and many watched, they went to her tent. Inside was lit up like a Christmas tree. Rose petals covered the pallet and champagne chilled in a bucket.

"Wow. Did you do this?" Tara asked.

"She did." Duncan dropped a bag on the bed with a frown. "Fill it quickly with whatever you think you need."

Tara wanted to question why his urgency was so great. She didn't. Instead, she shoved all her clothes and her purse into the bag. On impulse, she grabbed the bottle of champagne.

They exited the tent the same route they did the previous day. The brown muslin cape she had brought to the Faire hid her pale dress and red hair. Wordlessly, they walked behind tents and stuck to the shadows. When they reached the outskirts of camp they walked briskly until they reached the cover of trees.

Duncan kept silent, listening for any sound of alarm.

Tara however, was growing increasingly anxious and unsure of her decision to follow him without a better explanation as to why they were leaving in this manner. "Where exactly are we going?" she finally asked.

"Beyond this ridge. Fin is waiting with the horses." Assuming that meant the horses would be loaded in a trailer and they were driving to their next destination, she asked. "And then?"

"Home."

"I told you I didn't have a passport. How do you expect to get me out of the country?"

"The same way I came."

All right, that's a bit cryptic. "Do you have your own plane or something?"

"Something such as that."

A rustle in the bushes in front of them stopped them in their tracks. Duncan whistled a low hum, met with one from beyond the trees. "'Tis Fin."

Fin was atop his horse, with Durk's reins in his hand.

"Where's the truck?" Tara asked surprised to see there wasn't one.

Brother glanced at brother. Neither spoke. "Okay, what's going on? I've come along this far, but until I hear more I'm not budging another foot." To make her point Tara sat on a rock and crossed her arms around her chest. "Give!"

Damn! I'd hoped this could wait until we made our journey.

"Damn is right." Tara voiced his word to make sure he knew she was listening. "And I would appreciate a better explanation as to how we can do that."

"Do what?" Fin asked, obviously confused.

She eyed Duncan. *You tell him.*

Duncan cleared his throat and turned to his brother. "It seems Tara and I have the ability to talk to each other in our minds."

Tara waited for Fin to laugh and ask for details. She waited in vain. "Oh," was all he uttered.

"That's it? Your brother says he can read my mind and all you can say is oh?"

"It isn't uncommon amongst our people, Tara," Fin told her. "Our own parents have the ability to do it."

"You're kidding." Tara could tell by his look he wasn't joking. Her unease elevated.

"We can't stay here." Duncan tossed her belongings on the back of his horse. "Grainna will soon notice our absence and send a search party after us."

"Why exactly is that?"

"I told you she was evil, lass."

"I agree she gave me the creeps at first, but why would she care if we are gone now?"

"We don't have time for this." Duncan almost barked his response. He took her arm only to have her pull it away.

"That's too damn bad. You can make time, because without an explanation I'm not moving from this spot."

"Think, My Lady. Why would Grainna single out a virgin amongst everyone else? Why would it matter to her that you are one? No one would be the wiser if you weren't."

True. "Go on."

"Don't you think it strange she kept you away from all the men, only to thrust you and me together in the end?" Duncan looked her in the eye. "Your room screamed out for us to be together tonight."

True. "Why?"

"Grainna is a very powerful...person. She's very old." Duncan shot his brother a look, as if asking for his support. "She needs you, or what it is you are, to give her the ability to gain more power and strength."

Tara chuckled, "Are you saying she's some kind of a witch?"

"Aye, something like that." Duncan bent down on one knee and took her hand. "Now, we have to keep moving."

Tara snatched her hand away. "She's a witch and she wants to what, sacrifice a virgin? Me?"

Again, brother looked at brother with sober looks.

"You know something? I don't think it's me who's crazy." Tara stood up and started backing away. She mumbled a disbelief in magic and witches. "I think you are the ones who are nuts! So I tell you what. You two just go on your merry little way and I'll go mine." Tara tripped on a fallen branch in her haste to get away. Duncan caught her arm and kept her from tumbling.

"I can't let you do that."

"I don't see how you have a choice. This has all been fun and exciting. I appreciate the good time, really I do." She attempted to pull away. This time he didn't let her go.

"This isn't getting us anywhere," Fin spoke up. "If we could prove to you magic exists, would you wait to hear the rest of our tale once we are out of harm's way?"

Her nervous laugh echoed off the valley walls. "Okay, prove it."

"Not here. There's a place a few miles away that will help us prove magic exists." Fin pulled up the reins on his horse, signifying he was done talking.

Could they be luring me to a private spot to kill me? Tara asked herself.

"We won't harm you. Look at me," Duncan demanded when she refused. "Look through me. Tell me what you see."

Because she was scared and angry at herself for being so gullible, Tara did look into him. In his heart, she felt his fear for her safety. She saw his visions of the two of them kissing, felt the heat of the cord, which bound their wrists together during the handfasting ceremony.

Nowhere did she see malice or harm. *Trust me.* Duncan told her with his mind.

"If I go with you both, and end up dead, I'll never forgive you."

~~~~

Horns blew in the distance once they cleared the shelter of the forest.

"Grainna," Fin declared, then forced his horse into a full gallop.

Riding in front of Duncan was becoming commonplace for Tara. The darkness of the night and the speed of the horses made the ride less comfortable

She didn't have energy to concern herself about where they were going. They were traveling so fast, all she could think about was staying on the horse.

Duncan and Fin must have seen some type of
~~~~

landmark, because they took a sharp turn and were once again surrounded by trees. They stopped, but Tara saw and heard nothing. Even the breeze halted. The night music, which was made up of the crickets chirping and miscellaneous sounds of scurrying nocturnal animals, abruptly ended.

Both Fin and Duncan jumped from their horses. Duncan helped her to her feet and handed her both sets of reins. "What are we doing here?" Tara asked, fear shaking her voice.

Duncan brushed away dirt and branches covering an erect stone standing like a pillar on the ground. Similarly, Fin unearthed two more. There were six altogether when they finished. They circled the stones where they stood.

Voices carried through the forest. Their horses pranced and snorted the air. "We don't have much time." Duncan hurried Fin.

"You wanted to see magic, Tara McAllister." Fin led her over to one of the stones. "Touch it."

Tara hesitated. *This is crazy!*

But when she lifted her hand to the stone, she felt a pulse emanate from it. When her fingers touched the surface, etchings emerged and glowed in amber light. She pulled her hand back as if burned. "How?" she asked.

Fin placed a hand on her cheek. "Later, now we have to leave."

Duncan watched her examine her hand and stare at the glowing rock. Fin nudged him into action when the voices came closer.

One by one, both brothers touched each stone and set them alight with only a brush of their fingers, just as Tara had done. Once lit, the air inside the circle shimmered. There was no other way to describe how the air changed. It was like the fabric of space detached itself from the surrounding forest.

The horses responded and pulled against their tethers. Duncan laid his hand on Durk's side and spoke to him in Gaelic, instantly calming the animal. He turned and did the same to Fin's horse.

Fin started to chant in a sing-song rhythm in a language Tara didn't understand. She swore she saw trees shift outside the stones. Squinting her eyes, Tara searched harder to see what was happening. But the world outside the stones was changing and she began to hyperventilate.

Weak and unsure about how she felt, she grasped Duncan's hand. "What's happening?" She had to raise her voice because the air had grown thick, and the wind started to blow. Her skirts molded against her legs. The ground began to quake.

Seeing her panic, Duncan crushed her to his side. "I promise you everything will be all right," he yelled in her ear. Lightning shot out of the stones and converged together over their heads.

At the same time, Grainna appeared from the forest to witness their departure. "No!" Grainna shouted, throwing herself from her horse.

"Hold on!" Duncan yelled as the earth crumbled beneath their feet.

Plastered against him, Tara saw swirls of light in the air. Strong wind whipped all around. Thundering noise came out of nowhere. Gone were the trees, the stars or anything other than the three of them and the horses.

It was impossible to talk or even think. Tara's body threatened to crumble. She closed her eyes, buried her head in Duncan's chest, and prayed everything would stop.

~~~~

Unable to remain conscious during the journey, Tara had fainted in Duncan's arms. The cyclone ended. Rain pelted the travelers with the dying wind.
~~~~

When the world righted once again Duncan picked up his bride and climbed into his saddle with her in his arms, leaving Fin to collect the stones.

His bride, he mused. How the hell was he going to explain that to her once she woke up?

Chapter 9

Except for the peat and coals burning in the hearth, the room was dark when Tara woke up. The fresh smell of rain saturated her senses. A nice summer storm always lifted her spirits. They were so rare in Southern California. She kept her eyes closed, and let herself wake up slowly, snuggling beneath numerous blankets in the soft inviting bed.

When her eyes finally blinked open, she noticed the nightgown covering her arms. She usually slept in nothing more than a t-shirt and found it odd to feel sleeves reaching to her wrists. Tara picked up her arm, puzzled by the fabric. *"Ah well,"* she pondered as she shut her eyes again, *"it has been a strange few days."*

Her eyes flew open with the memory of the last few days.

Tara shot up in bed and looked around the room. The walls were made of stone, the kind that belonged on the outside of a house instead of inside it. The fireplace across the room gave off little heat, and the smell of peat and coal embers filled the air. Again, she smelled the rain and heard a slight patter of drops behind the curtains.

She tossed back the blankets and climbed from the huge bed. When her bare feet touched the carpet covering the stone floor, she realized how cold and damp the room was.

The hem of the full-length nightgown dropped to her heels when she stood. Tara had never seen the gown before and couldn't remember putting it on.

Her breath started to come in small pants. She

closed her eyes and wondered if she was still asleep and dreaming.

Heavy drapes framed a window with no glass. Shutters kept out some of the cold, but not much. Tara raised a shaky hand and opened the wooden frames. "Oh my God," she whispered. Rolling green hills, like she had never seen before, stretched out as far as she could see. Although it was morning, gray clouds blocked the sun and filled the sky with moisture.

Tara gaped down from where she stood and saw what had to be a three-story drop. To her right a stone turret pointed toward the sky with a flag of amber and black flying from the top.

She let the drape fall back in place and attempted to make sense of everything she saw.

A knot of panic took form in the back of her throat.

"Duncan!"

She screamed his name at the top of her voice. Her strides took her to the door of her room. Mad as hell, she threw open the heavy wood and yelled his name again.

~~~~

Downstairs in the main hall, Duncan gathered with Fin and his parents to explain their tale because they'd arrived too late last night to do so then.

Tara's voice bellowed through the Keep, just as the bulk of the story had been told. Duncan dared a look up the stairwell where he heard her cursing him.

Fin laughed in the face of Duncan's pain. "I don't envy you, brother."

~~~~

Tara rounded the corner of yet another hall, walking in circles. She bellowed his name again, positive he heard her. She followed her instincts, and headed down another corridor.

"Duncan!" She wanted to add a very colorful expletive, but found herself at a loss. "Damn it, Duncan. I don't even know your last name!"

A young girl peeked around a door. "Where is he?" Tara sniped at the child.

The girl shrank back and pointed down yet another hall.

Tara uttered her thanks and marched in the direction the child indicated. Her path led her to a small staircase emptying into a larger hall. Once there, she saw a light flickering and heard murmured voices below.

The main stairway into the great hall was massive. Five people could walk side by side and never so much as touch one of the others. It curved in an arc Tara hardly noticed as she flew down the steps in a fury.

Duncan sat with his brother and two other people, a man and a woman, near an enormous fireplace dominating the great room.

The dogs sitting at the base of the staircase stood, stared, and then scurried out of her way as she passed.

Duncan—" Dammit-to-hell, what was his last name? She wanted to throttle him.

"MacCoinnich, Duncan MacCoinnich," he answered her unasked question.

"Duncan MacCoinnich, what the hell is going on? Where am I? How did I get here? And who put me in this?" She grabbed a handful of the material she wore as a nightgown.

He shifted his weight from one foot to another. His look darted from her to the couple standing beside him. The older man held a smirk behind his hand. He wasn't successful.

Ignoring her question, Duncan pointed out the others in the room. "Tara, I would like you to meet my parents, Lora and Ian. Da, Ma, this is Tara, the one I have been telling you about."

Remembering her manners, Tara faced the others in the room as if seeing them for the first time. "It's a pleasure to meet you both, Mr. and Mrs. MacCoinnich," she replied by instinct. Once the words came out, she realized who she was addressing.

"A pleasure," Ian said, taking her hand in his and kissing it.

Her eyes didn't leave Ian's, but her head nodded in Duncan's direction. "We need to talk!"

"Why don't we find you something more suitable to wear before—"

Her eyes darted to him, cutting off his words. "The last thing you need to think about right now is what I am wearing." She rounded on him, ignoring everyone else. "The only reason you are still breathing is because I wouldn't want your parents to witness your death!"

She plastered on a fake smile and glanced at the couple in question. "All due respect."

Without giving Duncan a minute to consider her words, she turned back. "Talk!"

"On that score," Fin said to no one in general, "I'm sure there is some chore which needs tending."

"Aye. Right you are son. Let me help." Ian followed him out, calling the dogs that appeared all too happy to leave.

Duncan and Tara stared at each other while the men filed out of the room. Lora broke some of the tension. "Tara my dear, do leave a little skin on him so I have some to remove once you are finished." Lora gave her son a very unsympathetic look.

Lora MacCoinnich lifted her small frame from her chair and crossed over to them. She waited until Tara glanced in her direction before she spoke again. "I look forward to getting better acquainted. Let me know if there is anything you need." Lora left the hall.

"Maybe we should sit," Duncan said, stalling the inevitable.

Tara didn't feel like sitting, but thought she should so he wouldn't avoid his explanations any longer.

Tara took the seat his mother had vacated. She folded her hands in her lap in a display of calm she didn't feel.

"I don't know where I should start." He took the chair opposite her.

A vision of Julie Andrews twirling on an Austrian hillside flooded her mind. "Start at the very beginning."

"That might be more difficult to understand."

Steam would surely begin puffing from her ears if he didn't start talking. "Okay...Where am I?"

"My home, in Scotland."

Tara stared up at the ceiling. It soared thirty feet or more above her and was made entirely of stone. Tapestries hung on the walls. The fireplace was so big it was possible she could stand up inside of it.

"Because I can't explain all of this, or what I saw outside my bedroom window, I'll buy that." She took a deep breath, "How?"

"The stones. Do you remember the stones last night?"

"I remember touching a rock, the glow. You and Fin turned on the others. Everything is fuzzy after that. I think there was an earthquake."

"It does feel like the earth moves when the stones are working."

"What are they?"

Duncan grinned, but her frown kept it from staying on his face long. "The stones are older than time. They were entrusted to our family for keeping."

"And they are used to move people from one place to another?"

"Aye."

"A few rocks moved me to Scotland overnight?"

"Aye, they did."

Not quite believing, but not able to explain everything she saw the night before, Tara pushed on. "You told me I was in danger last night, and we had to hurry. Why?"

He explained again about Grainna being evil. Only this time he told her Grainna would have killed them if they hadn't left when they did.

Tara referred to her as a witch, a term Duncan didn't deny. He told her of the curse binding Grainna in an old and powerless body. But when Duncan repeated a rhyme about Druids and Virgins, Tara's head started to swim.

"Back up," she told him when he wanted to continue. "*A virgin's blood of Druid descent?* Grainna thought my ancestors were Druids?

"Aye."

"Druids?" Tara shook her head, "As in ancient people with mystical powers?"

"Aye."

She started to laugh. "That's rich. Really rich! My parents are from Orange County. Believe me, there is nothing mystical about Orange County."

"That may be, lass, but you are of Druid blood," Duncan told her with a straight face.

"Just because my last name is McAllister, doesn't mean I'm a Druid. Scottish yes, some, but Druid? That's a stretch. My great grand parents immigrated to the states at the turn of the century like so many others. No one in my family ever had... powers." She shook her head in disbelief.

"Druids are private with their abilities, because they are often misunderstood and feared. They keep to their own and hide what they do."

"How is it you know all of this?" Not that she

believed any of it.

"I am Druid."

This is bullshit!

Then how is it, love, we can read each other's thoughts?

"I don't know. I can't believe it's because I'm a Druid. Or that you are."

"You activated the stone last night by your own hand," he reminded her.

"That can be explained. Maybe it was the heat of my hand that turned the stone on. Anyone could have done it, if that's the case."

Duncan stood and crossed over to the hearth. The fire had burned down to an orange glow. "Fire is the first ability Druids have control over. It is the first they learn. The first to come and the last to leave." He reached both hands toward the hearth, flames leapt three feet high and out of the embers.

"Oh my God!"

Duncan lowered his hands. The flames died in the hearth.

Air rushed from her lungs. She gaped at the man who she scarcely recognized from the days at the Faire. "This is too much." She stood and paced the room. "I don't know what to believe."

"Accept we are both Druid, and the rest will fall into place."

Stressed, she ran her hands through her hair. "Fine, I'll play along. I'm a Druid. You're a Druid." *We are all Druids... I'm losing my mind.* "I'm a virgin of consensual age, and blood shed from the loss of my virginity would give Grainna her youth and powers, yadda, yadda, yadda. Do I have it right?"

"'Tis correct."

"You and Fin were what, sent to California to stop her from finding me?"

"Or others like you."

"Like there are hundreds of Druid virgins running around Southern California." Tara laughed at the thought.

"Not hundreds, but a few. Most lack true Druid blood making Grainna's curse almost impossible to break."

Dear God, he's serious. "So, you whisk the young virgins away when you find them?"

"You are the first to come to our home."

Tara sent him a questioning look. "If I'm the first one to come here, then how do you get them away from Grainna? You couldn't leave them. Otherwise, her curse would have been broken by now. How did you keep them away from her?"

He didn't answer her question. He didn't have to. A picture of the two of them, laying together and kissing, flashed in her head. Her eyes widened in panic, her mouth dropped open. "You have got to be kidding! You were sent to deflower the virgins?"

Tara's laughter verged on hysteria. "Then why didn't you?"

"I have never forced myself on a woman."

"How noble of you. Really, you should be given a medal." Anger overpowered her hysteria. "So, because I didn't fall into bed with you, you brought me here. Where she can't get to me? Is that it?"

Tears started to fall. And to think she liked this guy! Really liked him. All six foot four, two hundred plus pounds of him.

"Aye." Duncan watched as her rage consumed her.

"Fine," she bit out before heading toward the stairs. "That's just great."

Duncan touched her arm to stop her. She shrugged him away. "Where are you going, Tara?"

"To get my things and get dressed. Now that you've had your laugh, you can send me back." She put much needed space between them.

His eyes lowered to the floor. "I can't."

"Then you can drive me to the airport, and I'll catch the next flight home." She would have to max out her credit card paying for a flight, but she didn't have much choice.

"'Tis not possible." He dared another look at her.

"Why? Because I'm still a virgin? A threat? I'm sure I can find some stud willing to rid me of that, so don't spend any more time worrying about me."

His eyes snapped at hers in alarm. "Nay, Tara. *That* you will not do!"

She reached him in two strides. Her finger poked him in his chest with every word she spoke. "Who do you think you are? It wasn't your choice in California, and it isn't your choice here." She lifted her nightgown and fled his side.

Duncan reached her half way up the stairs. "You cannot leave."

"Watch me," she shouted at him and pulled away.

"There are no planes to take you home."

"I realize your home is remote, but I'm sure I can find an airport somewhere."

"No, you can't. There are none."

She dropped her hands at her side and released an exasperating sigh. "What are you trying to tell me? I'm tired of this game."

"The stones do more than move you from one shore to another. They move you through time. Even if you could go back to America, there would be nothing there for you."

She stopped, turned, and her eyes searched his. "You can't be serious?"

"Look around you, Tara. Is this a home of your century?"

She stopped struggling against his grasp and considered his question. She remembered how his mother was dressed. Her gown would have seemed perfect at the Faire they'd left. Tara studied him now as if seeing him for the first time.

He had changed his clothes, but what he wore now was similar in fashion to what he had worn the past few days. The colors were more vivid, and the fit suited him better, but the shirt drifted beyond his hips, and his legs were covered in leggings appropriate in any Shakespearian play.

Tara took in the room, noticed the chandelier hovering above the great hall. The pulley attached raised and lowered it so candles could be lit before hoisting it overhead. No modern lights, no lamps, nor anything requiring electricity was visible.

Pale and trembling, Tara uttered her question with a barely audible breath. "What year is it?"

"1576."

Blood dropped to her feet, and her head spun until she saw stars. Even when she was sure she would collapse, and he reached out to stop her from falling, she protested, "Don't touch me!" Her words were cold and deadly. Her mouth gaped in disbelief.

"You should sit." He stood near her side, but did as she told him.

"You brought me to Medieval Scotland without my permission."

"You told me you would return to my home."

"Not to the sixteenth century!" she yelled.

"I didn't have a choice."

Angry hands trembled through Tara's hair. "You always have a choice!"

Duncan put his hand out to touch her.

She flinched. "I told you, don't touch me."

"Tara, please. Try and understand..." He reached for her again.

She flung her hands toward him to push him away.

He ducked to avoid the sparks shooting from her fingers. Behind him, the wicks on the candles of the chandelier burst into flames.

Gasping for breath and frantic, Tara looked from her hands to the lit candles, producing flickering shadows on the wall.

She felt the anger and the heat pulse from her hands. She'd lit the candles like he had lit the fireplace.

He was telling the truth. Everything he said was true.

Tara was stuck in a time she knew nothing about, without her friends, family, or anything. School would start next week without her.

Gone were her plans, her dreams.

Every possible emotion passed through her while Duncan stood, staring, his mind ever present inside hers. But when he reached to comfort her, she screamed in her head.

Stay away from me.

His hand halted midair, then fell to his side.

"And stay out of my mind." She tried, unsuccessfully, to control her breathing.

"I don't know if I can."

"Try. You've taken everything from me. The least you can do is give me peace in my own mind."

Tears welled in her eyes. Her pain was enormous.

"I'll help you to your rooms and have one of the maids draw you a bath."

She blinked up at him through her tears. "Why don't you get one of the maids to show me the way?"

"I will show you."

Tara sent him a deadly look. "It wasn't a request."

Chapter 10

A hole started to wear into the carpet thrown on the floor. No matter how many times Tara sat down, she couldn't for more than a few minutes. It was a good thing the space was large and allowed her room to pace.

She heard the comings and goings of people beyond the door. When Duncan walked by, his thoughts were so loud she shouted at him, "Get the hell out."

No one talked with her. Even the upstairs maid who brought in a tray of food said nothing. The poor woman kept her eyes on the floor when she entered the room. Tara did notice her look at her out of the corner of her eyes. Refusing to wear the dresses set out for her, Tara assumed the woman stared at her shorts and t-shirt.

Outside her room, Tara heard the maid talking with Lora. Their muffled voices of concern over what she was and wasn't eating reached her ears.

Lora gave a stern warning that everything the maid saw behind Tara's bedroom door should be kept secret.

Tara shook her head at their conversation, and continued to stew over what she would do about Duncan's deceit.

~~~~

"What do you mean you didn't tell her?" Fin asked while putting the stone to his sword to sharpen its blade.

"She didn't give me a chance. Besides, she had all she could take in one sitting. Telling her we are bound together for eternity may have snapped her
~~~~

mind completely."

"I'm still not sure why you went through with it. How do you know if you will be compatible for this lifetime, let alone the next?" Fin enjoyed his women, but only one had gotten close enough for him to care for. He was never cruel to the many women who had been in his life, and when they parted ways he was always generous.

Duncan, however, was much more particular with his bedmates. Being the first born meant he shouldn't spread his seed throughout the land like so many men in their time did. It also meant he needed to choose his bride wisely, to assure the next generation of MacCoinnich's had a proper mother to raise them. Now his choice was made, even if the bride was oblivious to her new station in life.

Fin tossed his head and shrugged. "I don't think I want to be around when you tell her what's happened."

"I'm not going to tell her."

Fin dropped the stone to his lap, gave his brother his full attention. "What do you mean?"

"I'm keeping this information from her until we have had a chance to grow to know each other better."

"You mean until you bed her."

Duncan winced at how his brother's words sounded. He wanted to deny them, but couldn't. "Aye."

"Be careful, brother. Tara has already been deceived enough for one lifetime. Keeping this from her might be the cause of great misery for you both."

"Telling her now would send her fleeing in the night."

"If that is what worries you, then lock her in her rooms."

Duncan shook his head. "Have our trips to the

future left no impression on your brain? If you bind women from her century, they will despise you for a lifetime. No one wants to feel trapped."

"And you, brother, are daft if you don't realize Tara is already trapped. Both of you are duly trapped."

Still, Duncan wasn't going to tell her anything about their binding vows. Instead, he would woo her like he'd been doing in her time.

Of course he would have to wait for her to stop yelling, and throwing things at the walls. He had to stop picturing the imaginative ways she conjured torturing him, even if it was only in her head, before he could implement his plan.

Unlike Fin, Duncan was a patient man. He would wait as long as it took for Tara to see they were meant to be together.

Just as he started to relax, a tremor of dread went through him. Duncan stood abruptly, startling his brother.

"What is it?" Fin jumped around to see what caused Duncan to move so quickly.

"Damn it," Duncan cursed. Adding nothing in the way of an explanation, he ran out of the room at an alarming speed.

Not needing an invitation, Fin followed.

~~~~

The more she paced, the angrier she became. He'd lied. Over and over again, he had lied to her.

God he had made her want him. She desired him more than any other man she had ever dated.

Ever kissed.

Disgusted with the way her skin tingled thinking about being in his arms, Tara tossed a heavy tray at the wall.

Duncan had used her. What made him so different from the woman he called Grainna? Worse, Duncan had used her emotions and feelings, tossed them at her for his needs. Maybe
~~~~

that wasn't a fair assessment of the situation, but Tara didn't care. She was hurt and angry. She hadn't even begun to consider what life in his time would mean. She did realize she would never see Cassy or her sister and nephew again.

She yelled her frustration and noticed the heat of anger building all over again. With all that fury, the need to get outside overwhelmed her.

She grabbed her sweater off her bed and stormed out of her room. She didn't notice her own strength when she slammed the solid wood door behind her and it bounced off the wall.

The hallway was clear. Not that it mattered. She would likely punch anyone who blocked her path. She almost dared Duncan to get in her way.

She found the main hall where she had confronted Duncan and his parent's only hours before. The massive double doors towering over fifteen feet tall had to be the way out of the house.

Not that the MacCoinnich's residence resembled a mere home. The place was a friggin' castle! One she might appreciate, if she was on tour in Scotland with a bunch of old people enjoying their retirement. But no! She wasn't on tour. That fact was confirmed further when she crossed over the front door threshold.

She stepped into a huge courtyard where several men dressed in armor and kilts all stopped participating in their daily chores to gawk at the new arrival. A few horses were tied to posts, while others had riders on their backs.

"Take a picture!" she yelled before storming past them all.

She had no idea where she was going. Sunlight pooled down on her from above, through another set of doors, looking very much like they belonged on the set of a movie.

The doors were large enough to allow six or seven men to move through, side by side on horseback. It was obviously the way in and therefore her ticket out.

She tossed her hair over a shoulder, sucked in a deep breath, and damn near ran to her freedom.

~~~~

The front doors were left open, and by the look on the men's faces Duncan knew she had already crossed their paths.

"Where?" He barked the question to all who stood staring.

Several men pointed in the direction of the gate.

He could hear her curses in his head and knew she hadn't gotten very far.

Duncan held up a hand to his brother with an unspoken request to leave him alone.

He spotted her marching away and sighed in relief. He watched her for several minutes before shortening the distance between them.

Tara didn't turn to look when he came up behind her. "Where are you going, Tara?"

"Out!"

"I can see that, but where?"

She stopped and turned. "Far away from you."

He almost collided with her. But before he could react she was storming off again.

"A lady is not safe out here by herself."

She stopped again. This time he didn't stop in time and fell into her.

Hands at her sides, her chest thrust up next to his, she gritted the words between her teeth. "A lady isn't safe around you, either."

"Now, Tara." He tried pleading with her.

"Oh don't you even, 'now, Tara' me." She stepped to the side and started off in a different direction. Walking in circles.

He let her walk for several minutes before attempting to talk to her again. "I would be happy to escort you on a walk. But we need to get you
~~~~

more properly dressed." He knew the effect watching her walk was having on him. He could only imagine what his men must have thought when she had stormed the courtyard in her shorts.

"You're a bastard, you know that MacCoinnich?"

He wanted to counter what she said but cautioned himself against it. "Still, we need you in more fitting clothes. If someone were to come along, questions would be raised which would be most difficult to answer."

"You should have thought of that before you brought me here." She waved a hand in his general direction. "Right now I don't give a crap what questions *you* might have to answer."

"I told you how necessary it is for secrecy." He turned to the Keep and noticed some of the men watching to see what would happen. He needed to put a stop to this and soon.

"Bite me."

A completely inappropriate image of him doing exactly that popped in his head. A slow lazy smile inched over his lips.

Unfortunately for him, Tara read his thoughts. She didn't find them nearly as entertaining as he did. "You ass..." She raised her hand to slap his face.

He caught her hand before it made contact. "I've had enough of this."

Without warning and in complete disregard for what she might think, Duncan bent down and un-ceremoniously tossed Tara over his shoulder and started back to the Keep.

Once she caught her breath, and realized what he was doing, she started pounding on his back, demanding he let her down.

He ignored her every plea. Fin watched his brother approach and bit back the smirk on his lips.

"Let me down."

Quiet, Tara.

Let me down, and I'll be quiet.

He saw the image of her running away from him if he did as she asked. "I don't think that would be wise."

"Since when do you think?"

Duncan took the stares of his men and some of the jibes as he marched past them all. "Women," was his only explanation.

Many laughed. Some rolled their eyes and went back to their tasks. Fin closed the doors to the Keep once Duncan had Tara inside.

He didn't set her down until she was back in her room.

Her fury had calmed slightly, replaced by the humiliation of being carried around like a sack of potatoes. But she still dared him with her words. "You have to sleep sometime. And when you do, I'll make my way out of here, away from you."

Her words sobered him, and the words of his brother rang in his ears. "You cannot leave. Maybe when you've calmed down, we can discuss the why, but right now you simply need to trust—"

"Trust? You want me to trust you?" She flopped down in a chair. "Ha."

"I see you're not ready to talk about this."

"You think?"

Resigned with what he had to do in order to keep her there and safe, he walked to the door.

He glanced at her one last time before he left. All she awarded him with was her profile.

Fin stood in the hall, smiled, and calmly handed Duncan a key.

The second they heard the loud noise of the lock sliding in place, they both learned how colorful Tara's vocabulary could be.

~~~~

He didn't know which was worse, her wrathful
~~~~

vengeance or the silent misery he sensed when she realized she had no way out.

He sat staring into his cup, thankful that after two full days and nights, she had finally ceased crying. How many times had he stopped himself from going to her in that time? He couldn't count. The ale he drank wasn't potent enough to drown out her pain, pain overwhelming him in waves. He knew every time she cursed his name in her head, felt every insult she threw his way.

But of late he hadn't heard her voice. And that worried him more.

Every hour since their handfasting, he felt her more, sensing her every need. Even if the maid hadn't reported her activities, he knew what she did. He knew she refused to eat the meals he sent her, knew she existed on only a few hours sleep every night.

His mother's words stopped him from going to her when she went weak from hunger. Lora assured him Tara was drinking enough broth to survive, and told him she needed time to sort out her feelings. He risked her running away again if he cornered her now. And next time, he might not be able to stop her.

So instead of doing what he thought was best, he sat with his drink and, along with her, refused to eat.

~~~~

Lora entered the room with little more than a whisper. Tara, dressed in the shorts and tank top, sat in a chair pulled over next to the window. Her legs were tucked under her, and her head rested on the tall back of the wooden chair.

Her pale features worried Lora. It was time to pull Tara out of her depression.

She walked up behind her, yet Tara didn't take notice. Nor did she notice when Lora set a tray of food down and took a seat.
~~~~

"Beautiful, isn't it?"

Slowly, Tara moved her eyes, glanced over to her, and then continued to stare over the green rolling hills. "Yes."

"Have you ever been to Scotland before?"

"No."

Always patient, Lora gave pause between each question, each statement. "My sons tell me your California is hot and dry. This must be very different for you."

"It is."

Lora poured some tea and brought it to her. When Tara took it out of politeness, but didn't bring it to her lips, Lora thought it best to rile her enough to bring some fight back. She had overheard much of the argument Tara and Duncan had the first day. The woman sitting in front of her resembled little of the fiery lady her son had brought home. "He is riddled with guilt."

"Good."

A spark. Lora sensed it. "If there was any other way he wouldn't have brought you here."

Tara sighed. "Mrs. MacCoinnich..."

"Call me Lora."

"Lora, if you've come in here to defend your son, or his actions, you're wasting your breath." She sipped the tea with a trembling hand.

"I was quite angry at him when he told me his tale." Lora brought the bread and cheese over and pulled her chair closer. "Duncan was always one to act on impulse, no matter how hard I tried to get him to think everything out more thoroughly." She buttered the bread, handed Tara a piece, and broke off a small amount for herself.

"He certainly didn't think this one out." Tara absently nibbled on the bread in her hand.

Smiling, Lora went on, "Nay, he didn't. What's done is done however, and there is no way to reverse it."

"Are you sure?" Tara washed down her bread with more tea. "That there is no way I can go back?"

"Not safely. Your return would mean death to you." *Both of you*, she thought.

Tara ate in silence and continued to stare out the window. Lora saw her watching children playing with a puppy in the distance.

"I had a life you know." Her eyes swelled with tears. "I was almost finished with school. I was going to be a nurse. I shared an apartment with my best friend, Cassy. We were going to celebrate our graduation by going to Europe. Cassy will think I'm dead. She'll blame herself for convincing me to go to the Ren' Faire."

Tara wiped her eyes with the back of her hand. "Oh, God," she sobbed. "I was going to help my sister who is raising my nephew by herself. Help her, so she could go back to school." A choking sob burst from her lips.

Lora placed a gentle hand over Tara's in a form of comfort in her grief.

Grief for a life she would never live.

Grief for the family she would never see again.

Chapter 11

Light. Searing bright light pummeled the back of her eyelids. She lifted her hand shielding the rays from hitting her full force.

Lora's voice filled the room as much as the sunshine. "It is the most beautiful of days, Tara. In fact I don't think I've seen one much better." She stood by the drapes she had pulled open.

Lora came to the edge of the bed and sat. Tara wiped her hand across her face trying to shake the sleep from her head. She'd slept peacefully. Better than any of the other four nights since she'd arrived. "Please, Lora. I'm not even awake yet."

"Nonsense! You can't confine yourself to this room any longer. I absolutely forbid it!" Lora smiled. "Besides, flaunting yourself in front of my son will bring him much more pain than hiding in here all day long."

"You think so?" Tara liked the sound of pain and Duncan in the same sentence.

"I know so!" Lora bounced off the bed like someone half her age. "First, we need to heat up this room. Even with the sun shining, our summers are nothing like yours." Lora strode to the fireplace, tossed a small log on it, and then turned her hands up. Flames leapt where none were before.

"How do you do that?" Tara asked, stunned to see the wonder of magic again. "I tried it myself. All I got was tired."

"Practice my dear and a bit of skill I suppose. I'll teach you." She opened the door and allowed the maids to enter. "Let's get you ready for your day."

A couple of young men carried a trunk into the room. Inside the trunk, were several gowns, which paled anything she wore in the twenty-first century.

One by one, the maids sorted them into piles. Some needed alterations. Some were simply not the right color for Tara and her auburn hair. They finally settled on the one she would wear for the day.

The maids made quick work of the needed alterations. Within the time it took Tara to bathe, brush out and dry her hair, they had completed the dresses.

The gown she chose was made of fine, spun wool. The dark umber color blended beautifully with her hair and a hint of gold along its edges gave it a sense of elegance normally saved for special occasions. Tara had to admit the dress was stunning. *Eat your heart out, Duncan.* She let the thought escape when she saw her reflection in the mirror.

Pleased, Lora led her from the room.

The meal which broke the family's fast was beginning when they entered the dining area.

Ian, knowing what Lora was up to, sensed their presence before they came in the room. Fin took notice and dropped his food midway to his mouth. The others at the table sized up the woman who had caused so much talk and tension in the Keep.

Duncan, the last to realize something was amiss, turned only when everyone else grew silent.

Lora's hand on Tara's arm kept her focus. "Tara, I want you to meet the family. Amber is the youngest at ten." Amber stood and made a quick curtsey.

"Cian, who is trying not to drool in his food, is ten and six years of age." Cian sent his mother a wicked glance before coming to his feet and bowing at the waist. Tara started to squirm under the family's stare.

"Myra, our oldest daughter, is twenty and one last spring. I'm sure you both will get along well."

Myra stood, but instead of a bow, she tilted her head and smiled. "'Tis a pleasure to finally meet ye, I mean you." Her glance to her mother told Tara the line was rehearsed. But her effort was sincere.

"Of course, you've already met Finlay and Duncan."

Fin opened his mouth only to be cut off. "I'm not ready to talk to you," Tara interrupted. He wasn't without blame in the whole ordeal.

Tara's eyes traveled to Duncan. His face sported a look of awe and a five o'clock shadow.

"What is this?" Tara touched her own jaw, indicating the growth of beard he had managed since she had seen him last.

His hand reached out and scratched the growth. "I normally have it when I'm not...traveling."

It was a bit sexy, but she blocked the thought from her mind. "I guess some might like that *Brad Pitt* look."

"Who is this, Brad Pitt?" Duncan asked.

"No one you would know." *No matter, you won't be close enough to scratch my skin.* She cleared her throat, more confident by the second. "Have you heard of a shower, Duncan? Oh, that's right. Indoor plumbing hasn't been invented yet. Just one of the many pleasures you ripped from my life." She accepted the nod of approval from Lora. "You smell like a tavern. Maybe your mother won't tell you to give her respect at her table, but I will."

Duncan's younger siblings tried in vain to hide their mirth. Even Ian couldn't hold in his laugh.

Although her words were meant to sting, Tara

sensed a weight lifting from Duncan's shoulders. Their connection was so fierce, she nearly sighed when his mouth lifted into a small grin.

"Tara is right, *Mathair,*" he said to his mother in Gaelic. "I could use fresh water and a change of clothes."

Lora said nothing, and everyone watched as the eldest son left the room. Only when the women took their seats did the men sit down.

The conversation flowed after that.

Except for Finlay, who stared, with a smirk on his face and a twinkle in his eye.

~~~~

Duncan, on the other hand, struggled with the decision to shave his skin bare. He had done so before his journey, knowing he would blend more with the people. Now, he saw his reflection and heard Tara's voice vowing she wouldn't get close. He turned his blade over in his palm and considered his options.

He took his bath, replaying Tara's words in his mind. Her mere presence in the dining hall brought a smile to his face. He knew the pall hanging over their relationship had lifted slightly.

While water cooled around him, his eyes drifted down. Sleep was easy once he no longer sensed Tara's desire to leave.

~~~~

She didn't think it possible to adjust to Medieval Scotland. But adjust she did, and in a short amount of time.

About the time Tara would be settling into a new routine of classrooms and clinical work at a hospital, she was in a different type of school.

The school of the MacCoinnich clan.

As promised, Myra and Tara fell into a friendship more like a sisterhood. Myra was fascinated by Tara's stories of the twenty-first century. Her mind craved knowledge. She longed to know what the future would look like.

Tara spent her time observing everyone's behavior. She learned what was expected, what was proper, and what was not. Myra was Tara's personal sixteenth century encyclopedia.

The women wore dresses all the time. This wasn't a surprise to her, but getting used to it was. She longed for the simplicity of t-shirts and shorts. When she was alone in her room at night, she would slip into her twenty-first century clothes.

"Why do all of these men bow to your father?" Tara asked Myra while they watched the men train.

"My father is Laird over this land."

"What does that mean? Is he like a King or something?"

Myra laughed. "He might think he is at times, but nay. My father is the authority here, he and my brothers."

"Who gave him that title?"

"I suppose you could say it was his father, but in reality he earned it himself. My father has defended this land from the men who would take it. Although the sieges of the past are not as frequent of late."

Tara turned a worried look over to Myra. "Are you saying that at any time anyone could come along and take all of this from you? All they would have to do is fight you for it?"

Myra attempted a smile. "Aye. But don't worry. My family is strong. The men here would fight to the death to keep it from being occupied by another."

But Tara did worry. Being under siege might sound mysterious in a novel, but in her new reality it didn't seem the least bit romantic.

Myra explained that the people of the village depended on the MacCoinnich's for direction and safety. Ian and Lora would often counsel the population and, when needed, act as judge and jury to their troubles.

"How do you get used to all the people?" Tara rested her leg on a bench. "I can't go anywhere without running into someone."

"It was worse before my brothers started their journeys in the future. It was common for the knights and squires to spend their days and nights in the main hall."

"All of them?" Tara stared down at over two dozen men in the yard. All of them heaving heavy swords and sweating. Duncan's sweat didn't bother her, but the others... "I hope they bathed."

"They didn't!"

"Yuck!"

Myra chuckled. "It was quite horrible at times."

"I should be grateful I arrived when I did."

"My father needed privacy for this family, because of who we are. If you were to visit our neighbors in the North you would find their halls filled with men."

"These men here don't mind that they are treated differently?"

Myra nodded. "I think they prefer their privacy, as much as we do."

Tara scratched the nose of one of the dogs who prattled around after her. "What do they know about me?"

"That you are under Duncan's protection."

"Ha," Tara scoffed.

Myra went on, "They think you are distraught from the loss of a family member. They've been told to avoid approaching you at this time. Your accent will be difficult to explain. Even if you came from a neighboring village your speech wouldn't be as different as it is. You must keep who you are from them."

"I know. Your mom told me."

"It wouldn't hurt if you tried saying a few things as we do, aye and nay perhaps."

Tara smiled and took Myra's hand. "Now don't ye be worrying about me, lassie. I can hold me own."

Myra wiggled her nose. "That was much too Irish. I think it best you keep to your own accent. We wouldn't want the men to think you a spy."

Tara laughed.

Myra got up to leave. "I need to see to Amber and her studies. Would you like to join me?"

Tara skimmed her eyes over to Duncan and Fin who faced each other off. "I'll stay here if you don't mind. I could use a little time alone."

Myra nodded and went off.

Duncan and Finlay were quite literally, brothers in arms. They taught and exercised their fighting skills daily. Neighboring knights and their ladies sent their sons to train with them.

Duncan wielded his sword with little effort. He lifted it high above his head and twisted his body in all directions as if facing his enemy from all sides at once. There was none faster and more cunning on the battlefield. If his skill alone didn't set him apart in a crowd, his clean shaven face would have. He had kept it bare since she had emerged from her room weeks prior. He faced ridicule and jokes from his peers, but he didn't seem to mind.

She slipped from her perch and moved to get a closer look.

Tara sometimes caught him watching her, felt him trying to peer into her thoughts. Lora had provided valuable information advising her how to block him out of her mind. When Tara sensed Duncan peeking into her head, she purposely thought of a running river or some other body of water.

Sometimes, she pictured an animal playing or

running. These thoughts blocked and confused him. She even went so far as to sing rock songs in her head, which always brought a puzzled look to his face when she was near enough to see his expression.

At times like now, when he was busy training, he was too involved in what he was doing to notice her presence, or at least she hoped so. It wouldn't do any good to ignore him all day, and blow the effect by letting him know she was interested in how he spent his time.

So, she sat in the shadows of the massive Keep, sang a little Green Day, and watched the men sweat.

Life could be worse.

~~~~

Ian watched as his wife sat patiently with her needlework. "Have they even spoken two words since the first day?"

"Oh, one or two, but only when they cannot avoid it."

"I have to put an end to this nonsense. I hear rumblings from the men. Jacob asked if he could court her."

"We can tell the man Duncan is pursuing her, it's up to him to make it believable." She snipped off her thread and changed the color.

"How can he make it believable if they aren't even speaking?"

"Tara's needed this time, husband. Have a bit more faith in your son."

"I've never been as patient as you."

Lora nodded her head in agreement. "Growing up an only child has kept your patience short."

It was an age-old story, which bore repeating. "I grow tired, Lora. I want to see our children have families of their own."

"You make it sound like you're at death's door. We both know nothing could be further from the
~~~~

truth."

He ran his fingers through graying hair. "Myra is well past the age of eligibility. Why, by the time you were her age Duncan was almost two and Fin was well on his way to this world."

Lora removed her eyes from her embroidery and gazed at her husband. Stress and worry etched his face. She put her needlepoint aside and went to him. "My lord husband, do not take to heart these matters. I've seen the goodness ahead for our children. Myra's husband will come. Forcing her into a marriage was never an option and ye know it. All this needless concern will only remove precious years from them if you allow it to continue."

"What would I do without you?"

She laid her head in his lap and felt his hands stroking her hair. She wanted his apprehension over things he wasn't in control over to end. Because of her conviction, she kept from him the feeling she had been carrying with her since Tara had arrived. Lora sensed that after a short amount of happiness, turmoil would return.

Lora couldn't shake the feeling that something was coming.

Something evil.

~~~~

"How long are you going to give her?" Fin asked when he came up for air after sparring with his brother.

Duncan took a long drink from his cup. "As much as she needs."

"You've both been circling around each other for weeks. Even the men are starting to talk." He kept his voice low to keep their conversation private.

"Exactly what are they saying?"

Fin wasn't sure how much he should tell. "They ask if you have actually spoken for her, or if
~~~~

she's your leman."

Duncan whipped around catching his brother unaware, his eyes ablaze with anger. "Such gossip could ruin Tara's reputation. Who would question me?"

"Calm down." Fin spotted a beige skirt peaking from the shadows. "You must know how it looks from the outside. Neither one of you look to be the happy couple."

Fin formulated a plan in his mind to bring the couple in question closer. "I'm sure the talk is nothing. Come. Let us work with our swords."

Frustrated, and having a need to move, Duncan sparred with his brother. He worked out some necessary energy.

They danced around each other, practicing their blocking and agility. Duncan had pushed his brother twice into an un-defendable position. "You hesitate on that move every time. Any foe would see it as your weakness within a few minutes." Duncan helped his brother to his feet.

They started again.

Short of breath and giving under his brother's physical demand, Finlay glanced over his shoulder. "She watches us now."

Distracted, Duncan shot a look around to see where she was, knowing Fin spoke of Tara.

Fin took his opening and bested his brother. "Ahh...now I've found your weakness."

Again they circled. Each thrust and block more powerful than the last. "Women hate to see their men hurt or injured. I wonder how yours would act if you took a fall? Of course, it would have to look good."

"Most likely she'd thank the one who put me down."

Fin used his shield to block Duncan's blow. "Maybe. 'Tis only one way to find out." He didn't give his brother the chance to react. He kicked out his feet, tripping Duncan, and came upon him. Normally he would have stopped the sword from going near his skin. This time however, he let the blade connect enough to scratch and startle his brother, enough to bring blood to the surface.

Enough to rip a scream from the shadows of the Keep.

Tara came at a full run with skirts lifted to her knees. She pushed Fin aside. "Get out of my way, you big jerk."

Men stood back. Tara dropped to the ground, completely uncaring about the dirt or the scene she made in doing so.

She brushed aside Duncan's bloody hand clenching his side. "How bad is it?" She pushed away his chain mail to get a good look, but couldn't manage to see where the bleeding came from. Frantic, she struggled with his clothing.

Duncan stared at the top of her head. She smelled of roses. Her hands were soft on his skin, her voice purred concern for his well-being. He glanced at his brother and nodded his thanks.

The other men watched as Lady Tara took great care in helping Duncan to his feet. "We need to get you out of this thing."

Fin offered his help while holding back a smile.

"You've done enough already. You should be more careful. Save the actual blows for someone who deserves it."

"Aye, my lady." Fin bent in a mocking bow.

Tara noticed the men who gathered and watched. "The show's over cowboys. Why don't you all get back to work?"

The men watched her walk away. Daniel, Finlay's trusted friend, turned and asked, "What is a cowboy?"

Laughing, Fin shook his head, "I don't know."

Chapter 12

Duncan leaned on her as they slowly made their way up the stairs and she helped him into his rooms across the hall from hers.

When Megan saw them approach, she jumped to follow them.

"Fetch me hot water and clean cloths," Tara ordered.

Alone in his room, Tara pulled his chain mail over his head and helped him out of his tunic. Naked to the waist, he sat and watched her inspect his body. Small holes marred his skin.

Blood oozed making it difficult for her to see the damage. Megan soon returned with the supplies Tara requested. When she saw Duncan's half-naked body, she lowered her gaze and blushed like the virgin she was.

Tara rolled her eyes at the maid's blush and dismissed her with a flick of the hand.

Duncan shot her a quick grin she hardly noticed before she started to clean him up.

She drenched the cloth, rung it out and dabbed it over his wound. When he winced at her touch, she pulled back, warning him, "This is going to sting. Try and hold still."

He watched her clean away the already dried blood. Her touch was tender, even if her words had a bite to them. "Your brother should be more careful. He could have done some serious damage."

Tara leaned back and studied her handiwork. A small amount of bruising already formed, but none of the cuts were deep enough to cause any worry about infection. "The chain thing you wear helped keep this from being worse, even if it contributed to a bit of the damage."

She glanced at him, his eyes were shut, his fingers clenched. "Does it hurt that bad?" She reached a hand and touched his cheek.

"Nay, lass. Not so much."

"Still, I think you should take it slow for the rest of the day." She moved to take the bowl of grimy water away from the bed. "You don't want any dirt getting in your wound. Maybe your mother has some type of salve to put on the worst of them to keep out bacteria." She returned to his side, and sat on the edge of the bed.

"What is this thing you call bacteria?"

"Germs?"

He was still puzzled.

"Microscopic organisms that cause infection?"

"Microscopic?"

Her eyes narrowed. "Germs are small bugs that make you sick."

"What do you know about stopping these germs from making an infection?"

She leaned against the post of his bed and started to explain. "Keeping wounds clean makes a big difference. Staying healthy so your body's defenses have a chance to heal helps, but the biggest power against infection are antibiotics. You're going to have to wait until the 1800's before any of that will be available."

"We'll have to stay healthy and avoid cuts," he said.

She laughed at his conclusion. "Don't make me laugh. I'm still mad at you."

He forced his smile into submission. "As you wish."

They stared at each other, silent.

"I've missed you, Tara."

He sat across from her. His lazy smile melted her resistance. The sight of his rippled chest muscles made certain parts of her body clench. Her desire for him increased, growing with each moment. "I've missed you, too."

His hand, heavy and strong, reached for hers. "I hope you know if I could have done things differently, I would have."

His touch made her heart beat faster. His words reached out and touched her soul. "I know. Your mother explained everything to me." She let her thumb stroke his fingers. "It didn't change the outcome. I needed some time."

"Have you had enough time?"

Her eyes moved from their joined hands to his sexy mouth. From there, she sought his gaze. "It takes a lot of energy staying pissed-off at you."

"Am I forgiven?"

"I haven't heard an apology yet." She was half joking.

"Is that what you've been waiting for? An apology?" He moved closer. She didn't have any room to back away. Not that she would have.

"It wouldn't hurt."

He inched closer.

She moved in.

"I'm sorry to have caused you such grief, Tara. I'm not sorry for keeping you from Grainna, or for keeping you alive."

"I should be thanking you I suppose," she said against his lips.

He used her words. "It wouldn't hurt."

"Thank you, Duncan, for saving my life." She looked down at his smiling lips.

A lifetime could have passed in the moments before her lips met his.

Her mouth opened in silent invitation, which he accepted greedily. Their kiss was a homecoming. Much more than a meeting of their lips.

Her hands reached into his hair, hair she had dreamed of running her fingers through daily since they met. Even when she was angry at him she couldn't get him out of her mind. Every resistant bone in her body melted when he angled his head and deepened their kiss.

Duncan lowered her to his bed. Butterflies with wings the size of dragons filled her belly. Her hands drifted to his back and she pulled him on top of her so his weight pinned her in place. The long length of his body felt delicious against hers.

Tara dug her nails into his flesh. A moan of pleasure escaped him.

When his hand slid up her side, molded to her breast, a sob of pure pleasure burst from her throat.

The door flung open and banged against the stone wall.

They sprung apart.

The sensation of Duncan's lovely body heat, the sheer weight of him, suddenly disappeared. His absence left a cool breeze drifting across her bare breasts.

Stunned, they gaped at the open doorway where Lora stood inside the frame with wide eyes. Amusement rapidly replaced her look of worry.

Tara recovered first. She pushed Duncan back, attempting to adjust her clothing. "Ah..." *What's her name?* "Mrs. Mac Coin..."

Duncan's laugh didn't help.

"Lady..."

Lora took the lead and added to Tara's stress. "You can call me, hmmm..." She tapped her chin with a finger. "Let me see... what is the term you use? Mom. Aye, you can call me Mom, if this is what I should expect to discover when entering a room with you two within."

Unnerved, Tara scrambled to her feet. She felt like a teenager caught in a compromised position in the backseat of a car by her parents. "Duncan had a... Well he was, ah, hurt." The word came from Duncan's thoughts. "Aye hurt. I ah...came here to help him." *Yes, that's right.* "He could use any salve you might have to keep his..."

Wound, Duncan said in his mind.

"Thank you." She turned to Duncan's smiling face. "Wound, from getting infected."

Tara fled Duncan's room without further word.

Outside, Tara leaned against the closed door trying her best to catch her breath. She heard Lora.

"I never dreamt, in my wildest dreams, I would be happy to walk in on this..."

Tara shook her head and walked away before she heard more.

~~~~

At the evening meal everyone noticed the difference between Duncan and Tara.

Amber spoke up first. "They're not mad at each other anymore?" she asked her mother.

Duncan and Tara hid their grins. Fin sent a 'you owe me' smile to his brother.

Lora slid her hand under the table to her husband who had been given every detail about the encounter she had witnessed.

Myra's eyes darted back and forth between Tara and her brother. Her eyes widened in question, but she made no comment.

All in all, the meal was more pleasant than any since Tara had arrived. Even Cian had gotten over his infatuation with Tara enough to talk about joining in the practice of fighting the next day.

Especially with Duncan being hurt so bad.

Balance had been restored.

~~~~

Myra pounced on Tara's bed long before the cock crowed, her eyes ablaze with excitement.

"I do not want all the details, he *is* my brother, but I do want to know what happened?" She didn't give Tara time to talk. "I overheard my mother say she walked in on you both…" Myra grinned.

She may have been twenty-one years old, but she acted like a teenager, bouncing on the bed. Tara sighed and pushed herself up, shook the sleep from her head. Tara told her the bland facts withholding from Duncan's sister the gist of what she was asking.

"Duncan was hurt."

Myra nodded.

"It was a nasty abrasion that needed to be cleaned. I'm not sure those chain garments they wear are the best thing. I think they cause more harm than—"

Myra cut her off. "I don't care about that."

"Right, well, you know, Duncan and I were ahh, involved before he brought me here?"

"How involved?" Myra waited.

"Let's just say your brother is an expert kisser."

"Duncan?" She wrinkled her nose at the thought.

"Sorry to burst your bubble, but Duncan, your brother, sure knows how to kiss. I've never been so tempted to..." Tara stopped. Sex simply wasn't thought of the same way in this time as it was in her time. Telling Myra how tempted she was might give her the wrong ideas. Proper women in this age didn't lose their virginity until they were married. Especially when the woman was one of privilege and stature, as was Myra's case.

"...to what?" Myra asked.

"To keep on kissing him." That was lame, even to her. Myra didn't buy it either.

"Come on, Tara. Tell me more."

"All we did was kiss. I swear." Tara held up her right hand.

"But you wanted to do more, right?"

Would it hurt to tell the truth? "Yes, I did. For

the first time ever in my life, I considered…more." Was that too much information?

"You know what *more* is, don't you?" Myra asked.

"I do. But..."

"My ma won't tell me the details. Only that it shouldn't happen unless you are promised or married to the man."

Sighing with relief, Tara agreed. "She is so right." Her valley girl was coming out. "All men will want to. They can't help themselves. So make sure the one is...The One!" Tara wrinkled her nose at her words. She sounded like a prude.

"Tell me what the *more* is, Tara."

Shit! Shit! Shit! Myra wasn't about to let her off the hook. It wasn't her place. Or was it? Didn't she have a similar conversation with her sister growing up?

"Tell me what you think 'it' is."

"Well..." Myra blushed. Shyness crept over her, which hadn't been present before. "I've seen animals. Last year Durk was bred to one of the stable mares. I wasn't supposed to watch, but I snuck down and took a glimpse. The sheep in the fields have similar ways of mating."

The image of two rutting animals had Tara squeezing her eyes shut. "Well...the basics are the same from what I've heard. Remember I haven't... You know… But I do know many women who have made love and weren't afraid to tell me what they knew." Tara took Myra's hand and made sure she had her full attention. "It's supposed to be more magical, more special between people. Animals simply fill a need." She stopped and frowned. "I suppose some men fall in that category. To be fair some women do as well." She thought of her sister and her years of peril raising a child on her own. "Every time can mean you will…well, become with child. So you want to be with someone worthy of being a father to your children."

Myra squeezed her hand, and acknowledged her advice. "But, when you wanted *more,* it was wonderful? Right?"

Smiling, Tara flopped back on her bed. "Honey, you have no idea."

~~~~

They were finishing up the first meal of the day. Cian had already left the table, anxious to train with the men. Amber went to see if one of the expectant cats had given birth during the night.

"Well, brother," Fin said. "What will you do with this day since you have to rest your injuries?" He slid a smirk in Tara's direction.

"My *injuries* are not so great I can't join you. It seems I owe you." *In more ways than one.*

"Are you sure you wouldn't want to rest?" Fin tilted his head toward Tara.

Duncan debated his answer.

Ian saved him the trouble. "I have need of you for another task, Duncan," Ian told him. "It seems the widow and Haggart are once again fighting."

"Not again," Myra said. "Seldom has a day gone by where they don't have trouble. I've noticed their rife increasing since her daughter married."

"I'm told Haggart's dog trampled her garden, destroying her food supply. I need you to see if she has any claim. If so, see he compensates her accordingly."

Disappointed about not spending the day with Tara, Duncan sighed. "I'll see it done."

He was ready to leave the table when his father's next comment stopped him.

"Take Tara with you," Ian said and turned his focus to Tara. "I don't believe you've been to the village, lass. You're sure to enjoy the experience. Take Myra's mare. The ride will do you good."

"Oh," Tara said in alarm. "I—I don't know how to ride."
~~~~

Looks of disbelief came at her from all directions. "Other than riding along with Duncan, I have never been on a horse."

"Then today will be a wonderful adventure for you. Myra's is the most gentle among our mares. Duncan is an excellent horseman. He can teach you."

"What a lovely idea, Ian. I can't wait to see more of Scotland."

Ian took her hand. "You'll love our land."

"I'm sure I will and Myra, you won't mind me taking your horse?"

Myra waved away her concern. "Nay, Meg will treat you well."

Tara turned to Duncan, "And you, you're sure you won't mind me tagging along?"

"'Tis my pleasure."

How much pleasure? Tara wondered with a secret smile.

"You'll need a cloak," Myra said. "In case the weather turns before your return. Come with me. We'll find you one." Myra tugged on her arm, laughing.

Chapter 13

Within the hour Tara stood in front of Myra's horse. The massive animal had a beautiful chestnut coat with a tuft of white on her nose. She was calm, quiet, and huge. One of the stable hands tossed a small saddle over the blanket placed across her broad back as Tara watched.

Myra did the introductions. "Meg, this is my friend, Tara. Now, I have told her of your sweet disposition, so don't make me a liar." Myra turned to Tara. "She really is quite calm. I'm sure you'll be able to handle her well enough."

Tara wasn't so sure. Maybe she should ride with Duncan on Durk. It would be easier than riding Meg alone.

"Horses can sense when you're afraid." Duncan led his mount toward the women. "Let the horse know who you are, and that you are the master."

"I don't feel much like a master." Tara sent him a wry look. "And I'm scared to death."

He handed his reins to a squire who stood by. "Here," he took Tara's hand, and placed her palm on Meg's nose. "This way she can smell you and become familiar with you." He leaned in, sniffed her hair and sent a shot of awareness through her body. "Ahh, lass, like roses."

His attention brought a flush to her face.

"I see I'm no longer needed here." Myra's face turned red. "Have a wonderful ride."

Tara choked on a laugh. The word ride had so many meanings, and with Duncan sniffing her hair, it was hard to keep her mind on the horse instead of on erotic thoughts about him

Myra's eyes grew large. She laughed a nervous little sound and covered her smile with her hand. "I mean *time*... Have a wonderful time."

When Tara grinned, Myra's face turned scarlet before she scurried away.

Duncan watched his sister's haste. "What would she know of *that* kind of riding?"

Tara's laugh grew deeper. "About as much as me I'm afraid."

"How much is that?" His frown grew deeper.

"Enough to know the word 'riding' can have more than one meaning." She watched her words sink in.

"I doubt my sister knows any such thing."

"Men are so naïve," Tara said under her breath.

"Myra hasn't been exposed to the ways between a man and a woman."

"So, you assume she knows nothing?" They faced each other now. The squire holding Durk's reins took a step back.

"Of course she knows nothing. She's innocent." Anger dipped into his voice.

Tara rolled her eyes. "Let me ask you something. When you were *innocent,* how much did you know? How much had you been told or figured out on your own?"

Duncan started to squirm, clearly not comfortable with the direction the conversation had turned.

"Uhh huh, I thought so. I'll let you in on a little secret." She leaned in for effect and lowered her voice. "Women talk! Even us virgins. We also have hormones urging us toward certain needs. God made us that way so the world would repopulate. Or, don't you pay attention in church?"

His astounded look made her break out in laughter. "Come on, cowboy. We have somewhere to be." She took in the massive horse she was supposed to ride. “How do I get up on this thing?”

“Twenty-first century women,” he muttered, but the words came out with a tinge of humor.

“My Lady?” He made a grand gesture of bending down so she could put her foot in his hands to hoist herself up.

Enjoying the game, Tara replied, “My Lord.” A short bow and two attempts to get up into the saddle had Tara halfway there. “Now, how do I make it go?” She wiggled her butt, making sure she was secure on the animal. “I just kick, right?”

Before he could respond, she dug her heals into Meg, who responded with a jump, lunge, run combo. Duncan chased the horse and rider down as Tara hung on for dear life.

He caught up to Tara and poor Meg quickly. When he pulled up alongside, he took her reins, slowing the horse to a walk. He coaxed, “Easy.”

Slightly frightened and exhilarated at the same time, all Tara could manage was, “Wow!”

“You might be thinking a bit more than ‘wow,’ if she had tossed you on your arse. Don’t scare me like that again. Next time ask, before you do.”

Tara nodded. “Check, ask before I kick. Got it. Now what, boss?”

Flashes of her falling off the horse raced in his mind and translated to her. She had frightened him taking off as she did. Instead of commenting on her observation, Tara calmed her beating heart and waited patiently for his next command. She smiled at his gruff expression until his bottom lip wavered. Soon he smiled back.

“Why don’t you let Meg follow me?”

“How do you know...? Ohh...” Meg started after him without provocation. “All right, this is easy,” Tara agreed after a few minutes.

“Riding is not difficult, after a bit of practice.”

She couldn’t help herself. He did walk into it. “What riding would you be referring to, laddie?”

She added a bit of his accent.

His blush hit before his laughter.

"Sorry, I couldn't resist."

"I've never met anyone like you, lass." They rode side by side.

"Is that a compliment?"

"Aye, I think it is."

"Good."

Tara pulled up the skirt, freeing her ability to move more comfortably.

"You'll have to pull your dress down when we get closer to the village," he reminded her.

"I know. But I didn't think you would mind."

He traced her leg with his eyes. "Nay, I don't mind."

"Good."

They fell into a steady pace in silence before Duncan asked. "What do you think of my family?"

Glad to have him asking easy questions, she gave her answers freely. "Your mother is amazing. Strong, beautiful…you have her eyes. Wise. I really admire a woman who can be a mom and a wife and do both well."

Duncan smiled, obviously pleased with her praise. He listened when she went on.

"She hardly has any time for herself. She's either planning meals, directing the help, counseling villagers or handling any number of other tasks. Not to mention caring for Amber and Cian, who are both still very needy. Not Cian so much, but Amber still needs extra attention. Lora knows exactly when she's needed. It really is uncanny how she always knows what to do." She took a breath and continued. It was as if she stored up all the days of not talking, and she finally had the opportunity to express herself.

"Your dad can be a bit frightening. His power over everyone is eerie. He deserves everyone's respect, don't get me wrong, but I'm not used to seeing people bow down to anyone. His sense of justice is really honed. I guess it would have to be with so many people to watch over."

"My father is deserving of his title."

"I couldn't agree more. You'll follow in his footsteps. The men respect you like they do your father."

"I've fought by their sides many times in the past."

Tara ignored the chill running down her back at the mention of fighting. "Fin, now Fin's a player."

"What is a player?"

"A ladies' man. I'll bet he has women falling all over him wherever he goes. I guess that's why you were both sent to the future. The virgins didn't stand a chance."

Duncan laughed at her assessment.

"Now Myra," Tara went on. "She's like your mom. A hopeless romantic. I know arranged marriages are common for this time, but I tell you, she'd wither and die in a loveless marriage."

"What makes you say that?"

"She needs more, I don't know, more passion, romance. Anything less than a knight-in-shining armor and she'd turn up her nose."

"She's told you this?" he asked.

"Not in so many words. It's only my opinion."

"Is there anyone Myra has an eye for?"

"She hasn't told me if there is and I think she would." Tara took in the hillside, her thoughts grew distant. "She reminds me of my sister."

"I didn't know you had a sister."

"Lizzy. She's two years older than me. Now, she is a hopeless romantic. For all the good it did her."

"Tell me." His look was full of questions and concern.

"Lizzy had a hard start. She fell for her high

school sweetheart, her first real love. He was nice enough, in the beginning at least. They dated for awhile."

"What is dated?"

"Courted, is how you would say it."

"So your father approved of this man."

Tara laughed. "He was a boy, not a man. Only one year older than my sister. My dad was too busy working to notice his eldest daughter falling in love. My mother noticed, but she believed in the 'don't ask don't tell' theory. She figured she'd completed her job when she warned us about what boys want, and expected us not to do it."

"Ahh, it sounds like what mothers tell their daughters in this time as well."

"Lizzy did do *it*. She thought she loved him. He told her he loved her too, and before long they started sleeping together. Within a few months she was pregnant."

"Your time has protection against pregnancy, does it not?"

"Accidents still happen even with those precautions." Tara breathed in the cool air. "My dad flipped when he found out. My mom cried. Lizzy's boyfriend denied all responsibility."

"What? He was a coward."

Tara was surprised to hear resentment in his reply. "Yes, he was a coward, a kid. I imagine he was scared to death at the possibility of his life being over at seventeen. His parents moved out of state when they heard Lizzy was going to keep the baby."

"What do you mean?"

"Oh, that's right. You don't have abortions here. Well..."

She picked her words carefully. "If a woman doesn't want the baby, a doctor can stop the pregnancy. Lizzy never considered that an option. Giving the baby to someone else to raise wasn't an option for her either. So, she had Simon.

"He's Amber's age now. Lizzy found a job working in a daycare. She has always struggled to make it work. But she has, somehow."

"Your parents didn't help?" Disgust laced his words.

"No. As soon as she turned eighteen, they kicked her and Simon out." Tara narrowed her eyes at the painful memory. "I finished high school six months early and left home. Once I was out of the house, they moved somewhere in Arizona. I haven't heard or seen them since. But Lizzy and I were very close. Her son Simon is the greatest kid."

They rode is silence for awhile, both caught up in their own thoughts. Neither of them snuck into the other's mind.

Breaking the solemn mood, Tara asked, "How long will it take us to get to the village?"

"At this pace it will take us 'till mid-day."

"Which means we would be getting back after dark. Is it safe?" She glanced toward the woods and thought of thieves living in them.

"I can protect you, Tara."

She noted the massive sword strapped to his waist, his straight back and ruffled hair reminded her she had nothing to fear. No self-respecting criminal would willingly clash swords with him. He would protect her and look good while doing it! *He is the definition of eye candy.* She forgot to block the words from him.

An image of a child's sucker being popped into her mouth came straight from Duncan's mind. She watched his laughing eyes, their expression bordered on seductive. He drew his horse closer.

"Would you like a taste?"

Her teeth caught her bottom lip. "Maybe a little." What harm could come on the back of a horse?

He dropped his lips to hers, like every time they connected, Tara felt shudders of pleasure drifting down her body.

Unable to keep her thoughts to herself, Tara moaned inside and out. *I want more.* Her hand resting on his chest moved over his body, searching for skin-to-skin contact.

The horses pushed away from each other, breaking their contact.

Tara, feeling off balance, struggled to keep her seat.

Duncan struggled in a different way. The effect of their brief contact had his leggings tight, and his position on the back of his horse was uncomfortable.

Tara struggled to keep from smiling when she read what Duncan thought.

"You're thinking this funny are you?"

Not able to stop, Tara started laughing so hard she doubled over and had to hold her sides for support. "I'm sorry, really." His serious look made her laugh even harder. Tears fell with every renewed giggle. "Maybe you should go back to wearing a kilt."

"Perhaps I will."

Tara imagined his ease with seduction while wearing such clothing. She quickly stopped laughing after reading his thoughts.

He changed the subject and kept her busy with instructions on riding until they reached the edge of the village.

Tara gawked at the sights. The village was right off the pages of a novel. Thatched roofs on top of simple buildings blotted the landscape. Smoke from cooking fires rose out of pits both in and outside the dwellings. Children ran free along with dogs and an occasional chicken.

People stopped what they were doing and watched when they approached. Greetings came in the form of waves and an occasional bow.

Tara noticed a few mules corralled or hooked up to an occasional cart and asked, "Where are all their horses?"

"Not many villagers can afford the luxury of a mount. Those that do are in the outlying fields working the summer harvest or herding sheep. They prepare all spring and summer for our long winters."

"Oh." Long winters weren't something she thought much about after years of living in Southern California. Instead of dwelling on the unknown, Tara noticed a cart loaded with what looked like dirty cotton. "...and over there?" Tara pointed to the cart.

"Wool, from the sheep. The women will comb out the dirt, divide it up into colors. Some will be dipped and dyed for fabric, some will be spun for blankets." He had more to tell, but she was already moving on to the next question.

"...and that?"

"Our resident smith."

"And there, do you have someone who makes glass here?"

"Aye, we do."

"I remember reading once that people in this time often were sick from lead poisoning. I noticed most of the dishes and cooking surfaces are some type of iron. Do you know if they contain lead?"

"Some I suppose."

"You might consider having him make more of the cooking and eating surfaces."

Duncan nodded at her. "Aye, I will."

The scent of baked apples filled the air. "Mmm... what smells so good?"

"Mrs. Claunch. She makes the best sweet pies. Would you like one?" He signaled for a nearby lad to fetch the leads of his horse after he dismounted. Duncan took her by the waist, and helped her from the horse.

"Thank you, my Lord," she teased.

"The pleasure is mine, my Lady." He swept her fingers in his hand, and brushed the back of them with his lips.

They stared at each other.

You sure have the moves.

Are they working then, Tara love?

Instead of answering, she kept his hand from dropping hers and placed it above her rapidly beating heart. *You tell me?*

The clearing of someone's throat stopped him from capturing her lips. He turned to see Mrs. Claunch dusting flour from her hands.

"Lord Duncan, give the girl some room, lad. She looks a bit flushed to me."

Holding Tara possessively around the waist, he led her to Mrs. Claunch. "She smells the aroma of your lovely cakes, lass. Might you have some to spare for a pair of hungry travelers?"

Mrs. Claunch, long past her *lass* days, blushed at his words.

Tara sent Duncan a hidden *'you big flirt'* message. His hand squeezed hers signaling he heard her.

"Mrs. Claunch, I want you to meet Lady Tara."

"I had heard of a new Lady at the Keep. 'Tis nice to match a face to the name." Mrs. Claunch looked Tara up and down with a smile. "Come, come. No need to stand in the street."

They entered a large room with a cook's fire. It held a table with four wooden chairs. A larger chair laden down with blankets was obviously where Mrs. Claunch spent her days. A much smaller room appeared to hold a bed was toward the back.

"Sit please. Have ye eaten?"

"We ate before we left the Keep," Duncan told her.

"No wonder your Lady looks like she does. Starving her, are ye?" Mrs. Claunch moved to the fire and pulled out the skillet holding the object of the mouth-watering aroma.

It was some type of apple bread or cake, Tara thought. "Can I help you?"

"No, my lady. I have it."

"Call me Tara."

Pleased at the request, Mrs. Claunch moved to place her hot skillet on the table.

Tara noticed an iron trivet and quickly placed it down for their hostess.

Mrs. Claunch patted Tara's cheek and smiled. "I like your Lady, my Lord. Ye must bring her back to see me."

"Once she tastes your treats, I'll have a hard time keeping her away."

Mrs. Claunch set a kettle on for tea and then took a seat with her guests. "Tell me news of the Keep."

Duncan filled her in on the comings and goings of those in the main house. He talked of Amber's kittens and how she would be looking for homes for them when they were old enough.

Mrs. Claunch's movements were slow and well thought out. Tara thought she suffered from arthritis, and did her best to assist the woman while they enjoyed her apple cakes.

When the water boiled in the kettle, Tara moved quickly to pour the tea.

Duncan gave her a nod of approval.

When it was time for them to go, Tara helped Mrs. Claunch to her feet. "Thank you for the delicious cake. Perhaps you would show me how to make them sometime? I've never tasted anything quite like them."

"I would love to." Mrs. Claunch said her goodbyes and sent them off with a bag of cakes to take back.

"She was very nice." Tara said to Duncan when they walked away.

"Aye, she is. By day's end she'll have spoken to every woman in the village singing your praises."

"I doubt that."

"There is little to entertain our people. Your kindness will be talked about for weeks."

"My kindness? She was the one who cooked. All I did was eat. She wouldn't even let me help with the dishes."

"I believe you are the first Lady to volunteer to do her dishes."

"We both know I'm no more a 'Lady' than she is," Tara said.

"Nay, Tara. You are in every way a Lady."

The widow's cottage was like Mrs. Claunch's home. Straight across was Haggart's. His offensive dog slept peacefully by the door.

"We'll talk with the widow first." Duncan took stock of the darkening sky. The clouds forming overhead worried him. The time it would take to bring closure to the neighboring feud would mean they would return to the Keep in the rain.

"We could save a little time if we talk to each of them separately." Tara tapped her head. "We can use our special communication skills to work out a solution."

"Are you sure?" he asked. *You've been working hard to keep me out of your beautiful head.*

It's all the MacCoinnich charm you've been oozing today. It makes me want to try something new. "You'll need to introduce me first." Tara mimicked Duncan's actions when he tied his horse to a pole.

The widow was much younger than Tara was led to believe. She was incredibly beautiful and looked like she was less than forty-five years old. Even her name sounded young, Celeste.

Tara suspected, just as Myra thought, Celeste

was lonely after marrying her daughter off only two years before. Widowed when her daughter was only ten, she had spent many of her best years without male companionship, and her loneliness showed.

After Duncan introduced Tara, he made his way to Haggart's, where the horribly vicious dog licked him enthusiastically when he reached down to pet him in greeting.

"Ahh, Lord Duncan. To what honor do I owe your presence?"

"I've come to speak with ye on behalf of my father."

A small frown passed Haggart's face. "Come in, come in. I have an excellent ale I was about to pour." Haggart, shy of his fiftieth birthday, welcomed the future Laird of Coinnich into his home like he had many times in the past.

"What happened with the dog, Celeste?" Tara accepted the water she gave.

"He trampled my vegetables is what he did. I had one this big." She lifted her hands showing what she meant. "It was about to turn red."

"How did he get in your garden?" Tara had noticed the small fence surrounding her precious vegetables when she walked in.

"The gate was open while I tended the plants. That mangy mutt walked right in like he owned the place and made a mess. Haggart should keep better care of his dog." Tara sensed calm when Celeste talked of the dog and anger when she spoke of its owner.

Tara listened while Celeste went on and on of other times Haggart had neglected his animal and she was *forced* to care for it. "Who leaves their animals to themselves overnight with no one to feed them?"

Tara turned her thoughts into words, words she hoped Duncan would hear. *I think Celeste has the hots for your friend Haggart.*

Duncan's reply was instant. *What is* the hots?

Passion! I think she likes him. I'm sensing a love-hate vibe.

Duncan peered over his cup at Haggart.

"I'll tell ye she's impossible. She pets Max every chance she gets. The second he acts like a dog, she cries foul."

"Ye believe she invited this on herself? Max digging up her vegetables?"

"I wouldn't be surprised. Why the other day she had me hauling water for her, saying Max drank the supply she left on her step. Why put water on your step when a thirsty dog sat feet away? Answer me that?"

"Maybe the widow needed some help carrying the heavy load?" Duncan suggested.

"Her name is Celeste. A widow she is, but for over eight years now." Haggart's voice softened. "I don't think she appreciates the title."

Duncan sent his thoughts across the street. *Aye, love, I think you're right. Haggart has* the hots *for his neighbor.*

Poor Max is in the middle. Tara told him.

What shall we do?

They need a little nudge. Try and see if Haggart will come to her defense if you suggest she is accusing him falsely. I'll do the same. If they take the bait, I'll suggest she try befriending Haggart by fixing him a meal or something.

"Well my friend," Duncan said. "Perhaps 'tis time we move Celeste from her home. If she's accusing you falsely of foul play, she should be punished."

Haggart's eyes grew wide, his jovial smile vanished. "Ahh well, wait just a minute. True the woman exaggerates a fair bit, but there is no denying Max spent time in her garden. To punish her wouldn't be right. I think ye should leave this matter to me. I'd hate to see the poor, old widow suffer because of me."

Tara grinned over her cup. "If you really think Haggart deserves it, I'll see that Duncan moves him, and his terrible dog."

"What? Nay, 'tis not... I mean to say." Celeste took a breath. "I think my Lady, Haggart and I can come to some agreement on the animal. I shouldn't have left my gate open. Some fault lies with me."

Both parties met in the street when Tara and Duncan left. Neither spoke an unkind word to each other. Instead, they talked of the couple who trotted down the dirt road on their way back to the Keep.

"They make a lovely couple, don't you agree?" Celeste asked.

"A couple?" Haggard tilted his head, considered his Lord's actions. "Are ye sure?"

"Aye, I'm as sure of that as I am they will meet with rain before they get back to the Keep." She snuck a glance at her handsome neighbor.

"It does have the feel for rain." Haggart looked over to her cottage. "That roof looks in need of repair, Celeste. Maybe I could help with what needs fixin' before the rainy season begins again."

"I'd appreciate that." Celeste reached down to scratch Max behind his ears, a small smile pealed at the corners of her mouth. "If ye haven't any supper on the fire, I've made enough for two tonight. Ye could come by if ye had a mind to."

"I never was much of a cook I'm afraid."

"Fine then, bring Max. We wouldn't want him finding another garden to frolic in."

"Nay, we wouldn't be wanting that."

Chapter 14

Ian MacCoinnich stood on the highest point of his home and scanned the skies. Clouds had blown in from the sea during the day, hinting at the rain, which would come sometime in the night.

Tonight would be entirely too late for his needs.

He closed his eyes, opened his arms and lifted his palms to the sprinkling of sun he wanted to disappear. Then he called his gift.

The wind slowly started to shift. With more effort, Ian brought darker clouds and the rumble of thunder. The moisture sent a spray of feather soft mist into the air. The bones of the old and broken would feel the shift in pressure as it dropped.

Soon the mist turned to small droplets of water. When the sky was completely clouded over, and his hair dripped with rain, Ian let his hands drop. A satisfied smile broke across his face.

Below, Lora watched her husband with arms folded across her chest. She tried prying into his mind only to find herself shut out. When the air cooled and the wind started to blow, understanding dawned.

Duncan would be headed back by now with Tara in tow. If a storm kept them from making the entire journey, Duncan would seek shelter at one of the many cabins between the Keep and the village.

Lora laughed. Her husband was such a smart man.

~~~~

Duncan and Tara were smug in their accomplishment as they rode out of town.
~~~~

"I'll bet they're together within a week."

"It won't take that long. You should have seen Haggart when I suggested the widow was not telling the truth and needed to be punished."

"Celeste was ticked when I told her the vicious dog should be put down. Then when I told her you planned on moving Haggart to a different part of the village if things didn't settle, her story changed." Tara reached over, patted him on his shoulder. "We make a great team."

"That we do, lass. That we do."

Lightning split the sky, causing them both to look up and jump. "Looks like we're going to get wet." Tara pulled her cloak tighter and lifted the hood over her hair.

The next boom of thunder threatened a decent sized storm. Meg skipped a step when the sound filled the sky. Duncan's hand darted out, calming the animal instantly.

They rode in silence for a few minutes before the rain started to fall and Duncan shouted over the sounds of thunder, "I think we should find shelter." Already soaked to the skin in a few short minutes, Tara yelled her agreement.

They changed course while torrents of rain pelted down. Duncan kept the horses at a brisk trot, not wanting them to bolt when the lightning danced in the sky.

The cottage was small and dark. But most important, it was dry. Duncan quickly helped Tara inside, then rushed to care for the horses.

Tara shook out her cloak and hung it on a hook beside the door. The sack of food Mrs. Claunch had given them for Ian and Lora would have to do until the rain let up. After wiping off the only table, Tara set their provisions down and searched the cupboard for cups.

A small bed, covered with blankets, dominated the space. Tara fluffed off the collected dust, scattering any spiders from their would-be home.

Even inside, Tara could see her breath. She noticed the fireplace and pined for a match. There was wood outside stacked up on the porch so she knew once Duncan returned, they wouldn't be cold.

It was nice having a personal fire starter, she thought. Until he returned from dealing with the horses, she curled up under one of the blankets to keep from shivering.

~~~~

Duncan lingered outside longer than necessary. It didn't take him long to pen up the animals and feed them grain, but he dawdled.

Inside the small cabin was a woman he desired more than life itself. He accounted his rampant emotions to the vows they took, but somewhere deeper, he knew it was more. There would be no interruptions from anyone or anything once he passed through the door of the cottage.

As sure as the sun would shine the next day, he knew he would have her. Their passion had simmered long enough.

She was his wife, even if she didn't know it yet.

Duncan wondered if he should tell her, before... then decided against it. The knowledge would shock and anger her. He wanted her passionate, not irate. With a temper as lethal as the color of her hair, he wouldn't chance confronting her with the facts until she was his, completely.

Confident in his plan, he squared his shoulders and entered the cabin.

She sat balled up on the bed, shaking like a leaf in the wind.

"Why didn't you start a fire?"

"Withhh whaat?" she chattered.

He went to the fireplace with palms spread, called one flame, then another. He placed a log
~~~~

inside the hearth and kept his hands elevated until it caught.

The atmosphere in the room changed with the glowing light of the fire. "I should have started one before I left to do my chores."

"It's o-okay." Tara held her hands in an effort to stop her body from shaking. But with her hair and clothes drenched, her effort was useless. She shrugged off the blanket and stood near the fire. "D-do you think you can show me how you d-do that?"

He removed his own wet outer garments and hung them with hers. "Of course, maybe once you've warmed up." His hands rubbed the chill from her arms.

"You need to get out of this." He helped unlace her gown, trying not to notice her silky skin. Her chemise wasn't very wet and covered most of her.

Duncan pulled a chair close to the fire and encouraged her to sit. He took his boots off and laid them with her clothing to dry.

While Tara combed her fingers through her wet hair, Duncan wondered what she thought, and probed into her mind just a little.

The song she sang in her head made him smile. She avoided his eyes as he put his belongings in place for the night. Under lowered lids, her eyes shifted to the narrow bed. Her fists clenched.

"Why so nervous, love?"

"Nervous?" Warmer now, Tara played idly with her hair. "Who says I'm nervous?"

"If not nervous, than what?" He sat on the edge of the bed.

"I'm just...thinking, wondering really." She huffed out a breath, pulled in another and spit out the next words, "Yeah, I'm nervous!"

Her hands shook more, even though the chill had left the room.

"Why?"

"You. Me. Us."

"Why?"

"Because, we can't be alone together without jumping on each other, that's why."

He hid his smirk. "This is a problem?"

"Damn straight it is. Maybe not for you, you won't have to be the one raising the potential consequences of it. I will." Her words came out in one steady stream.

She was thinking beyond the now, and it scared her. And it cheapened him.

"You think so little of my honor? You believe I would leave you to 'raise the consequences' by yourself?"

"No. Yes. I don't know." She stood and put some space between them.

Her conclusion had angered him. He got up and paced while she talked.

"Listen, Duncan, I can't deny our strong physical attraction anymore than you can. But it isn't like we've made any promises to each other. Anything could happen when we..." Her eyes shot to the bed. Let the obvious go un-said.

He reached her in one step. Holding her face in his hands, he forced their eyes to meet. "Look at me," he demanded. "Into me. What do you see?"

Tara tried pulling away from him. Doubt crept over her, showing its ugly face in her mind. "I can't."

"Look!"

Smoldering eyes leveled to hers. Her body started to relax, her vision blurred and mixed with his. Duncan forced his thoughts into her mind. Finally, she saw herself through his eyes, passion churning in his blood, through his veins.

His vision overtook her. She saw herself standing in front of a mirror, holding a swollen stomach and smiling. Behind her Duncan smiled with a possessive hand around her waist.

The vision left her lightheaded. Tara swayed in his arms. "Wow."

He knelt down beside her. "I would never leave you to raise a child on your own, Tara. You have my word."

Believing he meant what he said, Tara gave a timid smile. "I didn't mean to question your honor."

"The men in your life have held little honor to you or your sister. I understand why you would question. I am not them."

"I know. You're right! I just..." She swallowed hard. "I don't think straight when I'm with you."

"We have that in common. I have not thought clearly since before I went to your time."

Really?

Duncan read her thoughts and smiled.

He pulled her hand to his cheek and snuggled into her warmth. "Do you know the pleasure I can give you, Tara?" His lips skirted over the inside of her wrist. "I have dreamed of how I would make you ache for me. How I would make you mine."

Oh God, Tara thought as her knees went weak. She could scarcely breathe, let alone move. His dark knowing eyes shimmered with desire. Lazy seductive lips moved over her pulse. Unable to do anything but whimper and watch, Tara let every ounce of fear leave her body. Duncan stepped closer, filling the empty space surrounding her. Hot breath fanned her cheek. He waited for her response.

This is what she wanted, what she desired.

Tara fanned her hands over his chest. He drew in one unsteady breath after another, but still he waited. Unable to hold back for even one more desperate moment, Tara pulled his head down to meet her lips. The air sizzled, his lips burned, promising to leave their mark.

Each caress of his tongue over hers felt like a homecoming, felt like completion. She knew he wanted her, but her need was just as combustible, just as hungry.

She had waited twenty-five years for this man to enter her life. She was desperate, more desperate than even he was, to feel the smooth texture of his tongue sliding over hers.

Without boundaries, she let her years of pent up passion and fantasies take over. His taste intoxicated her more than the vision he placed in her head. More than the taste of him she remembered from California. She sucked in a ragged breath, then eased back slightly.

"Ahh, love." He skirted his lips along her jaw, drew her head back exposing the long expanse of her neck. "Don't deny me. I could die with wanting you."

"To deny you would be to deny myself. I never wanted anyone, ever, until you." Her moan, when his teeth nibbled on her shoulder, broke off her words. His hands trailed down her sides. She arched toward them, wanting his touch.

"You kept me up at night. Visions of you, of this," he confessed. His hands filled with the weight of her breast. Her lips parted in anticipation.

Hearing her silent pleas only added to his need.

Her chemise was merely a thin layer between them, one he wasn't going to tolerate. He pushed it off her shoulder wanting her flesh against his. He expected a virgin's shyness, and was elated when she showed none as he lowered her clothing and caught her nipple between his fingers.

She all but collapsed from the chair. Her mind whimpered to his, *Yes. Please yes.* He saw her eyes close and her body go weak with wanting.

He picked her up, carried her to the bed, and

pressed her back against the mattress, hardly believing she was about to grant him his every dream.

His hands were quick to resume the exploration of her body. Hers clenched into his hair slowly at first, stroking it until he lowered his mouth to her taut nipple, begging to be claimed. His mouth closed over the tip and then her hands balled into fists, crushing him closer while she moaned.

Her frantic fingers suddenly started pulling at his clothing. He laughed at her struggle to remove his tunic.

"I want to feel you," she said, her lips trembling.

He helped her with his shirt and tossed it off the bed. His eyes closed when her delicate hands swept over the expanse of his chest.

You like that, he heard her say in her head.

"I crave your touch."

She took his nipple in her mouth, the sensation piercing them both with need and want. Their thoughts mingled in their minds. He couldn't tell if it was his pleasure or hers making their movements more desperate.

His body reacted to her slow quest. His need to disrobe and plunge into her warm folds overwhelmed his sense of right. She took away his control when he wanted to savor every moment, desperate to bring her complete pleasure in this first mating. He captured her head and brought it up to his, devouring her lips once again.

Tara felt his arousal strain against her. A gnawing urge formed in her stomach and its fingers reached lower bringing with it a need she had never experienced. She arched against him, instinct guiding her.

Her clothing dropped away from her body, as his hands passed over her, leaving her naked to his gaze. His lips and hands distracted her from her sudden and complete exposure to him for the first time. He held her hands away from her body and took a long awaited look.

He whispered, "Lovely. You are so beautiful."

She felt his eyes travel down her body, lower and lower. Embarrassed, she felt heat reach her face when his look stopped at the triangle of hair covering her core. "You are lovelier than I ever dreamt."

His eyes lifted, never leaving hers as his fingers drew a trail of fire from her lips down her neck. He stopped briefly at her breast, bringing another gasp from her as he squeezed her nipple.

She went pliant in his arms, while his hand dipped lower. Pressing his palm flat on her hip, kneading her flesh, he sent another wave of pleasure through her.

When he hesitated at her hip, she lifted herself to him, wanting more, knowing he could give her *more*. His hand moved slowly to her core. Once there, he cupped her fullness, rendering his name from her lips.

He demanded, "Open for me, my love."

She did, a little, her virginity showing.

He smiled at her sudden shyness. He ran his tongue along the expanse of her neck nibbling at her ear. Her body arched.

She felt heat searing her, melting her from the inside out. Her need beckoned him, she felt his hand, and still he made no move to possess. "Please..." she begged.

He whispered words to her in Gaelic. She heard them in her head in English. *Open, my love, I will not force you. Show me your trust.*

Her knees fell to the side giving him what he asked. His fingers found her heat, slipped inside. She turned her head away as the shock of his probing fingers thrilled her body, threatening to consume her with the cresting waves of pleasure.

Need built inside her at his gentle touch. Her breath mixed with his as he prepared her for him. One finger became two, stretching, filling. She arched further, faster. Her breathing ceased as he brought her over the first crest. Spasms shook her body, tightening around his fingers.

He crushed her mouth to his, refusing to allow her passion to ebb, for even a moment.

Her arms and hands ran down his broad muscular back, lower over his narrow waist and gripped his buttocks. His complete nakedness thrilled her. When had he removed his clothes? She'd been too enthralled to noticed.

She felt his full desire for her pressing against her entrance. He let her get used to his body, the weight and feel of him. She knew he was doing everything in his power to make her comfortable, wanting to ease the pain of her first time. Knowing this, had tears threatening, tears of joy for his compassion and tenderness.

Instead of weeping, her hands grew bolder, exploring his body with little of the shyness she held before. One hand slipped around his back and more thoroughly traced his hips. Slowly, she brought them to the front and found the long, thick, hard length of him.

His body stiffened to hold control as he enjoyed her touch. Her eyes widened when she felt his size, his girth. She was sure she blushed. A little frightened, she traced his length. His head fell forward as her hands explored his body.

She sensed him holding back, waiting for her to be ready. Tara caught his lips in another desperate kiss, feeling her need mounting again, unable to wait any longer.

His body jerked against hers. Neither could he.

Take me. She urged with her mind, wanting to

feel him inside her, wanting his fullness, and the sensation of having him fill her.

He moved above her, hovered over her. "Look at me, Tara. Let me see your eyes."

Lashes fluttered opened, her eyes locked with his. The tip of him sought entry where none had been before. He forced control he didn't know he had.

Slowly he lowered himself, she opened for him wider. He held back. "Make me yours, Duncan, I was meant to be yours."

She gasped as he entered her body, felt herself tightening at his intrusion. He paused, and stopped moving. "I'm sorry, lass, it won't happen the next time."

"I know."

He kissed her long and deep, waiting for her to adjust. Slowly his hips moved. With each slow stroke, she felt her body giving him the room he needed. The more they moved, the less pain she felt.

Each patient thrust brought her closer, closer to feeling his heart beat with hers.

Hunger replaced the pain. Patience, murmured words of encouragement, and friction brought a bigger and brighter need. Her hips moved, matching his rhythm. She raced with him, knowing the *more* was around the corner.

Higher and higher they climbed, and when she could hold back no longer, she wrapped her legs around his waist and let go. She exploded, becoming a thousand shimmering stars as she shuddered with her release. Tara called out, "Come with me, Duncan!"

Needing no further encouragement, he joined her mind, body and soul, his seed spilling deep inside her womb.

~~~~

Slowly, she floated back down to earth. He
~~~~

pulled her on top of him to keep from crushing her with his weight. Her cheek rested on his chest, as his hands stroked her hair down her back. Neither of them seemed to have the strength to move, to talk, or even open their eyes.

Finally, when Tara looked about, firelight flickered on the walls of the room casting romantic shadows in their wake. The rain outside still fell in steady sheets, but the lightning and thunder had stopped.

She felt his heart beating beneath her ear. Her body never felt so wonderfully used. *What does one say after such a satisfying experience?* Thank you *doesn't seem to cut it.*

His chest started to rumble.

"You heard that?" Embarrassed, she glanced up at his smiling face.

"Guilty."

Her lips tilted at his expression. His eyes were shut, but his grin was just this side of wicked.

"Well?"

He opened one eye, stared at her a moment, then shut it again. "Well what, lass?"

"You know exactly what." She hit a playful hand to his chest. "You're the teacher here, what does one say?"

He forced a slight snore, pretending.

"Duncan!" She swatted at him again.

Like a tiger on the prowl, he pounced, and with little effort, she was under him again, gasping. "The teacher says, you are the most beautiful creature alive, and I look forward to our many lessons on making love." He nipped her nose then caught her lower lip in his teeth. "And if it wasn't your first time I would take you again right now." He lowered his face to her neck, playfully tasting the salty aftermath of their passion.

On a moan she asked, "Why let this being my first time stop us?"

"I want you to be able to walk, my love." His teeth traveled lower.

"If I can't walk, I'll need to stay in bed all day." She arched when his lips met her breasts. "Doesn't sound like a bad idea to me."

"All day?" he asked.

She felt him grow hard. "I could think of worse things."

She lost herself in his warmth once again.

Chapter 15

Like a kitten, after lapping up all the cream, Tara stretched her limbs alongside Duncan's and settled into his arms. Even though the hours of accumulated sleep the night before could be counted on one hand, she couldn't remember ever being more rested.

He stirred, waking slowly to a beautiful day. The sun was bright through the window, the rain only a memory. A few smoldering embers gave way to a wispy trail of smoke up the fireplace.

"Good morning, love." She felt his lips kiss the top of her head.

"Morning."

They had slept most of the morning away, the sun was already high. "We must make our way back."

Smiling, she snuggled deeper. "I don't want to. Let's pretend it's still raining." An idea formed in her head. "Can you call the rain, like you do fire?"

He pulled her closer. "Not without at least a few dark clouds I'm afraid."

She lifted her head and gazed at him. "I was joking. But I can see by your face, you're not."

"And I can see by your blotched face that I need to shave." There were scratches on her skin from the evening's activities. He brushed her cheek with his hand. "I'm sorry to have marred your sweet skin." His eyes darkened slightly.

"Why don't you wear a beard like the other men?"

His brows drew together. "You told me you preferred a clean shaven face."

Hiding a grin she confessed, "I lied." When his

face pinched together, she continued. "What I mean is, I *thought* I liked a clean shaven face, until I saw you with a few days growth. Very sexy! But, I was angry and didn't want to be drawn to you."

He lifted up on his elbows forcing her back to the bed. "So I've been torturing my face with a blade daily, and you prefer it otherwise." His voice was strong, but his look was playful.

"Sorry?"

"You should be."

"I should be punished." The glint in her eyes betrayed her desired punishment.

"I know the perfect penalty for your offence." He held his mouth a fraction away from hers, waited for her breath to hold. Anticipating.

"No kisses." He drew away, as if leaving her side.

She caught his arm and pulled him back. "Oh, no you don't." She toppled him, straddling his chest. Her hair cascaded down, framing them both. "That," she said, poking his chest with every word, "would be considered cruel and unusual punishment, mister."

"Now, lass, I deserve to lay out the punishment since you did the lying."

She sat up giving him full view of her naked body, pulling her hair behind her back. "All right." She smiled a siren's smile, one full of knowledge and power. "Don't kiss me." Her hands flattened over his chest, circled his nipples. "But I can kiss..." She dipped her head and her lips led fire down his torso.

He struggled not to move. Her mouth moved lower, tasting along her path. His breath caught when she dropped below his navel, nearing his raging need.

She won't kiss me there. The thought escaped his mind and from the look on his face, he didn't know it. His body shuddered.

"Mmm, what is this?" He wasn't expecting it, she thought, all the better.

She let Duncan's body want a bit longer, moved her lips toward the inside of his thigh. He went rigid, his breath caught in his chest when she brushed against him. Longing. Hoping. But not saying a word, either aloud or in his head.

Tara smiled before taking him into her mouth.

Surprise, shock and consuming pleasure poured from his mind into hers. She swirled her tongue in circles over the tip of his sex, long wet strokes over his length, and pulled a moan from him that sounded only remotely human.

Enjoying his pleasure, she took the bulk of him inside of her mouth and added pressure. She used her hands to explore the parts she couldn't consume. His palms came to rest on her head, whether to guide or to stop, she didn't know.

Duncan read her thoughts and let her have her way. He didn't stop her, didn't want to, and didn't have the power to do so. He rode on the pleasure of her teeth and tongue until he could stand it no longer.

He tugged her away before he exploded. He flipped her over, savagely pressing her back on the bed and took back control. His lips possessed hers at the same time he thrust into her core.

She clung to him, fingers raking flesh, riding wave after wave of pleasure until neither could hold off. Her release was so powerful his had no choice but to follow.

He poured into her, shouting her name "Tara!"

~~~~

The sun was mid sky before they rode through the gates of MacCoinnich's Keep. Half a dozen men in the courtyard readied their horses and armed themselves. All the activity stopped when Duncan and Tara arrived.

Duncan was laughing at something she said
~~~~

when he noticed the men. Alarmed, he pushed his stallion forward. "What is about, Gregor?"

Gregor shifted a glance at Duncan and Tara, then back again. A smirk crested under his full beard. "Nothing now."

Confused, Tara watched as Duncan moved from one face to another. All hid grins before lowering their eyes.

Ian stepped into the courtyard, watched as Duncan lifted Tara from her horse, and raised his brow when Duncan's hand lingered on her hip.

"Duncan!" he bellowed. He made long anxious strides toward the couple. Everyone watching gave him a wide berth. "Where have you been? I was about to send a search party."

Duncan turned and answered his father. "We found shelter from yesterday's rain in the cabin by the old tree."

Feeling like a teenager who had been caught after curfew, Tara added, "We're sorry to have worried you, Laird Ian. But my experience at riding horses is limited...and it took us longer to get back."

"'Tis afternoon." He scrutinized them both. "It stopped raining before the sun rose."

"We over-slept," Duncan said.

"Slept, is it?" Ian stared them both down, his face stern.

Tara's face grew warm, and a tingle went up the back of her neck. None of the men looked her in the eye except Finlay, who smiled at his brother and winked at her. The rest of the family stood in the shadows of the Keep, staying out of Ian's way.

I think we're in trouble. She sent the thought to Duncan.

Duncan slid a hand around her waist in an effort to calm her fear.

"Aye, Father, we slept." Duncan stared at his sire. He stood his ground. He didn't look away even when the men started wrestling with quiet whispers all around them.

"Am I to understand, son, ye are speaking for Lady Tara?" Ian asked loud enough for everyone to hear.

"I am," Duncan said.

What are you doing? Tara asked Duncan suddenly feeling trapped.

"Very well." Ian turned to the crowd who had gathered. "Let it be known throughout our land this man," he said and took Duncan's hand, "has spoken for this woman." He took Tara's, and placed her fist in his son's. "From this day forward they are handfasted, and known as husband and wife until a man of the church can be brought forth to commence the ceremony."

Ian nodded to his son, clicked his tongue, and let a rare smile pass his lips before turning to a very shocked Tara.

"Welcome to the family." Ian kissed both her cheeks and walked off.

Wide eyed, she watched Ian march away. "Oh, my God. Did what I think just happen, happen?" She looked down at her hand still cupped in Duncan's. "Oh, my God!" Her knees, suddenly weak, started to give. Duncan kept her upright, while a steady flow of men came and congratulated them.

She couldn't form words or even thoughts. She didn't even think to try and read Duncan's. One by one, the men kissed her hand and pounded Duncan's back.

Smile, he told her.

The edges of her mouth lifted up. Her eyes moved from one face to another. *What the hell is happening?*

Well…

"Congratulation's, Lady Tara."

"I'm sure you will both be very happy."

"Duncan will make you a fine husband." This came from Fin who kissed her cheeks.

Husband? Did I miss the wedding? Her breath started to come in waves, her fingers tingled. *Oh my God! Oh my God! Oh my God!*

She saw Duncan's image swim in front of her, his face blurred a bit. The sun overhead made her eyes squint. It felt good to shut them. So very good to shut them...

Duncan caught her before she went down. His men cheered.

"Ah Duncan, 'tis just like ye to have the woman fall at your feet."

"I thought it would be ye hitting the dirt." Gregor's boast had the men laughing.

He took her to the main hall, laid her on a couch. Lora followed him in, sending servants to fetch water and a towel.

Tara's eyes fluttered open almost the minute he set her down. Duncan leaned over her, stroking the hair out of her eyes.

"I fainted, didn't I?"

"Aye, love, that you did."

It came back to her in a hurry. "What was that all about, Duncan? What did your father do?"

"He handfasted us." He watched for a reaction, saw none. "As Laird of the Keep it is within his right to do so for all who dwell on his land."

"Why?"

"Here." He helped her sit up and brought the water to her mouth, encouraged her to drink it.

"Are you well, Tara?" Lora asked.

"No. Yes, Oh God! Can one of you explain why the men acted as though we're married?" She looked to Lora and Duncan, who both exchanged glances.

"Handfasting is equal to marriage in this time." Lora told her. "The men will look at you as Duncan's wife from this day forward."

"What?" Tara moved to stand up, only to have Duncan hold her in her seat.

"Try and understand, the men will assume you and I, that we..." His words choked on themselves in the presence of his mother. "If a child were to come, its legitimacy will never be in question."

"Oh."

"I can see by your expressions, Ian was right in doing this," Lora said, eyeing them both.

"Mrs. MacCoinnich, may I speak with your son in private please?"

"Of course." She kissed Tara's cheeks. "Welcome to the family."

Tara took a long drink from the glass of water, wishing for something stronger. "You saw this coming? Didn't you?"

"When he asked if I was speaking for you, I knew."

"So they all think we're married? But we're not really? Right?"

He opened his mouth to say something, then shut it. "Duncan?"

"Well..."

"Duncan?"

"To everyone, we are married, Tara. Vows given before God are all that need to come." He looked at her now, into her.

"Don't we have any say in this?"

"My father gave me say. I chose you."

"What about me? Don't I have any say in any of this?" She took a small breath, his words sank in. "You chose me?" She stopped, took a breath and smiled. "Really?"

He nodded.

"I should have some say. Don't you think? I mean, I'm from the future, your dad knows that. In my time, we have a fifty, fifty say in marriage." She stood up and started to pace. "Shouldn't I have some say in whether or not I'm married to another person? Well?"

"Aye, love."

"Good. We agree. I should have a say."

"Do you know you're beautiful when you rant?"

She waved off his compliment. "Don't distract me. It's nice to know you're not pigheaded like your father, I mean..."

"Would you choose me, if you had a choice?"

"Of course I'd choose you. Didn't I already do that?" She rolled her eyes and flipped her hair back. She'd given him her virginity for goodness sake and he held a big clump of her heart in his hands. "Still, a woman should be asked. Given a choice. It's supposed to be the most defining moment in a woman's life. Well, maybe not mine. But then again how many women go back in time six or so centuries? Huh?"

"Tara?" He stood in front of her, stopping her pacing.

"What?" Her ranting had almost run out.

"Will you marry me?"

"...six centuries is a long time to... What?" Oh God, did she miss it? Her head started to clear.

Duncan stood holding her hands, looking in her eyes. "Will you marry me, Tara? Will you take me and my name and all it holds? Will you give any child that may even now be forming or any future children my name?" He placed his hand on her flat stomach. "Will you be my wife?"

She melted. Putty. A big fat pile of goo all over the floor in a sixteenth century castle in the middle of Scotland. "What?"

His hands caught her head, focused her eyes. "Marry me, Tara."

Tears caught behind her lids, "Really? You're not asking because your dad...?"

"Ian has nothing to do with this. There is always a choice."

Her world shifted. Everything, which was off

balance only minutes before, settled, much like dirt after an earthquake.

"Yes." Was there any other answer? "Yes, I'll marry you."

Chapter 16

The night was pitch black, not even a wayward star could be seen peeking through the clouds, sitting layer upon layer on themselves. The evening brought with it a cold, which settled into her bones, making her feel every aching joint and muscle. The leg she had broken from throwing herself into the vortex was almost healed.

Grainna thought of the night she returned to her homeland and the time of her reign. She was never one to believe in luck, but had no other word for how she escaped notice from Tara, Duncan and Fin. Rain and thunder met them when they had arrived, disguising her presence, and giving her a chance to flee.

The first days had been a scalding reminder of how harsh living in the sixteenth century was. Being immortal had its advantages, otherwise hunger would have weakened her body and claimed her existence.

Gypsies had found her and with little effort, Grainna willed their minds to take her with them. To her, gypsies were nothing but a pack of filthy thieves who could not be trusted. Their knowledge of the land, and the people in it, was what she sought. Once her body recovered, she would leave their side.

Without boundaries or markers, the caravan took to the west.

"Why have we changed direction?" she asked.

"We skirt outside of MacCoinnich's land, our presence there would not be tolerated." The driver spit a long dark stream from his lips. "Laird Ian would not allow our type anywhere near his people."

Grainna's eyes leveled in the direction they were leaving. "Does MacCoinnich have sons?"

"Aye, three, Duncan, Finlay, and Cian."

Vengeance formed into a ball of heat in her chest. Swallowing hard, Grainna studied the landscape in an effort to memorize her way back. The men who helped Tara escape would pay.

She settled back in her seat. Her weariness was fueled by pain and a lack of sleep. In her weariness, she plotted another's demise.

In the end, she would have her revenge. With every breath, she felt her strength returning. The forest was rich with the elements of her past spells, giving her all she needed to once again rule over this land...and destroy those she didn't want in it.

~~~~

Long summer nights drifted slowly into autumn. Leaves started to fall and a bite in the air brought with it a hint of a change in the weather.

The priest was due to arrive in less than two weeks. His time at the MacCoinnich's Keep would be filled with more than one exchange of vows. Two other couples had been handfasted over the year since the priest had been there. To no one's surprise, Haggart and Celeste asked the priest to wed them as well.

Tara's rooms were moved next to Duncan's. An adjoining door made their path each night less obvious to anyone watching the halls. Duncan often teased Tara about her ruse to keep their intimacies from the servants. "They are not stupid, my love. To them, we are married."

They sat in front of the dark fireplace in Duncan's room for the second lesson. Her first on calling a flame had ended within ten minutes of starting when Duncan developed other ideas on how to make heat that night. His sexy beard had
~~~~

grown in enough to be soft and welcoming, making him even more irresistible to Tara.

"I never said they're stupid. I look at handfasting as a fancy engagement. Once we're married, I'll move everything in here." She sat cross-legged on the floor, her eyes shut like he had suggested.

"Do you think they don't notice your bed isn't slept in?"

She peered at him out of one eye. "If they do, they don't say anything. Now, can we get on with this? You promised to show me how you do it."

He shook his head at his crazy wife.

Soon to be crazy wife. She corrected him.

Crazy beautiful wife, with plump moist lips, lips I need to kiss. He moved in to make good on his threat.

"Oh, no you don't! You promised." She put a hand up and stopped him from coming closer. "As soon as you show me this, you can do...that." She smiled, and closed her eyes again.

"Promise?" He teased.

"Yes. But no cheating. It has to be me lighting the fire this time. No twitchy fingers from you."

"Close your eyes."

"They're closed."

"Feel your breath. Slowly in, slowly out. Listen to the room. Let your mind go blank." His voice was calm and soothing. "Feel the energy surrounding you. The heat, hear the crackle of flames licking the logs. See the embers turning orange."

Sitting in a trance-like state listening to his voice, to his words, sweat started to bead on her brow. The air tingled with static electricity. The hair on her arms stood up. She rubbed her fingertips together, felt a snap. Each breath brought her closer, she could feel it.

"Pull the energy in. Now...look at where you

want it to go."

When her eyes opened, she saw only the dark fireplace, heard only his voice. Her fingers gathered strength. When she could bear the heat no longer she extended them toward the log in the hearth.

To her utter amazement flames leapt from the ashes. "Did you see that?" She jumped to her feet. "Did you see that?" She clapped her hands like a child receiving a gift on Christmas morning.

His lopsided grin answered her question. "Aye, lass. I saw it."

"I did it, right? You didn't help?" She turned an accusing look his way.

He mimicked a movement she had shown him a time or two over the last couple months. He crossed an X over his heart. "Promise."

"Oh man, that was great." She searched the room with excited eyes. "What else can I catch on fire?"

He caught her before she could reach for a candle. "Oh, no, you don't." He molded her body to his. "A promise is a promise." He kissed the grin off her face.

~~~~

"It's called indoor plumbing. Pipes bring water in. Bigger pipes take waste out." Tara stood in front of a closet trying to explain to Ian, Fin and Duncan the finer details of a modern day water closet.

"How is the water forced into the walls where the pipes are?"

"See now, that's where you come in, Finlay." She gave him a hefty pat on the back and tried not to laugh at the baffled look on his face. "You look bright to me. Why don't you think on it and come up with a solution. If hundreds of teenagers can siphon gasoline out of tanks, than you can figure out how to get water to flow into pipes." Putting
~~~~

her hands on her hips she said, "If you want to know about the four chambers of the heart or the way blood oxygenates, that's where I can provide you with details. Plumbing is a boy thing." She lifted her skirts and walked away from the men who stood around scratching their heads.

Lora and Myra waited for her in a small private courtyard. It was time for the women to give Tara a lesson in her Druid heritage.

"We're going to determine if you're able to move the wind. We all have the ability to a small extent. But some, like Myra, have mastered it. Show her."

Out of nowhere, and with no visible sign from Myra, Tara's skirt started to billow out from under her. As quick as it started, it stopped.

"I will try the same, feel the difference." Lora pointed a finger at Tara's legs. Slowly she felt the air stir, barely moving the fabric. "As much as I have practiced, I'm unable to do more, and not without channeling the energy with my hands. My daughter has more skill."

Myra demonstrated her talent in a more practical manner. "Let's sit down," she suggested. When she did, three chairs surrounding a small table pulled out by themselves.

"Wow. How did you do that?" Tara reached out to feel the weight of the chair.

"Air surrounds everything. Moving the air moves the objects. It was the first gift I knew I had. Da had taken away a sweet pie from me when I was only four, told me to finish my supper before I could have it. I don't care much for kidney stew, so instead of eating, I sat and brooded."

Tara poured tea and listened.

"I stared at the pie the whole meal. I noticed colors in the air, red, blue and white. Before I knew it, the pie flew across the table and ended up in my lap."

"We took our meals in private after that," Lora said. "At least until she was able to control the power."

"Do you actually see colors in the air?"

"Only when I want to move something. Let me show you." Myra picked up a fallen leaf and placed it on the table. "Sitting here, there are no colors. But when I think of how I want it to move, up let's say." The leaf started to levitate. "I see red below it, blue above. Like heat rising from a fire or vapor from a boiling kettle, I suppose. Now, if I want it to move faster, or in a different direction, the colors change blending orange with the red and white with the blue. The red and orange push."

Tara watched the leaf fly to the right of the table and back again. "The blue and white pull."

"Exactly."

"I have a difficult time seeing the colors," Lora admitted. "Then again, 'tis not my strongest gift."

"You try." The leaf settled on the table.

Mother and daughter worked with Tara for over an hour. The leaf did move, several times, but not in the direction Tara wanted. Lora said, "Don't be discouraged. You will find your true gift one day, the gift that will set you apart from all others.

Myra suggested they practice for a set time daily, and Tara enthusiastically agreed.

~~~~

When the lesson was finished, and the giggling over, what one of the knights decided to wear started to dominate the conversation, Lora took her leave.

"They were too tight," Tara went on. "It's like he was asking every maid and lady to look at his package."

"And not very impressive from what I could tell," Myra said, rolling her eyes.

Tara squealed. "Oh, you saucy wench. I can tell we'll have lots to talk about once you pick a
~~~~

husband."

Wistful, Myra glanced up at the sky, "Maybe someone will come to the wedding and catch my eye."

"It's coming so fast, at times I want to pinch myself. I want to remember every detail."

"The celebration will last for a week," Myra explained. "So I doubt you will remember everything. It can be quite exhausting."

"Why so long?"

"Traveling takes time. Knights from surrounding villages will bring their Lords and Ladies. Weddings are where many find future husbands and wives."

"Are there any knights invited who you have considered?"

"I wish! The Lancaster's will bring their son, Matthew and daughter, Regina. Regina has her eyes on Finlay, but in truth, I don't think he cares much for her. Matthew is too short, too shy, and unless he is talking about birds, he has nothing to say. The man can't stand up for himself if you ask me. He's the butt of every jest amongst his peers. I'd feel sorry for him, if they weren't so true."

"Why don't you tell me what you really think?"

"He is all that and more. You'll see. There are others, but none whom I fancy. Da promised he would give me a choice. I pray he keeps his word. Being un-married at twenty and one raises questions among the men."

"And if none are worth choosing?"

Myra watched the clouds part. "Someone will come. I'll know when he does."

~~~~

Brother Malloy made his life's work joining together sinners in matrimony. His arrival to the MacCoinnich Keep and the surrounding village was much anticipated and welcomed. His arrival also brought changes in sleeping arraignments, at
~~~~

least for Duncan and Tara.

He made it very clear the good book did not give excuse for lustful behavior in any form. A marital bed was only to be used for the sake of creating life. Therefore, the unmarried couple were to abstain from inappropriate behavior until after the nuptials. Then the life they would create would be right with God.

Duncan pissed and moaned to the point Brother Malloy threatened to leave without performing any service.

"Think of all the trouble Lora has gone through. Guests have already started to arrive," Tara pleaded with him.

"But we are already married." Duncan argued in hushed tones away from the meddling clergy and his parents who were trying to convince the priest to stay.

"Handfasting is not the same, and you know it. He even said there have been brides and grooms who have called off the actual marriage after being handfasted."

"Most of those are due to a woman being barren."

"Maybe so, but that doesn't make it right."

He knew the injustice of this fact. "I agree." He glared at the priest and looked back down at his bride.

They read each other's internal thoughts with ease.

Her brow had turned in. "Would you think differently about me if I were unable to have children?"

He was being foolish. His selfishness was concerning his wife. "Nay, my love." He cupped her face in his hands, brushed his lips over hers. "We are joined as few are, even without *his* vows."

"Good," she said a bit louder. "Then a few days in separate beds won't be such big a deal."

"This is what you want?" He searched her eyes.

"I want to be your wife, and if Brother Malloy leaves, it could take months before another will come in his place."

He hated her logic. "My bed will be lonely without you," he whispered against her parted lips.

"As will mine. Send me a warm thought or two." *He can't stop us from this. I can say completely inappropriate things in my mind.* "Besides, it will make the wedding night all the more exciting. Don't you think?"

He growled, placed his forehead against hers. *Your words make me so stiff I cannot move. Days of such talk will drive me mad.*

It'll be worth the pain. I promise to make it up. We will take to our bed after the wedding and stay there for a week. I'll put a white flag on the door when someone needs to bring us food.

She chuckled.

"Tsk, tsk, tsk." Brother Malloy said, giving them a look of stern disapproval.

~~~~

Duncan left with Fin on an errand before the guests started to arrive. He needed a diversion from his bride. Not that he didn't love how she taunted him with her secret words. He did. However, not being able to touch her was maddening.

No one would say they were growing apart by not sharing a bed. In fact, to the contrary, they grew closer every day. He didn't know exactly when he fell in love with her, but there was no denying he had.

He wondered now, as he often did, if she felt the same love for him. Was it only their Druid vows binding them so closely together? Would the deeper words of love bring them closer still?

He couldn't think of her without joy piercing
~~~~

his heart. Even now sitting on his horse with his brother at his side, his mind was on Tara and what she was doing. The farther away from the Keep they rode, the harder it was for him to hear her. But he felt her, and the happiness emanating from her.

Fin slowed his horse, peered at his brother, then rolled his eyes. "Good lord, get that blasted look off your face. Someone would think you daft if they saw it."

"Jealous, Brother?"

"Of how she has turned your brain to mush? I think not."

"You would be lucky to find a woman like mine." Duncan liked putting possession behind how he referred to Tara.

She was his!

"One as beautiful, I would agree. But her tongue can cut like a knife."

"But never undeservingly so."

Fin shifted his reins in his hands. "Still, I want my bride to be more subdued."

"Like Alyssa, from the village?"

Fin looked away. "She may be subdued in voice, but not in bed. There she has too many desires, which don't always require the same bed mate."

Duncan's brow creased with the weight of his brother's words. "'Tis unfortunate. She has Druid blood as well. I thought you two made a good match."

"As did I."

They rode in silence for a while, enjoying the quiet and opportunity to think.

"Have you spoken with Tara about the vows you took in California?"

"The subject hasn't come up."

"Are you content with leaving it?"

He shook his head. "Nay, but what am I to

say? I tell her constantly we are already wed. She knows we are connected with our thoughts."

"You are hoping she will come to the conclusion on her own?"

"Maybe."

"I hope you know what you are doing, brother. I wouldn't want to get on Tara's bad side. Something tells me she could bring down the Ancients themselves to fight for her if she pleased."

"I'll wait for the right time. Tara is a reasonable lass, she'll understand."

Fin kicked his horse to a faster pace. "I hope so."

Chapter 17

A few days, turned into five. Five long, painfully slow days, and even longer nights.

If not for the many guests distracting them, Duncan and Tara would never have been able to make good on their promise to stay away from each other.

Two nights before the ceremony, Tara sat opposite Duncan at the other end of the huge table set in the center of the main hall. She was surrounded by strangers who made polite conversation during supper.

Celeste and Haggart had married that day, along with several other couples from the village. All were asked to join the MacCoinnich's in celebration. Knights surrounded the table, their pages and squires sat at another.

Some of the men were none too happy about sharing their meal with commoners from the village, but none voiced this opinion to Ian or Lora. They wouldn't dare. Laird Ian ran his home as he saw fit and defied any to question him. He raised his sons to do the same. When Duncan's time came to rule, Tara knew the villagers and all their children would pledge their loyalty to him.

She listened to the daunting conversation between Myra and Matthew of Lancaster. He was attempting to impress Myra with his knowledge of the migrating birds near his home. He ignored the quips from some of the men and took advantage of the fact his father was seated several feet away and wasn't able to silence him.

Myra had been right about him, Tara mused. He was not at all her type. In fact, he was a chore to listen to and if the subject moved away from birds, he had nothing to say. Those around him, moved the discussion away from birds as often as possible. He was enthusiastic about his subject, and determined to return to it.

I'm going crazy down here. Tara sent a silent plea to Duncan.

Duncan glanced her way, looked around her, and smiled. *Ahh...Lancaster. Boring you to tears is he?*

It's Myra I worry about. If she could, she would spike his drink with arsenic just to shut him up.

Duncan choked on the ale he placed to his lips, drawing concern from those around him.

Tara hid a smile behind a napkin. *Sorry!*

You are not! He wiped liquid off his shirt.

Okay, you're right. I'm not sorry. She waited until he brought food to his mouth. *Guess what I am wearing underneath my dress.*

His eyes darted across the table. *What?*

Nothing at all.

Again, Duncan had difficulty with the food he tried to eat.

No one noticed when Duncan and Tara stopped engaging in conversation with anyone at the table. Except for Ian and Lora, who engaged in a full discussion as they speculated about what was going on between their son and daughter-in-law.

Once the meal was finished, and at the first opportunity, Tara begged Myra for assistance to get away from the others.

They both fell into chairs in the solar after closing and locking the door. "He's worse than you said."

"I told you. And did you see Regina? She was falling all over Fin."

"Do you think the two of them have ever..." Tara let Myra finish her sentence.

"Nay. Even Finlay has better sense than that. The Lancaster's may not be the brightest in the bunch, but even they would see that as a strike against their honor and force a marriage between the two of them."

"For his sake, I hope he keeps it in his pants."

Myra's laughter bubbled out. "You say the funniest things. How are you and Duncan handling sleeping separately?"

"It's awful," Tara sighed. "I thought it would be easy. I did sleep alone for the last twenty-five years, how hard can five days be?" She shook her head. "They feel like five hundred."

"I would guess they are even more difficult for him." Myra took lightly to her feet and poured them both some wine.

"Don't kid yourself. It isn't easier for me because I'm a woman."

Myra sipped. "I wouldn't know."

"Someday you will." Tara set her glass down, slipped her shoes off and crossed her legs under her. "I didn't think it was possible to love a man so much. I've tried telling him, but I can't get the words out."

"That you love him? Why?"

She shrugged her shoulders. "Fear, I guess. Fear he doesn't feel the same way. What if I tell him, and he chokes on a reply?"

"He calls you *love* all the time." Myra defended.

"He says the same to every child and woman in the village." She shifted in her chair. "I know he cares, and I think he loves me. But until he says those three small words, I will simply have to guess. And worry."

"Ludicrous. I've never seen my brother so enthralled with anyone until you. He loves you beyond measure."

"You think so?"

"I know so!" Myra took her hand in assurance. "You have nothing to fear."

"I hope you're right. I would hate to think he's doing all of this because his father forced him."

"Duncan would never allow that. He does nothing he's not in agreement with, no matter what the consequences."

Tara measured her words and found the truth in them. "I have been meaning to ask you something."

Suddenly serious Myra gave her a puzzled look. "What is it?"

"Will you stand up with me, during the ceremony?"

Moisture sprang up in Myra's eyes. "Oh, Tara, I would be honored. I know how you wish your own sister were here to stand with you." The women embraced, both brushing fallen tears from their cheeks.

"Lizzy would approve. Besides, you will be my sister after the ceremony."

"True, but blood is thicker. I'm sorry she can't be here."

"Me, too." Tara wished, knowing it was impossible.

"Hey, you know what? I have a way for us to be blood sisters." It was corny, Tara knew. But a sister held secrets, and this was one she wanted to share with Myra. "When Lizzy and I were ten and twelve, we were jealous of our girlfriends' friendships. As sisters, we were always close. It was almost unnatural how we never really fought or disagreed. Anyway, one night we sat up late gossiping about the mean girls we went to school with. Then we made up a special spell."

Tara moved to the sewing basket and took out a pair of scissors. "We had been reading books on witches, powers, and such."

"You mean a real spell?" Myra sat up in her

chair, riveted.

"I don't know how real it was, but it made us feel better."

"What was it?"

"It's kind of corny, completely juvenile."

"Great! What is it?"

"All right." Tara nicked her index finger with the scissors drawing a small amount of blood. "First we did this. Neither of us could bear more than a prick." Tara handed over the scissors.

Myra followed her lead.

"Then we became blood sisters." Tara placed her finger with Myra's.

"But, you were already blood sisters."

"I told you it was corny, besides we didn't choose to be born sisters, but we did choose to do this."

"Then what?" Myra sat palm-to-palm, fingers touching Tara's.

"Then, we wove our spell." Tara interlocked her fingers in Myra's. "In this day and in this hour, we call upon the sacred power. I choose to give my blood to thee, I choose you as a sister to me. Your turn."

Myra repeated her chant. Tara felt a slight tingle in her hand, but didn't comment on it.

"I told you it was corny."

"I don't think so. Now, I have two more sisters." She continued when Tara appeared confused. "You and Lizzy, we are all three sisters now."

"I'll buy that." They each wiped the blood from their fingertips and both moved to leave the room, rested and ready to face the crowd outside the doors. "What is the *sacred power*?" Myra asked.

"I have no idea. But it rhymed well."

Before she closed the door behind them, something caught her eye. The scissors, which held only a drop of their blood, glittered and shone in the darkened room. She peered closer and noticed a strange magical dust fall, from the blade. She opened her mouth to tell Myra what she saw, but her new sister had already left her side.

She shook her head and decided to keep her observation to herself. When she left the room, Tara felt like a teenager.

~~~~

Preparing the Keep for the wedding was no small undertaking. Extra candles had been made and placed in newly erected chandeliers. Yards and yards of amber and cream colored material draped the archways and walls to warm up the rooms.

The cooks prepared the food for the feast. Duck, pheasant, and wild turkey rounded out the choices of poultry. A roasting pig took up a large amount of space in the kitchen. Butter was churned and plastered over Mrs. Claunch's many baked goods. To her astonishment, Tara witnessed the maids whipping cream to sweeten the pies.

Tara made certain she thanked each and every servant for their assistance.

Musicians played in the great hall, entertaining the guests. The strings of a harp caught Tara's attention. She stopped, listened and let the music pull at her heart. Emotion choked her. Misty eyed, she surveyed the transformed room.

Lizzy would love all of this, and Cassy would be patting herself on the back for being the reason Duncan and I met.

Tara swept the back of her hand across her eyes brushing the tears from her face.

Duncan entered the hall, his eyes fell to her. His expression quickly turned from excited to concern. Tara grinned, but she knew he read her thoughts.

Slowly, he came to her side. There, he
~~~~

wrapped his arms around her waist and rocked her back and forth. A simple twist, and they appeared to be dancing.

They danced together with their eyes closed. It could have been only the two of them in the room as far as they were concerned.

Don't be sad, Tara.

I wish they could be here.

Do you regret being here?

She stopped moving, pulled away far enough to look him in the eye. "There is nowhere else I want to be. How can you ask?"

"I want you to be happy."

"*You* make me happy." Unable to stop the words from coming she let them tremble out of her hoping they would come back. "I love you, Duncan, more than life, more than time or place. There is nowhere else I want to be."

Tara held her breath and waited while his face sparkled and his eyes glistened.

"I will spend every day showing you how much I love you." He crushed his lips to hers, demonstrating to everyone who watched, the love he felt for the woman in his arms.

Tara didn't think she could get any happier than she was at that moment. She felt his love for her in his kiss. In her heart, she knew it had always been there.

Her arms wound around his neck, pulling him closer. The sparks building in the core of the couple, flickered into flames on top of the candles overhead.

The musicians stopped playing and without provocation the crowd applauded.

Laughing against each other's lips, they ignored the crowd and kept their lips glued to each other. Bringing hoots and cheers from the men.

"Okay you two. Take it outside." Fin shuffled them apart. "You're about to light the hall on fire," he whispered under his breath.

Tara glanced at the candles burning brightly above them. With a flash of drama she fanned herself, calling a small wind like Myra had taught her, and blew out the candles before others noticed they lit themselves. "You take my breath away." She said loud enough to call attention to her instead of the flames.

Laughter came from many directions.

Outside, the cool breeze helped bay the fire burning inside the bride and groom.

"I have a surprise for you."

"Really? What is it?" Her hand in his, he tugged her along the courtyard.

"My wedding present to you."

"A wedding present?" She stopped. "But I've nothing for you."

He placed a hand aside her face. "You are my wedding gift. The love you give me."

She melted. "Do they give you guy's lessons in this time?"

"Lessons in what, lass?"

She laughed. "Never mind. Where's my present?"

He laughed keeping pace with her. "Over here."

"Is it big or small?"

"You'll see."

"Did you wrap it? We women like to unwrap presents you know," she said, getting into the spirit of things.

"It can't be wrapped."

"Can I close my eyes and shake it? Guess what it is?"

Duncan kept laughing. "You could try."

"Okay, I'm closing my eyes. Don't let me fall."

Tara stumbled along beside him. They slowed their pace once she heard other voices. She heard Duncan shush those who were around them.

"Give me both hands," he said.

Under her fingers she felt the warm fur of what had to be a horse. A small noise and movement from the animal brought Tara's eyes open.

Tara caught her breath. The mare was beautiful. Her tan coat was the color of caramel, her mane as rich as chocolate. Her big brown eyes flittered with trust.

"Hello," Tara said in a soft greeting. "Look at you, so strong and regal." Stroking her neck, Tara glanced at Duncan. "For me?"

"Aye."

"You're making me cry again." She looked at her horse with awe.

"Sorry." Duncan gave a half apology.

"No, you're not." She moved in to thank him.

Even Finlay started to blush before he broke the lovebirds apart. "You two are making me ill with this. Brother Malloy had better not dawdle in his ceremony on the morrow, lest you announce a birth before a marriage."

Everyone in earshot agreed.

~~~~

The village was brimming with activity everywhere. Anyone within a fifty-mile radius filled the tiny streets, adding to the purses of the local merchants.

Grainna couldn't have picked a better time to come into the small parish of people and blend in. No one noticed an old woman walking with a cane.

Again, she considered luck was on her side, a luck that hadn't been with her for centuries. The Ancients must be asleep at the wheel, she thought. There was no other explanation for why her presence had yet to be discovered. They were so damn proficient at banishing her the first time. Calling attention to herself by using her black magic would certainly make her presence known.
~~~~

Their lack of diligence kept her more subdued than she would be normally.

She made her way to the village merchant who bartered and sold any and everything the town had to offer. Provisions of food, candles, and cloth woven from the wool of the sheep littering the landscape of the surrounding hills, were for sale.

She waited for a few of the gentry to finish with the man, while she kept to the back of his small home, which doubled as his store. "How can I be of assistance to ye?" he kindly asked, obviously happy with his burgeoning business.

"Only a few little things if you will, sir." Grainna put her old woman smile of kindness on her face. "A few candles and a measure of salt pork if ye have it."

It didn't take long for the man to start talking. "Are ye here for the wedding?"

"My grandson and I are passing through." She had guessed the nature of the festivities, but she kept herself from slipping into the minds of the people to confirm her assumption, again to keep her presence concealed for as long as possible. "It looks to be a grand wedding."

"Lord Duncan, the eldest son of the Laird, is marrying on the 'morrow. 'Tis good ye came today for these." He set the items she requested down on the counter.

"Quite lucky for me then."

The man kept up with the gossip, happy to have someone who didn't know his stories. "Now if only his daughter would pick a husband. Methinks she may find one during the celebrations. The village is filled with so many eligible men who would suit."

"How old is the lass?"

"Almost an old maid if ye ask me. She is twenty and one on her last day marking her birth. Why Laird Ian has not bound her to someone is always a question asked at dinner tables." He looked up and caught Grainna's gaze. Confusion crossed his brow and she felt his skin start to crawl. *You should squirm you lower than life bit of a man.* Grainna shook his trance away, realizing she had slipped into his mind without trying to.

He moved away in obvious discomfort. She would have to be more careful in the future.

They bartered with a bit of her jewelry, and because it's worth was more than what she had purchased, he gave her some coin.

She walked the streets, keeping her eyes and ears open. She didn't fear any of the MacCoinnich's coming into the village with the wedding the next day. So she took advantage of her *luck* and gathered more information.

An eligible daughter? A wicked smile curved at her lips. *And dwelling only a few miles away?* She contained her laugh. *How poetic.*

Grainna stopped at the smith and bartered for a pot. There she saw a young woman, not more than eighteen, smiling up at a man dressed in knight's clothing. She eavesdropped on their conversation.

"So, ye are Matthew of Lancaster. I've heard many stories of ye, my Lord."

"Ahhh." The knight searched the busy street. "I'm sorry, ye have me at a disadvantage, and ye are?"

"Alyssa." She flashed him a smile.

"'Tis a pleasure." He gave a quick bow, his eyes skirting to the street, obviously looking for someone.

Alyssa smiled and leaned into him enough to show off the curve of her breast and caught his eye with the necklace she wore. In whispered tones she asked, "I hope ye will not be leaving so soon after the wedding. I would like to get to know ye better."

Grainna noticed the exchange and the small

amount of power the woman used over the man.

Quietly and with swift skill, Grainna slipped into the man's mind. Yes, the woman speaking with him was Druid, and she was using her gifts on him. From what she could tell, the lass was looking for a husband, and wasting her time with the man in front of her.

"Maybe I could stay for a day or two." His hands twitched at his side. "Or return at a later date."

"That would be lovely, Sir Lancaster." She touched his arm, sending a path of red to his cheek. "Until then."

Grainna gathered her things and walked out of the village from the opposite way she came. Once hidden in the woods, she picked up her cane and moved with speed to the horse she took from one of the gypsies.

~~~~

With a little help from Ian, the sky cooperated the next day. The ceremony was to take place outside, overlooking the field of green where benches had been prepared so the guests could sit. The maids tied strands of heather together forming sprays of flowers everywhere.

Duncan had been kept from seeing Tara since they parted the night before. It was a frustrating custom Tara wanted to follow, even if it wasn't his.

He adjusted the plaid of his clan until it sat perfectly upon his frame. His bride had jested with him about his kilt. She would see him in it for the first time when they exchanged vows.

The beauty of a kilt was the ease in which he would bed his wife. Perhaps he would take to wearing the kilt more often if his bride enjoyed his pursuits in the outfit.

~~~~

Tara fidgeted while the women, maids, and in-laws fussed over her. They wove tiny flowers in her hair, and a small wreath sat like a halo on top of her head. The effect was magnificent.

The amber gown, adorned with pearls and gold ribbons, made every feature Tara had glow. The gown dipped low, and her breasts thrust high enough against the bodice to enchant her husband. The full, flowing sleeves cascaded over the tips of her fingers.

The most defining part of the gown was the material made entirely of silk, impossible to come by in this time and place. Someone told her, Duncan and Fin brought it back with them from one of their trips into the future. Its worth was immeasurable and admired by all who saw it.

The servants filed out of the room, leaving only Lora and Myra.

"Stunning," Lora said, looking at her reflection in the mirror. "You will make my son a fine wife."

Tara put her arms around her mother-in-law. "Thank you for everything."

"No, my dear, thank you for loving my son." Lora's voice cracked. "I should go, check on everything one last time."

Myra stayed behind to keep Tara company before she walked down the aisle. "Are you nervous?"

"Not like I thought I would be," she said. "I remembered the vows Duncan and I pledged in California, and I'm more comfortable with what I want to say."

"Tell me."

Tara closed her eyes and remembered. "They started out with North, South, East and West. There was something about following his light, I'm fuzzy on that part, but then it went on about me giving him my love past my dying day."

Myra stopped her by finishing her words, "Where two hearts beat, there is now but one. This tie that binds us together shall never be undone."

"Yes, exactly! How do you know?"

"You said those vows to him before?" Myra paled. Her eyes shifted to Tara.

"Yes." Tara's spine started to tingle.

"And he to you?"

"Yeah, why?" Tara felt a shimmer pass over her at the memory.

"You are already wed to my brother."

"That's what he keeps saying." Tara waved her off.

"Nay. You are truly wed already. Those vows are sacred wedding vows, Tara. When spoken by one with Druid blood, they are binding beyond any which could be said in a church or in front of a priest."

"I don't understand."

Myra sat. "Druid wedding vows can never be undone. Once pledged, they will bind you to the person you said them to, instantly. If the two of you part, your soul will reach out for the other. Without the other one, you would die. These vows bind for eternity, in this life and the next. There is no 'til death do we part."

Tara knew the color washed from her face when she felt the blood drain from her head. Her knees hit the back of a chair. Sinking into it, she spoke with trembling lips. "And Duncan knows this?"

"Of course. We are all taught this early on. Few Druids make this vow, because of the bind it makes. My parents shared the same vows which is why they can talk to each other with their minds." Myra placed a hand on her head. "I should have known you did the same. It all makes sense now."

Tara wrung her hands together, remembered the cord that burned when they said the vows to each other. Remembered the flash and the instant she could read his thoughts. "Why didn't he say anything?" she asked. "Oh God, maybe he doesn't love me. Maybe he is simply drawn to me?" Her hands started to tremble.

"Nay, Tara." Myra caught her hands and made her look her in the eye when she spoke. "The vows bind you. Aye. But they don't make you love. That is free will." Myra fumbled. "Don't you see? Duncan chose you before he brought you back. He could have stopped you and didn't. He knew what he was doing. Grainna would have bound you to a stranger, and flesh to flesh maybe you would have given into him, but when he left, you would have been empty. You would have died, only to dwell in eternity looking for a man you did not love."

"I had no idea." How could anyone damn another to such a fate?

"She is evil beyond anything we can imagine." Myra pulled the bulk of her black hair behind her. "Now, enough of this. Let us change a few words in your vows. Sacred vows should not be spoken in a ceremony like this, it is entirely too public and would bring to light who we are."

"It all seems unnecessary, knowing we are already wed."

"Nonsense. You look so lovely. My parents want to see their son wed properly. And look at all the happiness, which has surrounded the hall these last weeks. I know it's your day, but the rest of us are enjoying it as well."

"I need to talk to Duncan. We can't go forward without..." She stood and started to the door.

Myra stopped her. "Do you love my brother?"

"More than life." Her heart jolted with the reality of her words.

"Do you believe he loves you?" Myra stopped her pacing by standing in front of her.

Flashes from her time and his, passed in her head. The moment he made her his, the moment he vowed to be with her for eternity. The smile he gave her when they last saw each other. "Yes. He loves me."

"Then what does it matter? Vows said today or months ago? Your love will survive eternity if given a chance."

Tara looked in her sister's eyes. "You're right. You're right. I'm nervous." She put a hand to her fluttering stomach. "So very nervous."

Chapter 18

The music changed and announced Tara's arrival. She had asked Ian to walk her down the aisle. She would have been too apprehensive to walk alone. Besides, she still held Ian responsible. He had shoved her hand into Duncan's and started all this.

Thank God.

Behind her, Amber held the long train of her dress and smiled at the attention bestowed upon her.

Duncan looked proud and a bit stern as he stood before Brother Malloy, who seemed anxious to unite the couple in front of him. He made little rolling gestures with his fingers in an attempt to move Tara along.

But today was her wedding day and nothing was going to rush this moment for her. Nothing!

Duncan looked dashing in his kilt. She knew he owned one, and had even attempted to get him in it a time or two, simply so she could get it off of him. Today, she was marrying a man in a skirt. Who would have figured? The thought had her hiding a grin.

He wore his plaid, as did his brother who stood at his side. Even Ian bared his knees for everyone to see. They were a proud lot of men.

And she was proud to be aligning herself with them.

Duncan held his arms in front of him with clasped fingers.

Tara placed a gentle kiss on Ian's cheek when he handed her over to his son. He beamed his approval, then took his place with Lora to watch the ceremony.

Brother Malloy cleared his throat and began, "Lords and Ladies..."

~~~~

It took Brother Malloy's angry cough to separate the couple after their vows had been exchanged. Even then, the kiss went on until the crowd clapped their approval. Only then did Duncan release Tara.

At the reception, the lights of a thousand flames brightened the hall long into the night. Musicians played and people danced.

Amber led the children in games and ran them throughout the rooms, keeping them entertained. Cian plotted with friends he would one day ride with into battle. Tonight, however, he conspired with them about the young maidens they planned to corner in the yard.

Myra and Finlay toasted the couple, wishing them long and fruitful lives. Bets were placed on how soon it would take for the future heir to be announced.

Ian and Lora held hands and secretly conversed about their future grandchildren.

I pray a child comes soon. Ian spoke without words.

Not long by the look of them. Lora assured her husband. They both glanced to where their eldest son stood with their newest daughter.

Duncan stole a kiss in the middle of the dance floor.

~~~~

The Keep's females escorted Tara to the bridal chamber, previously known as his bedroom. The exit took place with as much pomp and circumstance as the wedding ceremony itself, while Duncan held back, entertained by the boasting of the men. All ranted on about how he should perform his marital duties. Or better yet, how to make sure his wife awakened on the morrow with a smile upon her lips.

Being apart from her had been torture. Her thoughts, swimming in his head, kept him in a state of constant arousal. Even during their wedding feast, she'd asked him mentally what he wore under his kilt, while she playfully placed a buttered vegetable to her lips. Slowly she swirled her tongue around the morsel of food until his need bordered on pain.

How lucky he was to have found such a seductive prize. Giggling women and maids bounded down the stairs, letting Duncan and the men know the bride awaited her groom.

"At last," he said, half to himself but loud enough for those standing close by to hear.

"Much wine was poured here tonight. Go man, lest she falls asleep," Sir William urged.

"I doubt that will be the case," Gregor said.

The men cheered and chanted when Duncan mounted the stairs. Once outside the doors, Duncan hushed them all and waved them away.

None would dare to peek at what lay beyond.

With the excitement of a man starved for release, Duncan slowly opened the door and peered into the room.

The glow of the firelight and candles flickered shadows on the walls. His eyes wandered the room. That was until he stepped inside and saw her standing next to the hearth in a billowing night dress. Her hair brushed free of all adornments framed her face and body.

"Hello, wife," he managed, his voice already choking on his desire. It had been a painful week without her in his bed.

"Hello, husband."

Tara watched him walk toward her, but put up a hand to halt him from getting too close. A little baffled, he slowed his pace and accepted the goblet of wine she handed him.

"Sit. I have a wedding present for you."

Her mischievous smile had him searching her mind for the secret she held. But inside he only saw the vision of him in her head. Visions of his kilt and the constant question as to what he wore underneath. "You are all the present I need."

She turned, took a few paces away from him, and then turned back. "I'm so pleased you think that." Her delicate fingers traced the length of her body from navel to throat.

His mouth gaped slightly when she started pulling on the strings of her dressing gown.

He sipped his wine and sat back, enjoying her show. Never had a woman stripped for him in such a fashion. Confident in her seduction, she gently tugged at her sleeves letting a glimpse of her shoulder come through. She turned away where he could only see her backside. Her gown slipped to her waist. Underneath, she wore something else but from where he sat, he couldn't tell what.

Her tongue darted out and moistened her lips when she caught his eye. In silent warning, he set his goblet down and leaned forward to see what she wore. He saw more flesh than dress. He could see her holding her breath, her breasts pushed forward and scraping against only a scrap of material.

Her gown hit the floor with a silent whoosh. Shock, passion and outright lust hit him hard. If he hadn't put his goblet down it would have hit the floor, much like his chin.

The silk material she wore was unlike anything he had seen in the past. Small straps held it up where the material hugged her curves like a glove to a hand. Small bits of lace trimmed the edges and plunged low. But the center, Dear God, the center was nothing more than a V of material gathered at the apex of her thighs, her sex hardly concealed.

His smoldering eyes took her in and followed her hands as they traced her own form. Tara turned giving him another glimpse of her back end. His breath drew in when her hands molded to her buttocks.

"Do you like it?" she purred.

"Aye," he choked out.

She came to him, stretched out one very long leg and slid her hand up its length, then placed her foot between his thighs. She bent forward to give him the full view of his present.

"I like it too," she confided.

His hand stroked her thigh. Slowly he let his fingers journey to where the scrap of fabric met between her legs. He slipped a finger under the silk.

A sound of pleasure escaped from Tara. She trembled when he found the moisture already pooling, her desire evident on the tips of his fingers.

"I think 'tis time I repay you for all your teasing."

Her fingers clenched. *Promise?*

Aye! In a single fluid motion he lifted her up, carried her to their waiting bed. There, she stretched out in a shameless display of legs and arms.

"What's under that kilt?"

His smile teased. "Need."

Only a clasp held his plaid in place. One quick tug and he showed her. He wore only the kilt and nothing else.

His *need* looked ready and wanting.

"Now, dear wife, how will I unwrap this present of mine?" he asked as he stretched out beside her. His lips caught her throat. "Slowly, I think."

His hands traveled the path hers had. The silk

was cool in his hands. Under it, her nipples displayed her passion, pushing against the cloth.

He spread his fingers along her stomach, letting them dip lower.

She arched up, aching for more contact.

He stopped short of where she wanted his hand to go, and traveled back up to cup the fullness of her breast. He would tease her, and make her want before he possessed.

Her hands made their own journey across his naked back, detouring to make bold strokes over his hips and thighs.

Five long days, Duncan. I thought I would die.

Death could never be so sweet.

He peeled the silk from her shoulders. With her arms freed, he lowered it inch by painful inch, murmuring how much he loved his gift and how he would savor each layer. *Ah now, look at this. Such a lovely navel.*

His lips explored her abdomen, his beard scraped her skin. She bucked beneath his touch. The silk dipped lower, exposing the swatch of hair covering her sex.

"And this," his accent thickened, "this I need to explore more thoroughly."

Please. He lowered the silk to her ankles. With a slight kick of her legs, the small piece of cloth sailed to the side of the bed.

His lips traced her hips, her thighs. An ocean of desire threatened to flood her before he finally found her center.

Tara wanted to tease him. Had done so shamelessly, but now he was the one in control, and his slow pace maddened her. He devoured her, lick by lick. He flooded her thoughts with images of his mouth covering her core, a pleasure she had yet to experience. "You're driving me mad," she told him.

"The longer I take, the more pleasure I will

bring."

Tantalizing kisses explored her thighs. Heart racing, she pleaded with him to find her. His mouth moved over her sex, breathing puffs of hot air onto her sensitive skin.

When he pressed his mouth forward and found her nub of pleasure, his tongue and teeth drove circles around her.

Cries of pleasure at the intimacy of such a caress wailed from her lungs. Her hands clenched the sheets balling them in desperation. Currents of pleasure coursed through her blood.

With every moan, he moved faster.

She thrashed, lust pouring through her limbs. When she thought she could take it no longer she begged him to take her. "Please, Duncan, I need you in me. All of you."

He pulled up and in one swift motion drove himself home. The waiting did have its advantages.

"Heaven," he murmured, sheathing himself to the hilt in her warmth. With each thrust he branded her his.

Mine. He chanted in his head.

Tara heard him and smiled. He possessed her mind, body, and soul, and she would have it no other way. Love poured out of her when they crested together.

Love floated over them as they fell asleep still joined.

~~~~

It took several days for the wedding festivities to end, and even longer for the last of the guests to leave.

Several times during the celebrations, Duncan and Tara rode off together for a few hours of alone time. They often returned to heckling.

Settling into a routine once the Keep was rid of its guests had a calming effect on Tara. She
~~~~

worked in the gardens tending the vegetables and herbs.

"I'm telling you, malnutrition is the death of so many people in this century. We need every vitamin and mineral we can grow." She dug into the soil with the help of a small wooden hand tool. Duncan stood over her with a scowl.

"We have servants to do this, lass. I don't want to see you covered in dirt."

Tara glanced up, sent him a chaste smile. "You didn't mind a few days ago."

She referred to the day when they didn't make it all the way into the cabin where they had first made love. It was a good thing the cabin was sheltered by a grouping of trees. Otherwise, anyone could have seen the future Laird of Coinnich rolling around in the grass with his wife. She didn't even try and explain the dirt stains on her dress when they came back to the Keep.

"Still..." Duncan bent down and stopped her from digging.

"Try to understand. I'm not good at needle point and every time I go to the kitchens someone chases me away. At least out here I can do something useful."

"But..."

"And I like it, I really do. Just look at this." She stood and walked him to a plant with huge green leaves and a bright yellow flower. "It's my first Zucchini. I never had time to do this before, now I have more time than I know what to do with."

"I don't know."

She saw a crack in his resolve, and drove her point further. "If I can have a little help from my big powerful husband, and his special gift, I'll be able to keep this garden going all winter. Or at least most of it."

"What kind of help?" he asked.

"Oh, just a little heating of the soil." Tara had learned Duncan's most powerful Druid gift was fire. Not simply the ability to light one, but control it. He could apply heat without a flame as well. If he wanted hot water for tea he merely placed a finger in the glass and bingo. Hot water. Just as Myra could move the wind without any external sign from her, Duncan could burn anything with barely a thought.

"You want me to heat the soil?"

"Yes, and maybe a quick little dehydrating of a few seeds."

"Tara..."

"I'll make it worth your while." She moved closer, until she felt her breasts push up against his chest. "Very worth your while." She nibbled a sexy little spot on his neck.

You're wicked.

And you love it!

By the time Duncan walked away, a small section of Tara's garden had a lovely warm temperature that would germinate the seeds placed under a layer of rich soil.

Tara talked to the plants while she finished up her work for the day. "Now you be sure and grow quickly. I have an appetite for a rich tomato sauce, and the garlic is almost ready." She picked a wayward weed and tossed it aside. She added a splash of water before brushing off her hands for the last time. "There." She looked down at her handiwork. "Not bad for a day's labor."

Several rows of newly planted seeds waited for a bit of sun to peak into the courtyard. "Hmmm." She clapped her hands together as the idea formed in her head, then went in search for her father-in-law.

Chapter 19

Fall closed in, bringing the bite of winter to the morning hours. The family gathered around the fire after Amber and Cian had gone to bed.

"Your mother has had another vision," Ian said with dread in his voice.

Lora's greatest Druid gift was one of premonition. It was one of the ways the Ancients spoke to them, and how they knew of Grainna's threat so far into the future.

At times Lora's visions were heavy in detail while others were cryptic and vague. Each brought a strong emotion none of them could ignore.

Tara watched as Lora surveyed the faces of her children.

Everyone grew quiet.

"Winter solstice is coming," she said.

"With it, the need to keep Grainna from regaining her powers," Fin stated.

"Only this time, it will be different. I no longer believe the solstice has anything to do with Grainna." Lora glanced at her children and took Ian's hand.

The gesture wasn't lost on Tara. Lora was worried.

Fin agreed with his mother. "I don't think Grainna would wait for the solstice if she found another virgin."

"I agree," Duncan said.

"Our stay in the future might be longer." Fin concluded, while looking toward his brother.

Tara's heart tore a fraction. "Duncan can't go." She tightened her grip on Duncan's hand. "First of all, we're married. And although I understand the situation, I think it's a bit much to expect me to allow my husband to be with another woman."

"True," Ian said.

"And second, I don't think it would be safe for him to go back. The authorities would be looking for him. Cassy would have gone to the police by now. He'd be put in jail." The thought frazzled her, panic pushed goose bumps to her arms. She often worried about how her friend and sister would handle her disappearance. Now, her fears turned to how her husband would survive the future.

"Duncan is not to return," Lora announced, bringing peace to Tara's mind.

"Well then," Fin sighed. "Since Duncan and I look so much alike, I will have to disguise myself when I return."

Tara shook her head. "I don't know, Fin. The law would look for you, too. You don't know how easily you would be picked up in my time. It isn't like here. Every cop will have a picture of both of you. If they think I'm dead, they'll keep you in jail. We'll have to come up with a very good disguise. Have you ever wanted to be a blond?"

He arched his brow and gave a disapproving scowl. "No."

"Nay," Lora's voice rose above the others, interrupting their debate. "Finlay will not be returning either."

"What?" Myra, Fin, Duncan and Tara all said at once.

"Then who?" Myra asked.

Lora took a deep breath. "My vision was clear, more so than ever before. I've searched for a better interpretation for it, but there is none." She lifted her head, leveled her eyes to her daughter. "'Tis you who must go."

Both Duncan and Fin came to their feet in protest. "You must be mistaken. Sending Myra isn't an option."

"She would be put directly in harm's way," Duncan said.

"There is no mistake. My vision was clear. If Myra stays here during the next solstice, she would die."

Eyes shifted around the room. No one spoke as gnawing fear crept into everyone.

Myra broke the silence. "What else did your vision tell?"

"The threat to you is here, now. I couldn't tell by who or what."

"Do you think Grainna's here?" Tara asked.

"I don't know."

"Is there another Druid like her out there?"

Ian nodded to his eldest son. "I only know of the legends."

"Didn't you tell me she converted Druids to her ways?" Tara asked Duncan.

"Aye."

"Then it must be one of them." Myra walked to the fireplace deep in thought.

"But why, Myra?" Tara asked. "Any virgin blood will break Grainna's curse. Or am I missing something?"

"Virgin blood is powerful to anyone in the wrong hands." Ian told her.

"Any Druid who wants to do harm."

"Oh."

A collective sigh went through the room. They all kept their thoughts to themselves. Each of them watched Myra beneath lowered lids.

"When can I return?" Myra gazed into the fire. "After the solstice?"

"I am not... I don't know." Lora's eyes filled with unshed tears.

Silence came over them like the heavy down of a comforter. The fire cracked, sending sparks above it. The smoke lifted weightless and silent, up and out of the Keep.

Tara asked what no one else dared. "When will she go?"

"On the next full moon," Lora stated as if it was nothing more than a flight to Vegas.

Forcing a smile, Tara spoke with a confidence she only half felt. "Well, that doesn't give us much time now, does it?" She kissed Duncan's hand, let it go, and stood.

"Time for what?" Myra asked.

"Time to prepare you for the twenty-first century." Tara stated as if the answer were obvious. "Lucky for you, I know all there is to know about my time. You're going to love it." As her words came out, she knew they were true.

Myra let a small grin break through as she wiped her eyes dry. "You jest."

"I'm not joking. And that is the word by the way, *joke*. If you go around saying words like *jest* you'll stick out like a sore thumb."

"I don't know."

"No, you don't. But you will, and I'll teach you." Tara turned to Lora. "She has to go with all her gifts. Nothing can be stripped."

"Of course she will," Ian proclaimed.

"She will need every possible weapon against Grainna," Duncan said.

"You mustn't go near Grainna," Lora's command was direct. "My vision told me of your death if you stayed here, and safety for you in Tara's time. But that doesn't mean Grainna isn't a threat. We all know if she finds you, she could..."

Myra put a hand up. "I won't go near her. I have no wish to die."

"But how are we to stop her from finding another virgin to end her curse?"

"We don't have to concern ourselves with that now. It may be I'll have another vision showing me the path to stop her. It's hard to say what the future holds. No one saw this change in events."

Tara took Myra's hand. "We need to get started. Lora, we need your help."

"With what?"

"Making clothes." Tara spun her newest sister around, giving Myra's skirts a bit of wind. "Beautiful as it is, this simply won't do."

Tara placed a quick kiss on Duncan's lips and smiled. *Everything is going to be fine.* "Don't wait up."

The women left the room in search of material and thread.

The men poured large amounts of ale, seeking another plan.

~~~~

Dressed in what looked like Capri pants and a young man's tunic shortened and taken in, Myra looked more the part of a modern day woman.

To make her feel more comfortable, Tara put on her own shorts and t-shirt for the training session.

Tara sent for Duncan who had yet to arrive.

"Self-defense is essential for a woman to know in L.A. There are no knights who will come to your rescue if you're in a bad situation."

"You mean if someone wants to harm me?"

"There are bad guys in every time. Knowing how to get away from them can save your life, and your virtue. Unless he's cute, then maybe you won't mind getting rid of your virtue," Tara teased.

Myra blushed.

"And none of that. Talk about a dead giveaway. Twenty-one year old virgins are few and far between. If you go around turning red at every crass remark, Grainna will smell you a mile away. Say the word sex," Tara coached.

"Nay, I couldn't." Myra giggled and turned away.

"Sex, sex, sex." Tara bombarded her. "Making love, doing it, horizontal bop. Come on, the more
~~~~

you hear it, say it, etcetera the better."

"Sex," Myra whispered.

"Louder."

"Sex!"

"Better. Look, the blush is starting to fade."

A knock on the door signaled Duncan's arrival. "Now, don't say a thing. Surprise is essential for over powering someone bigger and stronger than you."

Tara opened the door enough to see if Duncan came alone. She ushered him inside and slid a chair under the door knob to keep out curious eyes.

Instantly, Duncan's eyes went to his sister. "I hardly recognize you in those."

Myra turned to the mirror and slid her hands over her hips, smiling. "The clothes do allow more freedom. I see why women would want to wear them."

"They do reveal more." Duncan skirted his eyes away. Tara took pity on him. It was as if he was noticing his sister as a woman for the first time in his life. And he didn't like the feeling. Tara didn't need their special connection to see that.

Myra's hair was tucked back in a ponytail. Her arms were bare as were her feet and ankles.

Will she be safe in your future? None of us will be there to protect her.

Instead of answering him, Tara moved to the center of the room, which had been cleared of furniture and extra rugs were tossed on the floor. "Duncan my love, come here. I have a surprise for you." Tara pointed to the space beside her.

"I do like a surprise." He shot a glance at his sister who watched and grinned.

"Put your arm over my shoulders." Tara instructed. "Good, now tell me, Duncan. Are you bigger than me?"

He looked at his playful wife, confused by her question. "Of course."

"Are you stronger than me?" She reached up, traced his chin with her finger.

"What are you getting at?"

"Do you think there is any way I, your weaker, smaller wife, could best you in hand to hand combat or even get you to the floor?"

He laughed at the thought. "I'm sorry, love. But there is no way..."

Tara's leg shot out and at the same time she brought up both of her hands and grabbed his free arm. Surprise and momentum was her weapon. He tripped across her leg and found himself flat on his back, with the wind knocked out of his lungs. "God's teeth!" he hissed between breaths.

"Sorry, love." Her smile was less than sincere. "I had to prove my point." She reached out a hand to help him to his feet.

He took it, but instead of hoisting himself up, he quickly maneuvered himself and Tara to where she was now on her back, he above her.

"Touché." Tara glanced at Myra. "The moral to this is, once you have your opponent on the ground, run like hell. Surprise only works once, unless they're really stupid."

Duncan kissed her before releasing her.

Tara demonstrated how to get out of a chokehold, how to remove a vice grip, and most important, exactly where to place her knee on a man if he got too close. "...and once you've done that, he won't be able to do anything with it. Right, honey?"

Duncan turned a bit green at the thought. "Aye."

"You can always use your powers, but it'll call attention to you. If your life is in jeopardy don't hesitate. It won't matter if someone finds out you're a Druid if you're dead."

Duncan played the guinea pig as they practiced their maneuvers. He gave his own tips along the way, most required more strength than either of them could muster. But a few they managed to maneuver with some skill after a fair amount of practice.

~~~~

An hour later, Duncan left to fetch the unsuspecting Fin. It was Myra's turn to practice on fresh prey. He rubbed his slightly bruised ego and instructed his brother to join the women.

Duncan took great pleasure in escorting Fin to Tara's room. Shortly after the door closed behind him, a loud curse, one similar to what Duncan had used, came through the walls.

He laughed all the way down the stairs.
~~~~

Chapter 20

Grainna kept constant surveillance on the Keep. She hoped to find a weak-minded servant working there, someone she could obtain information from about what transpired inside. But her *luck* wavered. As was her ability to read people as easily as she had in the future. Not practicing her magic daily cost her.

She kept her short visits to the village very quiet and only when other strangers passed through. She wore pauper's clothing and leaned heavily on a cane although her bones had completely mended.

She seldom saw the same people of the village twice, but had managed to watch the Druid girl, Alyssa. To her complete surprise, Matthew of Lancaster started making regular visits.

Grainna prided herself on changing strategies when the need arose. And it was time she started procuring help in her quest. The winter solstice was coming fast, but she wouldn't wait until then if a Druid virgin crossed her path again. She had learned her lesson with Tara.

Alyssa could be a virgin. Although not as powerful as the MacCoinnich's, she was more accessible than the daughter, Myra. Lancaster's attention would make getting her blood effortless.

She staged herself outside the girl's home and waited for Lancaster to emerge.

Leaning on her cane, she walked directly in his path. "I'm so sorry," she pleaded when he tripped over her frame. "I've barely the sight to see, forgive me, sir."

"'Tis quite all right, no harm done." Matthew

dusted off his shirt.

"Ye're so kind, Sir Knight, so very kind." Grainna waved her hand in front of his eyes, catching his gaze and settling it on her ruby necklace.

Slowly, she moved the pendent until she saw his eyes flicker. "Yes, ye are so kind, Sir Lancaster. Would ye help a poor woman such as me to my home? 'Tisn't far." She slipped a smile, innocent and pure onto her face, his mind opened for her to possess.

"Ahhh yes, there are many beautiful birds near my home. So many different species. Ye could watch them all day and never see the same two twice."

"Oh, how wonderful. I do like our feathered friends."

She took his arm as he led her to his horse.

So easy, she smiled. So very easy.

In the thick of the woods they took to a faster speed. By nightfall, she had him sitting in the one room cottage abandoned long ago. It was deep in the forest where few traveled, making discovery nearly impossible.

With a small amount of her magical potion, she liquefied his mind, molding him to her needs. Once sleep took over, she finished what she had started, and by morning, he was like the men of the future.

She circled the small hovel with the same protective spell she used in her youth. Only this time she placed the same protection around several other dwellings she had come across in an effort to keep her identity secret from the Ancients.

As much as she hated her weakness, she jumped at any noise, big or small which came in the night.

Now that she had someone to do her bidding,

she wouldn't have to leave as often.

Victory was close and tasted bittersweet. The Ancients had cursed her once, and according to Druid law, could not do so twice.

Without the threat of them descending on her again, she would wreak havoc over the land, relishing with great pleasure in the revenge she would take on the MacCoinnich's...starting with Tara. No, she wouldn't kill her. She'd keep her alive long enough to witness her husband's death. Even then, she might let her live so she could feel the grief of a Druid wed woman left without her love.

A vindictive grin in the form of a thin line pulled at her lips. With her powers restored, Grainna would end them all.

~~~~

Myra's planned departure was less than a week away. Nerves were jumbled and everyone was ill-tempered.

Because of the unknown threat, no one outside the family had been told Myra was leaving. A plan was in place to keep her absence undetected until long after the winter solstice. By then, with any luck, Lora would know when she was coming back. And the charade could be dropped.

Tara coached Myra about how to approach her sister. She gave her intimate details of their youth so Lizzy would believe her enough to listen to her story.

Tara had written a very long letter to Lizzy explaining where she was and how she had gotten there. Hopefully, it would open the door for Myra.

"Her biggest concern will be for Simon. She'll need to trust you, or she'll never let you in."

"How will I get to your sister?"

They didn't know where the stones would take Myra. There was no guarantee she'd be dropped in the same place where Duncan and Fin had been.
~~~~

The stones answered to a higher power. Time travel wasn't an exact science. It was impossible to know exactly where Myra would end up.

Tara walked with Myra outside the Keep walls and over the hills. The sun shone, but the air held the chill of the coming winter. Both women wore heavy cloaks over their wool gowns.

"The only thing I think will work is finding help from someone of authority, the police, hospital, something. You need to fake amnesia." Tara reached down, picked up a flat rock from the ground.

"What is amnesia?"

"Pretend you have no memory."

"No memory? How could I do that?"

"Well, if the police pick you up, tell them you don't remember anything except waking up wherever it is you end up." Tara went on. "Tell them your head hurts and that you think you fell. They'll probably take you to a hospital, run tests."

"A hospital is where they treat the sick?"

"Right."

"But I won't be sick. Won't they be able to tell?"

"Maybe." Tara tossed the stone, reached for another.

"I don't like to lie."

Tara laughed. "Well, get use to it, sister. You'll be lying through your teeth the whole time you're there."

"Couldn't I tell the truth?"

"They'd lock you up so fast your head would spin clean off your shoulders. Or worse, someone would believe you and use the stones for something horrible. Then how would you get back?"

Myra let out a long sigh. "I'm so worried. I'm trying to be brave on the outside so everyone will think I'm strong." A sob tore from the back of her throat. "But I'm not, Tara. I'm not strong like you."

Tara reached for her and let the tears come. When Myra cried out in anguish Tara pulled away. "Now you listen here. You're one of the strongest women I know. You have learned so much about my time in only a few short weeks. You're ready for this, Myra, ready to go to the future, meet my sister, and stay long enough for the danger to pass." Tara wiped her cheeks with her hand. "And you're going to eat great food and meet so many types of people your head will want to explode." Her nervous laugh suffered a smile from Myra. "And the technology will make you crazy! You'll love it."

"Are you sure?"

"I am, Myra. Everything will work out. Tell whoever finds you Lizzy's name. Once they find my sister, the rest will be easy. Make sure Lizzy tells Cassy everything. I don't want Cassy spending her life thinking she caused my death."

The plan was solid. Tara secretly thanked God that her friend and sister would finally know what happened.

"Do you think I'll come back?" Myra asked when they stopped and sat on a fallen tree.

"God, I hope so." Tara took her hand without looking at her. "I don't think I could bear losing two sisters in one year."

"How will I know when to return? It isn't like Ma can tell me. I've never had any premonitions like her. Amber seems to have that gift, but I don't."

"We have to believe something more powerful than us is pulling these strings. Have faith if nothing else. And pray." It was all Tara had to offer.

"The real question is if you'll want to return. Between the indoor plumbing, clothes and food, we may lose you because you'll want to stay."

"I'd miss my family too much."

Tara squeezed her hand. "Good. The list I'm making is growing by the hour." The list was what Tara wanted Myra to bring back with her. It was loaded with everything from medication, to seeds for every plant available, and books about how things are made in the future.

Including one on plumbing.

~~~~

The night before her expected departure, and exactly three weeks before the winter solstice, the family gathered for their evening meal. Even though everyone tried making the conversation and mood light, they failed.

Everyone agreed that Duncan, Tara, and Myra would go together outside the walls of the Keep where they would activate the stones without notice. If the entire family were to leave, someone would certainly notice and might question where they were all going.

This night was for goodbyes and final thoughts.

The servants were sent away for the night. The knights who guarded the keep while the family slept were asked to remain on watch in the towers. Even the dogs slept outside the main hall.

"How long should I wait before I return?"

"A month, maybe two. After that..." Lora cast her eyes to her plate of food that sat untouched.

"I'll return in two months." Myra sighed with relief saying this out loud.

"Nay, Myra. Wait for a sign," Lora encouraged. "I want your safe return. Not one which will put you in harm's way."

Ian MacCoinnich glanced at his daughter with fear in his eyes. "If you're ever in danger in that time you must return."

"I will, father."

"Has anyone thought of how we could go to her
~~~~

if needed?" Tara asked.

No one answered. No one could.

"I see." Tara's hand found Duncan's under the table. *Are we doing the right thing?*

His reassuring smile helped lift her spirits. *My mother's visions have never lead us wrong before.*

Amber and Cian went to bed near midnight.

Duncan and Tara returned to their bedchamber shortly afterward.

Myra stayed up late talking to her parents. Over and over she told them her plans. Each time she listened to the advice they gave, grateful for their council.

When she left their side, she had a family heirloom that would be worth currency in Tara's time and afford her a way to take care of herself if Lizzy was difficult to locate.

Fin caught her in the hall when she made her way to bed. "I didn't want the others to hear what I have to say. They'd worry too much."

"What is it?" She and Fin had always spoken so candidly and yet he hadn't said anything of importance since Lora announced she had to leave.

"If Grainna learns of you, she will stop at nothing to..." He turned away, his words trailed off.

Myra read him so easily. "Use me," she said, finishing for him.

"Aye." Fin sought her eyes and held them firm. "Unless you are of no use to her."

His implication would have shocked her if she hadn't already thought of it.

He took her hands. "Dammit, Myra. How can I be saying this to you?"

"Tara and I have already talked of this. When I return, if I haven't been given a sign that I'm safe from Grainna... I will be of no use to her one way or another."

"Oh God." He pulled her into his arms. "If you

don't return, I'll find a way to go to you. If it takes the whole of my life, I will know you are well."

Myra hated the fear that crept inside her heart. "When I return, if I'm no longer... chaste, what then, Fin?"

He took her head in his hands. "Any man would be lucky to have you as a wife, chaste or not."

He lied she knew, but she didn't call him on it. There was no purpose. Besides, life was more important to live than chastity was to keep.

~~~~

The three of them rode in silence. The fog covered the land and cloaked the riders in the perfect cover.

The sun peaked over the horizon, slightly burning off the fog when they stopped and set the stones in a circle.

"Remember, Lizzy is short for Elizabeth. Elizabeth McAllister. If for any reason she won't listen, find Cassy. Cassandra Ross." Tara thought she was missing something, and found herself rambling.

"You've told me all of this. I won't forget." Myra pulled off the cloak covering the modern clothing she wore. "Here, I won't be needing this."

Tara held her tears back and smiled like she meant it.

Duncan held his sister for one last moment, listened as she whispered, "Congratulations, brother."

"For what?" he asked.

She smiled and said, "You'll see."

One by one they touched the stones activating them until they glowed and pulsed.

"God's speed," Duncan called.

The wind started to turn and light shimmered and burned.

"Hey, Myra?" Tara called out distracting her
~~~~

from what was to come after sensing her fear.

"What?" she yelled over the noise.

"Have Lizzy take you to Magicland. The rides don't compare to this, but you'll love it."

Myra held onto her sack and waved with her free hand. "Magicland. I'll remember." Myra started the chant.

Duncan pulled Tara back when the ground began to shake. In a flash of light and a thunderous roar, Myra vanished.

The earth was scarred where the stones had been placed.

Both of them couldn't help but wonder if they would ever see Myra again.

So this is what it's like to say goodbye, Duncan thought.

At least you know where she's going. Lizzy never knew. Maybe now she will.

Duncan kissed the back of his wife's hand and made their way back home.

Chapter 21

The family went from *operation LA,* to *operation cover up.*

When anyone asked about Myra, the family would say, "You just missed her." Or, "If you run, you might be able to catch her."

But this grew tiresome and proved difficult.

On the third day after Myra's departure, they concocted a story about an illness she contracted, which would keep her confined to her room. This was much easier to maintain.

Tara and Lora were in charge of minding the sick, so there was no need for anyone else to bother. When a knock came at the door, Tara would jump under the covers, pull up the sheets, and pretend to be Myra.

The ploy worked and no one suspected a thing.

As winter set in, the nights grew longer. The newlyweds enjoyed the longer nights for their lovemaking. It was easy to forget the troubles of the household in Duncan's arms. Tara sought them constantly. Passion filled nights often led to late mornings.

Tara enjoyed the winter weather and snuggled into their bed after Duncan went off to train with the men. She slept more than usual. She thought her worry for Myra was partly the cause.

The door to the bedroom opened with a crash, startling Tara awake.

"I'm sorry, my lady. I didn't know ye'd still be abed at this time of day." Megan scurried into the room, closing the door behind her.

Tara's pulse pounded at an alarming speed as her body responded to the intrusion. Her stomach gave protest. She bit back the bitter taste of bile.

"My lady, are ye well?" Megan asked.

Tara leaned back in the bed, waited for the nausea to pass. "I'm fine, Megan. Maybe some water."

The maid hurried to get what she requested. "I hope ye're not getting ill from Myra. She's been a bed for the better part of the week." She handed Tara her drink. "This room has such a chill. Had I known you weren't well, I would have brought more wood to warm the room."

The fire was all but out, yet Tara could have sworn Duncan had hocus-pocused it before he left her. "What time is it?"

"Nearly mid-day." Megan drew the drapes back to let the light shine in.

"It's late. I should check on Myra," Tara lied.

"I can do that, my lady. Ye look like ye should stay abed."

"No! I mean nay." Pulling back the covers, Tara started to get up. Her stomach clenched again, this time in earnest.

She ran to the pot on the other side of the room and retched. When she finished, Megan handed her a towel and took the pot away.

As Megan left the room, Tara said, "Have Lora check on her daughter. You wouldn't want to catch this."

Tara settled back in bed and recalled what she'd eaten the night before.

It didn't take long for Lora to seek her out.

"It's nerves." Tara excused her illness away. "We've all been jumpy since Myra left."

"Still, it would be best if you rested today."

Tara shook her head. "I'm feeling better already." Lora's look of concern made her add, "But I'll take it easy."

"Good. We don't need more bad rumors about illness in the Keep."

"What are you talking about?"

"I overheard Megan speaking with Alice. She thinks Myra has a grave illness. That perhaps the illness has spread to you."

Tara's shoulders slumped. "We need to come up with another plan."

"Aye, I agree." Lora tucked in the blankets around her. "Not today. Today you rest."

"Yes, mother."

Lora's hand came up to her cheek. "That warms my heart."

Tara smiled before snuggling into the bed.

~~~~

Edgy. It was the only way to describe the mood over the Keep. In the shadow of the upcoming solstice, Ian had knights patrolling more frequently and in greater numbers.

Although Lora's premonition was specific to Myra, the threat was still out there and everyone knew it.

No one left the Keep alone. If a medical need came up in which either Lora or Tara was needed, at least two knights went with them. Even when Duncan and Fin went to the village to pick up the commissioned dishes which Tara had insisted be changed, they left together.

With Duncan on her errand, and the rest of the family busy, Tara settled into an overstuffed chair by the fire and dozed off.

Amber nudged her awake. Huge brown eyes smiled down on her, warming Tara's heart. Amber had spent a lot of time searching out Tara since Myra's departure. She missed her sister, and had no problem letting Tara take her place.

"Hey, sweetie, what are you doing?" Tara pulled back the blanket she had thrown over her lap so Amber could snuggle in.

"I was bored with the dolls." She made herself comfortable and continued to talk. "Megan wanted
~~~~

the dolls to sit and watch while she cleaned the room. It was tiresome."

Tara laughed. "I wasn't into dolls at your age either. I liked trucks better."

"What are those?" Amber's big eyes and long lashes fluttered against her cheeks.

"Well, trucks are like carts that are pulled by horses, only they aren't pulled by horses."

"How do they move?"

"By an engine."

"What kind of animal is an engine?"

"An engine isn't an animal." Tara snickered. "Oh never mind. When Myra comes back maybe she can explain them better." She purposely said when and not if.

"She is safe," Amber declared as if reading her thoughts. "I know she is."

"Did you have a vision like your mom?"

"Nay, not like that. I simply know, like you know Duncan is well, I know Myra is well."

Tara doubted it was possible for Amber to have such a strong connection with Myra. Maybe her desires for assurance was clouding her thoughts and making her pretend. Much like a child with an imaginary friend, it wouldn't be harmful to let her go on believing this. At least until a time there was no doubt of Myra's fate. "I hope so, Amber. I hope so."

"I know it," she said with pride. "Ever since we became blood sisters the night before she left, I can tell." Amber turned her palm up to Tara's face. "See, blood sisters."

Tara noticed a healed notch on one of her fingertips. "Did Myra tell you we did that?"

"Mum hum," she smiled. "We should do it too, that way we can all be real sisters." The words flew out of her mouth in a rush.

Sentimental, Tara draped an arm around her shoulders. "I'd like that."

Wasting no time, Amber jumped off her lap and ran for a knife.

It took only a few seconds to complete their chant and mixing of blood. Tara had to hold back a laugh at the seriousness in which Amber did the deed. Once done, they both smiled and nursed their sore fingertips.

"Now, I will know you are safe too." Amber snuggled back into Tara's lap, resting her arm over her waist. "You and the baby."

Tara settled into the chair before Amber's words registered. "What baby?"

"Yours silly." Amber's giggle had her entire body shaking.

"But, I don't have a baby."

"This one," she put her small hand on Tara's flat stomach.

Tara laughed at her, a nervous little laugh that had her pushing her brows together in a thoughtful frown. She shook her head and closed her eyes.

"No," she told Amber. "That's not possible..."

Amber continued to chuckle.

Tara stood up, tossing Amber out of her lap in the process. "That's not..." Using her fingers, Tara started to count. "It's not..." Then it hit her. It had been well over seven weeks since her last cycle.

"I'm pregnant." Tara stared off, completely ignoring the young girl who watched her every move. *How could I have been so blind? Morning sickness and sleeping all day. I would have made a terrible nurse.* She sucked in her lower lip. "A baby," she whispered. *I'm going to be a Mom.*

~~~~

Fin didn't protest Tara's request that all the metal dishes be done away with to make way for ceramic and glass. But he would have preferred Duncan drag someone else on his errand.

The bathroom she insisted on building was
~~~~

mind-boggling. Mainly because he was having a hard time making it happen. He hoped Myra would return sooner than later with the book on plumbing Tara told her to get.

He voiced his complaints to Duncan as they worked their way back to the Keep. The cart was loaded down with dishes and pans making the ride slow, thus allowing them time to talk. Or in Fin's case, complain.

"The Keep has not had a central place to bathe since it was built. Why does it need one now?"

Duncan clicked his tongue. "'Tis a simple request, Fin. One you would like, if you could make it happen."

"I haven't seen you scratching your head on this."

"I've been busy."

"Busy?" Fin and Duncan rode their horses alongside the cart that was driven by one of the Keep's servants. "Ah yes, busy—busy counting the spiders in the cabins outside the Keep's walls with your bride." He rolled his eyes. "Such *busy* work."

Duncan rode in silence.

"What? Nothing to say? No retort?"

Duncan reined his horse behind the cart to stay out of earshot of the driver.

"I worry, Fin. Tara's not been well. She tells me she's fine, but she's not."

Duncan's sobering words wiped the smile off Fin's face. "Worried is all she is. We all are."

"I hope 'tis all it is."

Fin changed the subject to distract his brother from fretting over much. "Do you know the advice she gave to our sister before she left?"

"Which advice do you speak of?"

"Tara suggested Myra lose her virginity if she gets desperate."

"I'm not surprised at Tara's words. I should have thought to say the same thing."

"Your wife is very open with our sister."

"You don't approve?"

"It's not that, it's... Dammit, Duncan, doesn't it bother you that Myra could right now be—"

"Nay, it doesn't," Duncan said, cutting him off. "Myra is very wise and will take care of herself. I'm grateful for Tara's coaching."

"I hope her knowledge is helpful to Myra now."

"I think it is. One of us would know if she were in trouble."

"What about the risk here?" Fin asked. "Do you think 'tis great?"

"If it drove Myra from us, than it should be thought of as such."

"I want her back," Fin exclaimed.

"We all do." Duncan looked toward the Keep and smiled.

"What is it?"

"Tara is singing again."

~~~~

Fin went to the kitchens through one of the back doors. Duncan led the horses to the stables. He made sure they were compensated well for their journey before making his way inside.

He scarcely got in the door before Tara leapt into his arms, squealing and nearly knocking him off his feet.

"I thought you'd never get home." Tara pecked kisses all over his face, while he held her off the floor. She latched her legs around his waist and took advantage of the fact it took both of his hands to hold her up. "I missed you."

He laughed.

The maids who rushed to the hall when they heard her squeal, wore shocked expressions.

His dismissive glance had them scurrying out of the room.

"Feeling better, I see," Duncan said, holding her butt with both hands trying to ignore his
~~~~

physical reaction to their intimate embrace.

"I feel great." She caught his lips in a deeper kiss. She slid down his frame almost as quickly as she had jumped on it. "And hungry. I could eat a horse."

"No more sickness then?"

"I could only hope. But my guess is I'll have to deal with that for a little longer." She smiled, leading him to the dining hall.

"Deal with what? You'd tell me if you were ill, wouldn't you, Tara?"

"I'm not ill." She turned to him now. "In fact, I've never felt better." She made a show of holding both his hands and gazed up at him with misty eyes. "I have a surprise for you."

"What surprise, my playful wife?"

Her body wiggled closer, her mind and thoughts slipped in as well. *We're going to have a baby!*

Duncan's eyes flew open wide. He skimmed over her thin waist. His jaw dropped.

He stared, and said nothing, bending his head to study her. "Are you certain?"

She nodded, and did a little happy dance.

Duncan's heart burst with happiness. He crushed her into his arms. A primal howl escaped as he twirled her in circles.

Every maid, servant, knight, and family member within earshot ran to the room. "What happened?" several voices asked.

He seared her lips with a soulful kiss.

She stumbled backward.

He caught her at the elbows, heart still soaring with gaiety.

"God's teeth, son. Take it to your chambers," Ian bellowed. "You had us all worried." Ian stood surrounded by faces, all saying the same thing.

Can I tell him? Tara asked bouncing with excitement.

Be my guest.

"Sorry, 'Grandpa', we got carried away." Tara put her head down in mock shame. "We won't do it again."

"As well you should be. Such displays are... 'Grandpa'?" Ian stopped speaking, his voice lowered with suppressed happiness.

Tara looked up through strands of hair, which had fallen, in front of her eyes, obviously trying hard to keep a straight face. She failed miserably.

Duncan applauded her efforts.

"Grandpa?" Ian asked with a robust laugh.

Tara did the happy dance again.

Ian swooped her in the air as Duncan had done a moment ago. His beaming grin twinkled in his eyes.

By the time Fin had his turn, Tara looked green.

Duncan, Ian and Fin apologized at the same time.

When Lora led Tara to the kitchens for food, Duncan accepted the knocks of congratulations on his back.

A new life to celebrate, Duncan pondered. *'tis exactly what we needed. Worries can wait for another day.*

~~~~

Because the family wanted to talk of the new arrival until all hours of the morning, it was late when Tara and Duncan finally made their way to their chambers. Duncan helped her out of her gown. He pulled loose the strings binding the gown together, while she held her long vibrant hair back. It was a husbandly chore he enjoyed fully.

"Are you truly happy?" Tara asked.

Her question surprised him. How could she not know how pleased he was? He caught her reflection in the mirror, and gathered her against him. His hand trailed down her side and settled on
~~~~

her flat stomach. "I couldn't love you any more than I do right now."

Duncan remembered the vision he had placed in her head right before he had made love to her the first time. Looking at her now was as if the vision was a premonition to their future.

"Are you sure it isn't because of the vows we took in California?"

His brows narrowed. He caught his breath.

"The handfasting?" Tara turned to stare him in the face. "You haven't forgotten have you?"

"Nay but..." *How does she know...*

She read his thoughts, almost before they formed. "You don't really think I don't know what happened back there, do you?"

"Ah," He searched deeper to see if she was angry or hurt. It was the only secret he kept. He feared what she was going to say. He swallowed and waited, but neither fear nor anger emerged.

"Even if Myra hadn't told me, I would have figured it out. We started..." *Talking to each other like this the instant our vows were spoken. You had to think I'd know.*

Myra told you?

"Yes, the day of our wedding. I told her the vows we took in California, and she explained what they were." Her breath hitched. "Why didn't you tell me?"

"I couldn't have told you then, you wouldn't have believed me."

"What about later? When we came here?"

"There were so many things for you to take in at first. I didn't think it was wise to give you more."

"What about after we were engaged?"

He rolled his head back. "I didn't want to lose you. When you ran off that first day you scared me."

"I could never leave you." She put her arms

around him, placed her head on his chest. "When I think of how Grainna must have planned my demise, our demise, it sickens me. You didn't have to bind with me. You could have let me say my vows and left."

"That was never an option." He held her tighter and shot her a look. "You have flooded my mind every moment from the minute I sat on you."

She chuckled at the memory, then turned toward the mirror and watched as his hands slid down her hips. "A baby, Duncan. We're going to have a child."

He enjoyed the slim curve of her hip. "Do you think our child would mind sharing you tonight?" His hands circled in front of her turning from love to passion.

"I think our child has little to say at this moment."

He lifted her and carried her to the bed.

Chapter 22

Rumors began circulating throughout the Keep and leaked to the village. Talk of Myra having some deathly illness grew. Some rumored she'd run off with one of the men who had visited at the wedding.

Excitement over the announcement of Tara's pregnancy halted some of the gossip surrounding Myra. However, the MacCoinnich's thought it best to give some explanation to Myra's disappearance. It wasn't known how long she would be gone, and keeping up the ruse of her nonexistent presence was taxing on everyone.

One afternoon, Ian stood in the courtyard with Fin to set up their newest scam.

"She's unreasonable. Every suitor she denies!" Ian yelled.

"Calm down, father. Myra is willful and knows what she wants."

"Blah." He tossed his hands in the air. "She does not know what is good for her. Perhaps the convent will give her the solitude and time to regard my request for her to marry."

"Are ye certain?" Fin's voice carried to the men standing guard in the towers.

"Aye, tomorrow Duncan will escort her before the cock crows. She can return when she's more reasonable." Ian turned on his heel and left.

"Poor Myra." Fin announced to the growing crowd.

Mumbles of agreement ran amongst the men.

~~~~

Tara hated seeing Duncan leave, even if only for a few days. *I'll miss you.* She held him fast.
~~~~

"I'll be back in less than a week, my love. Stay close to the Keep."

"I will." She leaned close and whispered, "I'll think of all kinds of wicked ways to show you how much I missed you." *And your body.*

His eyes clouded with passion, a low groan emerged from his lips. *Witch! Now I'm sure not to sleep.*

"Good." With a final kiss, Tara watched as Duncan rode away with Lora, posing as Myra hidden beneath a long cape.

~~~~

Gregor kept watch in the early hours of the morning. The rain let up in the night, a relief for him and the men who patrolled.

He considered himself a faithful servant to Laird Ian and his family, and never thought to question why the men were placed on alert.

Whenever his laird sensed trouble, trouble came. He watched the hillsides with a keen eye, and investigated every noise.

He noticed the farmer long before the farmer saw him. He was running fast for a man his age, as if the Devil himself was on his heels.

As much as he would have liked to meet him half way, Gregor knew better than to leave his post and waited for the man to flag his attention.

Gasping for air, the man opened his mouth to speak. It took him several minutes to tell him what he found.

The nature of his tale had the hair on Gregor's neck standing on end. He hurried the man into the courtyard and bid him water from one of the maids, and then told his squire to ready a second horse.

The commotion in the courtyard brought Ian and Fin at a run. Gregor jumped off his horse before it came to a stop. His quick bow to Laird Ian was brushed aside, he kept his voice low. "The
~~~~

body of a young woman from town has been found by the edge of the village." He pointed to the farmer who was still catching his breath. "He found her, and begs that we come."

Ian and Fin exchanged looks. "Could he determine the cause of death?"

Gregor visibly swallowed. "Her neck was cut."

"A murder," Fin said aloud.

"And something else. Her blood was used to circle her body. The villagers will think demons are amongst us if they find her. The man was sensible enough to come here first."

Ian looked up at the walls of his home, several men were poised on the lookouts, and no alarm was being raised. "Quickly, Fin, and only us four." He nodded to Gregor as Fin ran off to get their mounts.

"Is this the trouble ye thought was coming?"

"I hoped to avoid any trouble."

~~~~

Tara slept in late. Again. Pleased she wasn't suffering with morning sickness, she took her time getting ready.

When she made it downstairs to the main hall it was all but abandoned.

"Where is everyone?" Tara asked the kitchen maid Alice.

"Laird Ian and Lord Fin rode off in a hurry, a problem methinks. Young Amber is out with the kittens. Lady Lora is in her chambers, mournin' her daughter's departure still. I'm not sure where Lord Cian is."

Tara tensed with Alice's words. The blank stare the woman wore on her face had goose flesh rising on her arms. Reading people was easier for Tara these days and Alice seemed scared. "Do you know what the problem is?"

"Nay, my lady. They don't tell me these things. I'm sure 'tis nothing ye can do. Sit, sit." Alice
~~~~

shuffled her to a chair. "Let me feed ye and the wee lass or lad ye're carrying."

Dutifully, Tara sat.

Alice hurried off to the kitchen and returned with a plate full of food.

Eating it proved difficult, despite her hunger.

Something was wrong. She could feel it.

~~~~

They smelled the scene long before they came upon it. Over the scent of rain soaked trees, surrounding the clearing in the woods, fresh blood and the stench of death penetrated the air.

"Who would do such a thing?" Ian absorbed the pathetic waste of life spread out before him.

"I know not, my Lord. Whoever did this must be mad." Gregor held back a gag.

She had been dead for at least a day, no more or the animals in the woods would have found her. Her limbs were stiff and grey as the clouds above.

All three men had seen their share of death, on the battlefield and in life. But what lay before them was beyond any carnage they had experienced.

The young woman's hands were bound. A dark cloth concealed her face and eyes. Bruising was evident on her exposed legs and arms. Her ripped and bloody clothing lay in shreds. Her neck had been slit exactly as the farmer had said. But the blood did not pool where she lay.

Instead, it had been used.

A circle had been carved in the soil. The woman's blood filled the groove. The points of a star jutted from beneath her corpse. The smell of sulfur choked the air.

It was the scene of a ritual, a horror not seen in this land for decades.

Fin noticed the small chain on the woman's neck and felt the fleeting sickness of recognition.

Behind them, the young squire accompanying
~~~~

them made sounds of fear.

The old farmer diverted his eyes. He jumped at the sound of a squirrel in a tree.

The wind rustled leaves from the forest floor. Their eyes shot in every direction and both appeared ready to flee at the first sign of trouble.

"Gregor, go." Ian nodded to the boy and farmer. "Calm their fears while I consult with my son."

"Aye, my lord."

Fin took off the dark cloth covering the lass's face. He closed his eyes and swallowed hard.

Alyssa.

"Father," he said in hushed tones. "I know this girl."

"Aye, I recognize her." Ian clicked his tongue. "Her grandfather was one of us."

They spoke her name together as soon as the thought emerged. "Grainna."

"It has to be, but how?" Fin stood and removed his cloak.

"I know not. But this is exactly what's described when stories of Grainna are told. If Grainna is here, then your mother's vision and Myra's need to leave all makes sense."

Fin glanced at his father. "Thank God, Myra's safe!"

"Do you think Grainna broke her curse?" Ian asked.

Fin remembered the last time he had been with Alyssa, her smile. "Nay, if the curse is broken, 'twas not done with this lass."

"How can you be sure?" Ian glanced at him.

Loss punched Fin hard in the gut. "She was no virgin." He turned from his father, strode to his horse, removed the blanket, and laid it on her. "I will tell her parents."

Ian put a reassuring hand on his shoulder. "I can see this done, Fin."

"I have to do this."

His father didn't ask questions or press for information.

"We should clean this up. We don't want folk to panic."

Ian instructed Gregor to escort the farmer back to his home, then return with his squire so a grave could be dug.

Finlay and Ian set fire to the grass once the others had gone, burning all evidence of the ritual away.

Unwilling to let Alyssa's parents witness the violence of her death, Fin removed her necklace to give to them. Once Gregor had returned, and her grave was dug, he set out to deliver the shocking news.

~~~~

Tara, acting as lady of the house, consulted with Alice about preparations for dinner. She spent a good portion of her day directing servants. They needed to remove tapestries and take them outside for winter cleaning before bad weather set in.

Once everyone was busy with her instructions she tried her hand at knitting to keep busy. She was all too happy to put it down when young Jacob, Duncan's squire, announced a visitor.

"Lady MacCoinnich, sorry to barge in on ye." Behind him stood Matthew of Lancaster.

"That's quite all right, Jacob. Sir Matthew, what can I do for you? Were we expecting you?" Tara hadn't been told he was coming. A silent alarm went off in her head.

"Nay, my lady, I was traveling this way when I ran into Lords Ian and Fin. 'Tis a problem." He looked around the room, lowered his voice. "A problem they need ye for."

Her unease from earlier returned. "What kind of problem?"
~~~~

"I was asked to bring ye to them. They didn't want me to announce what I've seen. They said 'tis a private *family matter.*" His eyes shifted to the door. "We should hurry."

"Of course. Jacob, have my horse readied." She turned to Lancaster. "I'll grab my cloak."

Outside Jacob held her horse with a nervous hand.

She pulled herself into the saddle.

"My lady," Jacob said, looking up at her with worry etched on his features. "Lord Duncan asked that ye not leave the Keep."

Tara smiled to give him some ease. Ease she didn't feel. "I'm on my way to Laird Ian now. Don't fret. I'm safe with Sir Lancaster."

"Mayhap another knight should also escort ye, my lady?"

Tara considered the lad's suggestion, then remembered the words 'family matter,' and thought twice about bringing more people to witness the problem.

"I won't be long, Jacob." She didn't give him more time to talk or question. She turned her horse and followed Lancaster. Worry and fear filled her.

Duncan was so far away she couldn't sense him, let alone speak to him with her mind. She cursed their decision to send him away.

They set out toward the village. Once under the cover of woods, Lancaster changed direction to one she wasn't familiar with.

So many things raced through her head. She pleaded in her mind for Duncan to return. She couldn't tell if her thoughts reached him. "What did you see?"

Matthew looked at her and speeded up his mount, making talk impossible. "We should hurry," he told her again.

They journeyed deeper into the forest.

~~~~

Duncan and Lora moved daily to keep anyone who might notice off their track. Not that they thought anyone watched. If anything, all had been quiet.

Too quiet. Lora fretted within.

Neither of them was able to talk with their spouses because of the distance. And on this day, they moved well beyond emotions, as well.

They both felt the pull to go back, yet neither acted on it. Instead, they made camp by a stream and waited another day before they started home.

Duncan fished by the stream while Lora dozed. A dream swept her away until it erupted into a vision.

In her head, she saw Tara riding into the woods. Above her, faces of the Ancients floated, all of them yelling warnings.

Warnings Tara didn't hear.

A cabin emerged. Inside was a presence Lora instantly knew was Grainna. A darkened mass threw its shadow over Grainna's evil form and choked off her vision. But not before she saw Tara in the woman's clutches.

Lora woke screaming, shivering in a sweat.

Panicked, she jumped to her feet and ran to her son.

~~~~

Duncan turned in alarm at the sound crashing through the brush. His mother ran to him, out of breath and collapsed at his feet. She warned him, "We have to return. I had a vision."

Alarm slithered through him like a snake in tall grass. In an instant, he knew his mother was about to reveal his worst nightmare. "What is it? Is Myra returning?"

She shook her head. "Nay, 'tis Tara. Duncan..." A sob burst forth. "Grainna has Tara!"

Duncan grabbed hold of his mother's

shoulders, his eyes searching hers. "Are you sure?" His jaw clenched on the emotion and bile bubbling in his throat.

She nodded, tears streaming down her face.

He should never have left. They knew there was danger and still they acted though there was none. Primal rage and terror broiled within. It left cold emptiness in his soul. He cursed his foolishness and prayed Tara's life would be spared.

Wasting little time, they mounted their horses, leaving most of their provisions behind in their haste.

A howl retched from his gut. He kicked Durk into a faster pace.

~~~~

"How much farther?" Tara asked, trying to stay in the saddle, which wasn't easy considering their speed. Tara wasn't convinced the rate they traveled was good for her baby and started to voice her concern.

They'd been riding for over two hours, and she was beginning to think they were lost. Matthew hadn't said a word during their journey. He ignored most of her questions, making the time even more uncomfortable. The weight of his silence sat heavy on her shoulders.

"Matthew, I need to slow down," she said, tugging at the reins.

He rounded back to her. "We should hurry." He forced her horse to a faster pace.

"Matthew, enough! Laird MacCoinnich knows I'm pregnant. He wouldn't want harm to come to me or the baby."

He continued to pull on her horse's reins.

"I insist we slow our pace," she yelled. She kept the words she wanted to toss at him in her head.

To Tara's relief, Matthew resigned and rode beside her.
~~~~

He said nothing.

She watched him out the corner of her eye. His back was rod straight, his gaze glossed over. His look was familiar, but she was having a hard time placing it. Was he angry? In shock? What had he seen to make him so stoic? “Do you know why they sent for me?”

He sneered at her, then moved his eyes forward. “I think it best they tell ye.”

“That bad huh?”

He said nothing.

The woods were so thick she could barely see the sun through the trees. The smell of rain blanketed the forest and rotting vegetation. Tara thought she heard a waterfall in the distance. That meant a stream must be nearby. She wondered if it was the same stream that followed along the village border.

Most times she would love the heavy scent of oak and moss, mixed with the pine. But the knowledge that she rode toward danger kept her from enjoying the forest. She wished Duncan was here. Despite the knight beside her, she was desperately alone.

Tara needed a distraction from the silence. She glanced at Matthew and picked a topic she knew he would ramble on about. “What species of birds do you find in these woods, Sir Lancaster?”

He stared ahead in utter silence.

“Did you hear me, Sir Matthew?”

“We’re almost there. See the cottage?”

Thank God. Matthew was wigging her out. She couldn’t wait to see her in-laws.

A clearing gave a glimpse of a structure that was close to shambles. The walls leaned and the roof appeared as if it hadn’t been thatched in years.

Why on earth would Ian and Fin be here? More to the point, how had Lancaster come upon them like he said? There was no noticeable path leading this way, and it certainly wasn't in the direction of any neighboring village. At least none she knew about.

The closer they got, the more uneasy she became. "Ian? Finlay?" she called out.

No answer. Alarm bells started to chime inside her head.

"They must be inside," Matthew said.

Her eyes darted all around. She stood up in her saddle to get a better look. "Ian? Finlay?" she yelled louder, cringing at the panic she heard in her voice.

There were no horses. No sign of the men. She was close enough to the cottage that whoever was inside would hear her.

But no one came out with her calls.

It wasn't right. An icy cold crept over her entire body, except for her hand, which started to burn with a radiant heat. The tips of her fingers grew hot where she had pricked them with Myra's and Amber's.

Something is wrong.

Something told her to get away. Tara turned her mount and kicked her into a full run.

Matthew came after her.

Over her shoulder, she saw his expression change from catatonic to murderous.

She didn't get far before Lancaster was beside her.

He grabbed her, dragged her off her horse and across his lap. Within seconds, he held her hands in a grip like a vice.

She kicked and screamed. The horse bucked, sending them both to the forest floor.

Winded and frantic, she scrambled to her feet. Skirts lifted to her thighs, she bolted. She made it a few yards before Matthew tackled her to the ground.

Spitting dirt from her mouth, Tara struggled to get up. His knee planted firmly in her back, held her in place. She had no leverage to fight off her attacker.

Tara managed to turn her head just in time to see him raise a fallen branch over her.

His blow to her skull stopped her fight. Her last thought before darkness overtook her was of Duncan.

Chapter 23

Tara woke face down on a musty dirt floor. Her head ached. Blood had dried on the back of her neck.

Rough rope bound her hands and feet. Cloth covered her eyes. A small slit in the bottom of the fabric afforded her a glimpse of light from a fireplace.

Laughter, wicked and familiar, filled the room. "Look what the cat dragged in."

Oh God! A wave of nausea hit her hard. She bit back nasty bile. She'd never forget that voice. "Grainna!"

"Well, well. Know my real name, do you?"

"What do you want?" Tara struggled to sit up.

A heavy boot pushed her to the floor.

"I'm no use to you, now."

"That is debatable." Grainna moved away.

The foot still held her. *Lancaster!*

Tara struggled to see Grainna, but caught only a bit of her image between the slits in the fabric.

Grainna glared down at her, cocked her head to one side, as if in debate. "You ran from me, after everything I did for you."

"You were plumping me up for the kill. No better than a turkey on Thanksgiving."

"True. Still, your ungrateful behavior has led to this."

"You're twisted."

Grainna laughed. "You're stupid if you think I'll put up with your insults for long."

Tara realized how vulnerable she was. No one knew she was here. Duncan wasn't due back for two more days. She couldn't use their telepathic link to plead for his help. "What do you want from me?"

"It pains you. Not knowing."

Tara heard her shuffling and saw the hem of a filthy skirt under the cloth covering her eyes. She heard the sound of old bones popping when Grainna knelt closer. "Where is she?"

"Who?" Tara asked. The foot holding her lifted and came down hard, pain raced up her spine.

"The virgin? What have you done with her?" Grainna said, spit coming out with each word.

"I don't know who you mean." Tara cloaked her thoughts as Lora had taught her.

Grainna pulled her up by the hair. "The sister?" she hissed. "Where is the sister?"

Tara screamed. The cloth covering her eyes was yanked off. Grainna stood over her. Hate and fury burned in her eyes. Red blazed from them, intense as the flames within the hearth. She somehow looked different—younger.

"Duncan took her to the convent."

Grainna raised her hand and brought it down hard. Tara tasted blood. Pain burst in her cheek.

"Try again."

Tara glared and kept silent.

Grainna flicked a finger.

Lancaster kicked her side.

She screamed. *My baby!* Tara huddled away from the pain of his boot. Fear for her child clenched her gut.

Grainna's grin widened. "Well now. Isn't that interesting?" She reached out and pinched at Tara's stomach.

Tara pushed herself back and away from Grainna until the wall stopped her.

Grainna pushed forward, reached and twisted her grip on Tara's waist.

A wrenching sob escaped her throat. Tara pleaded, "Please, no."

"New life has such power, even now. Yes, I feel the heart." Grainna loosened her grip, leveled her blood shot eyes upon her. "Your lover will try hard to find you."

The stench of her breath was nauseating. Tara turned her head away.

"Where is she, Tara?" Her hand gripped her stomach, nails bit into her flesh.

"Gone! Out of your reach, out of this time!" *Please leave me alone. Leave my baby alone. I'm telling the truth.*

Reading her thoughts, Grainna shrieked in rage.

Tara curled into a ball as objects around the room flew, hitting anything in their path.

Grainna vented her magical wrath.

~~~~

Megan met Ian and Fin at the door, frantic. She had difficulty putting her words together. "Please, Lord Ian, I dinna know what to do. Amber won't come out of her room, she locked herself in. She keeps calling for Lady Tara."

Ian looked at Fin in alarm. "How come Tara isn't with her?"

Megan's eyes grew large. "She is with ye, is she not?"

"Why do you think that?" Fin shouted.

"Sir Lancaster came to fetch her for ye. She left with him hours ago."

Father and son took the stairs two at a time.

Ian's foot knocked Amber's door off its lock. Amber rocked and cowered in the corner of her room. He ran to his youngest child, took her into his arms.

"Tara... Tara... The mean woman has her, Da." She hit her hand to her head. "They keep kicking her and hitting her. Tara is so scared."

"Who has her, Amber?" He wiped away the fallen tears. "Who is the mean woman?"
~~~~

"Grainna."

Amber held her hand in front of her, as if she could stop Tara's pain from afar. "No!"

Ian signaled to Fin to ready the men. It took a half hour, but Ian coaxed what information he could out of Amber. He calmed her enough to leave her with Megan and Cian, so he could direct the men.

"Why does Lancaster do her biding? He is not Druid," Ian asked his son.

"Grainna had many men who followed her. She had power over their minds." Fin sheathed his sword and prepared to mount his horse. "Alyssa's parents told me Lancaster was last seen with their daughter."

"We've no way of knowing if there are others who Grainna controls. If Lancaster did what we saw earlier, then there is nothing he would not do for her."

A search party formed and before the sun set they, along with Fin, moved out in the direction Jacob saw Lady Tara depart.

Ian had the daunting task of waiting. Cian slumbered in the chair beside him. Amber finally fell to sleep in her room.

With every hour, he felt his wife's presence draw nearer. He sensed her fatigue at the long hard ride and kept their internal conversation minimal, knowing there was very little good to say.

As his son and wife rode closer, Ian called off the guard. Completely unconcerned at the questions which would arise about why his wife was with Duncan, he ordered the gate lowered. He would fix those problems later. For now, he thought only of how he would explain to Duncan how he failed in keeping his wife safe.

A fate he never foresaw, and as God as his witness, would never allow to happen again.

~~~~
~~~~

Like the pot above the fire, Grainna's anger simmered. She should kill Tara now, and use her blood like she had the other.

Grainna killed the village girl to vent her rage when she realized she was not innocent. She would have killed her anyway, but that was no matter. The power, which surged while the girl slid slowly into the abyss, was enough to try one of her old rituals, a ritual which had brought some amount of power to her in the past.

It worked, to a small degree. Her face lost ten years of age, and her body felt a bit of strength returning. Very little of the girl's powers transmitted to her, but a part of her youth did.

Perhaps her luck was returning.

Lancaster's weak mind was easy to control. Even now the fool stared off into space. His mind only saw birds, stupid ugly birds. With a simple motion or thought, Grainna could have him snap Tara's neck.

Tara's sanity had started to waver, she thought. When Grainna reached into Tara's mind, all she heard were nursery songs. Fear for her unborn child kept her singing. There was no sign she reached out for help from her husband, or his family. Grainna had plenty of time before Duncan would find her. And she knew, without any doubt, he would come.

For now, she weighed her options carefully. The virgin was gone. But Scotland was littered with virgins and Druids. If killing one weak Druid gave her back ten years, than killing others could do the same. Slowly, she would gain back what she had lost. The Ancients left a loophole in their curse, one she would exploit.

She would wait to kill the sniveling woman in the corner. Wait until her mate could watch. Destroying love and life was her sweetest revenge.

~~~~
~~~~

Tara never took her eyes off of her. Her hours of clinical work in the psychiatric ward at the hospital were coming in handy. She rocked back and forth sometimes singing quietly, always singing in her head.

Grainna's probing into her mind wasn't gentle. She slammed inside bringing pain and leaving anguish in her wake.

Why she hadn't made a move on her in hours, Tara couldn't fathom. She sure as hell wasn't going to ask.

As much as she wanted to peek into Grainna's head, she didn't dare. To do so would invite her into hers, and Tara didn't want that.

So, she rocked and sang. All the while her hands struggled, pulling at the bindings on her wrists. Strength wasn't working, so she used little sparks of fire like Duncan had taught her when lighting a candle. She winced when the fire singed her skin and missed the rope. Despite burning her flesh, she kept at it. What choice did she have? Her unborn child's life depended on her escape.

She couldn't feel Duncan, couldn't hear him. For a short time Tara thought she had, but then realized it was Amber in her thoughts. Afraid to speak outright to Amber with her thoughts, Tara sang her hints and clues.

Hush little Amber don't say a word, Tara is hidden in the woods. I can hear a stream nearby. I need to sing this lullaby.

~~~~

The sun on the new day was cresting the horizon when Duncan and Lora rode into the yard.

Silently, Lora went straight to Amber.

Duncan cornered his father. "Tell me."

Duncan listened to his father relay the day's events, starting with Alyssa's death and ending with Lancaster taking Tara. Duncan kept his fear in check, even when it threatened to take him
~~~~

over. "She must be far away. I can only sense her."

"Amber acts as though she can hear her."

"How?"

"She mumbled something about a secret spell her and Tara had shared. Do you know what she speaks of?"

"Nay." But his clever wife wasn't afraid of anything, so he wasn't surprised to hear his father talk of spells.

They went to Amber's room. Lora was in bed beside her and stroking her long hair, soothing her as mothers do.

Amber's eyes fluttered open. Seeing her brother at the end of her bed, she crawled over the covers and circled her arms around him. "She's waiting for you, Duncan. She's in the woods by the falls."

"Can you hear her?"

She nodded. "She sings to keep the other one out. She doesn't want me to talk with her for fear Grainna will hear. But she's frightened."

That he knew, but to hear his youngest sister's tearful report made him restless to be on his way.

"The falls? Do you know which ones?"

Amber closed her eyes and repeated what Tara was singing.

"The woods are deep and thick by me. Lots of great big tall, tall trees. The cottage has an old thatched roof. The smoke will give off big black soot. I can hear the stream nearby. I need to sing this lullaby. Keep my baby safe in me, bring me help oh please, please, please."

Amber held her brother's hand. "She keeps repeating it over and over. Can I tell her you're coming?"

"Nay. Don't." He smiled at his sister. "You've done all you can, go to sleep. I'll have her home before dinner."

He nodded to his mother and left the room.

Outside, his father stopped him. “Take more men with you.”

“I do this alone.”

Ian grabbed his arm. “I’m not asking.”

Duncan, who could count on one hand the times he defied his father, did so now, with no regret. “I will not be witnessed in what has to be done. I will use every power at my disposal to bring my wife home. I do it alone.”

Ian relented. “God’s speed.”

Duncan gathered his weapons and packed up his father’s horse which was readied and waiting.

He kicked the horse into a full run in the route he believed his wife to be.

The farther away from the Keep he rode, the stronger her pull became. He headed in the direction of the falls, the opposite way Fin had set out.

~~~~

Her wrists burned and blistered, she finally managed to loosen the bindings.

Lancaster stared off in a catatonic trance. Grainna gazed into a glass sphere and chanted.

This is so surreal. Hansel and Gretel came to mind. She felt like the little girl who was going to be eaten by the mean, ugly witch.

She closed her eyes, attempting to rest. Her body was so tired. Even the pain of all the kicks and hits faded in her crushing need for sleep. She planned, all the while singing lullabies, but the multitasking proved too difficult.

She drifted into uneasy slumber. Her breathing slowed and evened out. It was then she felt him. Her eyes darted open, certain Grainna felt him too. But she remained unmoving, hunched over an old crystal ball.

A glimmer of hope filled Tara’s mind. She couldn’t stop the reaction no matter how hard she tried. She let out one thought, *I love you!*
~~~~

It came back. *I love you, too.*

Her heart sang! She looked up and knew her mistake.

Grainna's sneer pierced her soul. "Let him come."

Trembling with horror, Tara asked, "Why? You can't overpower him." She tossed her head at Matthew. "Not even with your gnome here."

"You wouldn't be so arrogant if you knew what I could do." Grainna moved from the chair to where Tara sat on the dirt floor. "I wonder what they told you of me."

With the bindings gone from her wrists, Tara felt more confident in her ability to get away. "They told me you were a vengeful witch who took pleasure in other people's pain."

"True. So true. You see, however, the key word there is *witch*. The Ancients took away my Druid powers, but they couldn't touch those of my black magic."

She walked to Matthew, put her palm to his face, and drew his blood with the tip of her nail.

Lancaster didn't flinch.

"I'm a very powerful black witch. I should thank you for leading me back here. With the small taste of Druid blood, I have regained more strength than in our future. Before this day is done, yours and Duncan's will be added to the mix."

"So you see yourself as a vampire?" Tara kept her talking. She knew Duncan was getting closer.

"I've been called worse."

"Why? Do you want to rule the world?"

"That, and rid it of every Druid. The whole lot of you."

"Why?"

Grainna stood close. "Because I can."

She broke off when the sound of a horse grabbed her attention. "You!" Grainna snapped

Matthew out of his catatonic state. "Look."

Lancaster drew his sword and left the cottage.

Tara yelled to her husband, *Watch out!*

Grainna moved quickly and struck the warnings from Tara's head.

Her head snapped back. She tasted blood again.

The rope on Tara's ankles restricted her movements. She cowered in the corner, rocking and singing—hiding her true intention. She let tears slip from her eyes in a look of desperation, which wasn't difficult to do.

Grainna turned to the sphere and searched inside. Swirls of smoke billowed beneath glass.

Tara saw Duncan and Lancaster, sparring under the glistening glass.

~~~~

Duncan circled the cottage, listening to his wife sing. *She is standing by the door.*

Lancaster barged out of the small home.

Duncan waited, his back pressed to the cottage.

Sunlight reflected off Lancaster's blade. Steel swooped down.

Duncan missed its weight by an inch. He somersaulted away, landed on his feet and leveled his weapon.

Matthew appeared as a warrior ready for battle. His build, however, was no match for Duncan's.

"You don't want to do this, Matthew. She's controlling your mind and actions."

Lancaster said nothing. His eyes darted around, searching for a way to attack.

They both crouched and waited for the other to lunge.

"'Tis time for you to go home, Matthew. Everyone is looking for you." Duncan's soothing words were an effort to snap the man out of his
~~~~

trance. The steel grip Grainna held on him proved too powerful. Duncan tried slipping into the man's mind. But the witch kept him out.

Lancaster glanced away.

Duncan took advantage and moved forward.

Surprisingly, Matthew raised his sword and retaliated with much more strength than Duncan anticipated.

Still, Duncan had him panting with only a few minutes of sparring. He didn't want to kill the man who had no ability to stop himself.

Duncan lifted a hand and pushed a wind through the tops of the trees. A large branch cracked under the force of air and dropped across Lancaster's back.

He went to his knees.

Duncan pounced and brought the blunt end of his sword down.

Lancaster crumpled to the ground unconscious.

~~~~

Grainna roared in anger when Lancaster's body hit the ground. The vision in the glass globe incited her rage. She pulled a knife off the table and advanced upon Tara.

Grainna's sudden movement forced Tara to slide up the wall and onto her feet. She swung her hands toward the witch. Sparks and flames flew from her fingertips.

Startled, Grainna stood back, brushing at the flames caught on her skirt.

Tara fumbled with the ropes binding her feet, desperate to get loose.

Grainna stood tall, no longer aggressing with her body. Instead she started to chant in a language all her own.

Just as she kicked the ropes around her ankles free, Tara felt the air leaving her lungs and couldn't draw it back in. She clenched her throat
~~~~

trying to breathe. But no air came. She panicked. Tara screamed in her mind, pleading with Duncan to hurry.

Tara stood between Grainna and the door. In a swift movement, Grainna grabbed her from behind and placed the knife to her throat.

The knife didn't scare her, but the lack of oxygen did. The room started to swirl and dim.

Duncan heard her cry and left Lancaster.

The walls shook with the weight of the door flying out. He stopped and took notice of the blade Grainna held at Tara's neck.

Smiling, Grainna leered down at Tara. "One breath, my dear."

Tara felt air return to her lungs, her vision cleared.

Duncan stood paralyzed at the door.

"Come no closer, Druid warrior, or you will watch her die."

Tara's eyes glossed over again, she could think of nothing but air. *I can't breathe.*

"Leave her, 'tis me you want. I took her from you. Your fight is with me."

"I will have you both. Your family has caused me so much time in this retched body. Stealing the virgins right out from under me." She spat at Duncan's feet.

Tara was slipping out of consciousness. Her body started to fall.

"Not yet, my dear," Grainna whispered in her ear. "He hasn't suffered nearly enough."

Tara managed one breath.

Duncan moved toward them.

"Uh, uh, uh." Grainna pressed the blade into Tara's flesh. Duncan froze. His jaw set in a deadly lock. Tara saw the scene through his eyes. His heart and body ached.

Tara's eyes swirled in a dizzying haze. Faces she didn't recognize mixed with the colors of the room, floating in circles. The dark oblivion threatened to envelope her.

Amber's voice slipped into the fog. "*On this day and in this hour, call upon the sacred power.*"

I'm hallucinating. I'm going to die. Tara closed her eyes and hoped it would be painless.

Amber's words whispered faintly in her head. "*On this day and in this hour, call upon the sacred power.*" Over and over Amber's voice rang in her ears.

Suddenly, Tara's lungs filled with life giving oxygen.

Surprise sprung her eyes open. Another breath came. It wasn't Grainna granting it.

Grainna continued to taunt Duncan. "I'll see each of you dead and bleeding before I leave this land. One by one, I will eliminate every member of your family."

The blade she held nicked Tara's skin, warm trickling blood caressed her skin on its journey downward.

Duncan moved forward, face filled with wrath.

The blade cut deeper.

He halted.

Stand back! Tara told him.

The faces she thought were a hallucination told her to listen.

Amber chanted.

Air filled her body again, and as thankful as she was for it, she did her best to conceal her feelings.

When the knife lifted away, enough to where she had a chance to survive, Tara let her legs go out from under her.

Now! Duncan, now!

Caught unaware, Grainna struggled to keep Tara on her feet.

Tara pushed at her with every ounce of strength she had.

Duncan flung his hand out.

The knife flew out of Grainna's hands and skidded across the floor.

Duncan moved in, putting his body between Tara and Grainna's. His eyes never left their enemy. He brought his hand up again. This time a ball of flame hovered in his palm.

Grainna stood in defiance.

Tara felt Grainna's hold on her weaken.

Grainna's lips lifted in a sneer.

Tara's eyes shifted between her husband and Grainna.

The flame diminished. Duncan's hands moved and clung to his throat.

When he hit the floor with his knees, Tara knew he was struggling for air. "NO!"

Grainna's wicked laughter filled the room.

Tara dropped next to Duncan.

Wonderful eyes which always gave her so much love glazed over with terror. The blood from her neck dripped on his chest.

Amber's voice grew more insistent. "*On this day and in this hour, call upon the sacred power.*"

The vision of faces still hovered in the room. "*Hurry,*" they said. "*It is up to you to banish her. We cannot do it a second time.*"

Tara laid her hands on Duncan's face. "On this day and in this hour, I call upon the sacred power." She kissed his lips. "Breathe, Duncan!" she yelled. "Breathe, dammit."

His head rolled back.

Grainna cackled.

"On this day and in this hour, I call upon the sacred power. Release the hold she has on thee, make it now that he can breathe."

One staggering breath followed quickly by a second.

Tara gasped. "Thank you!"

"No!" Grainna screamed. "How dare you?" She

found her knife and came at them.

Tara turned to see her approach. She lifted her bloodied hand. "Stop." She was shocked to see that Grainna did.

But it was brief, and Grainna came at them again.

Hand still raised, Tara started again. "On this day and in this hour, I ask the Ancients for more power."

Grainna hit an invisible force which kept her in place. Stunned, she hit her hands against an unseen wall.

Beside her, Tara felt Duncan move, gasping for each breath he pulled into his body. "Are you okay?" she asked, keeping her eyes on Grainna.

"Aye," he choked out.

Tara stood, shaking and took a step toward her enemy. "You were never meant to come back here, Grainna."

Duncan stumbled to his feet.

"None of us want you here."

The air in the cabin stirred. Velocity picked up. Objects in the room flew helter-skelter, landing on the floor.

The air thinned. The world shifted.

"I'll come back for you."

"You'll try." Tara circled Grainna. Tara placed a hand to her neck to capture the blood from her wound. She spread her fingers out, her blood dripped to the floor.

With each step she took, one of the Ancient's nodded and disappeared. Somehow, she knew exactly what she was meant to do.

Grainna chanted and beat against the invisible wall.

"Light the ring." Tara placed a hand on Duncan's arm.

A flick of Duncan's wrist, and Grainna was surrounded by a ring of fire.

"The Ancients banned you once before," Tara said.

"You haven't the power to do it again." Grainna's hand slipped through the magical force which held her in place. A triumphant smile spread over her face.

Heat surged from Tara's hands. She raised them.

Grainna stopped, motionless in her place.

"Forces of good will overpower the forces of evil. Take my advice, Grainna, change your ways." Tara held Grainna's blood red eyes fixed on hers. "You've been banned from this time and place. You've been banned from the Druid race. No more threats from you to me. I send you now across the sea. If the Ancients will it so, I bid it now that you must go."

Fire surged toward the ceiling, circling and lifting, engulfing Grainna.

Tara stood with her hands extended and her eyes closed. The force of the wind blew her hair back.

Duncan stood at her side and watched in awe.

A swirling vortex opened above the flames. Pitch black, the current pulled Grainna away. Her scream went with her through it and beyond, sucking the flames with her. The fiery cyclone shut the vortex as quickly as it opened, but with a deafening silence.

Everything went still.

Emptied, Tara stumbled back. Duncan's arms kept her from falling.

When her eyes opened, he was all she saw. They held to each other, assuring themselves the other was whole.

"'Tis over," he said.

She couldn't get close enough to him. She held him hard and refused to let go. "I thought I was going to lose you."

He pulled back and kissed her bruised and battered lips. "Never," he said when he moved away. He kissed her again, long and deep. When she winced, he released her lips.

"How did you know how to banish her?"

Puzzled, Tara shook her head. "The Ancients. Didn't you see them?"

"Here? You saw them here?"

She nodded. "You mean you didn't see them?"

Duncan surveyed the damaged room. "Nay, my love, I didn't see them. No one has seen them outside of dreams."

"Then they must have really wanted her gone, because they were here, guiding me."

"Then it is finished."

"For today." Her hand went to her neck where blood still trickled. *For today.* She released a long sigh, stepped back and looked at the burned mark on the floor, then up at her husband. "Take us home. Our baby is hungry." She passed a hand over her stomach and smiled.

Outside the cottage, Duncan gathered the horses, tossed Lancaster's still unconscious body on the back of his mount and watched after his wife who stood staring at the building that had been her prison.

It was only wood and stone, but the cottage held the essence of Grainna.

Her undying evil.

Tara raised her hands again. Branches around the building blew in, leaves covering the ground rose up and encompassed the dwelling. Vines grew at a rapid rate, twisting and turning until no sign of the cottage beneath could be seen. Within minutes the cottage was camouflaged by the underbrush. Anyone passing would only see overgrown forest and not think to stop.

Duncan helped Tara upon her horse and slowly made their way out of the forest.

She rode in silence on the way back to the Keep. He let her have the solitude of her thoughts. His own plagued him while he reviewed everything that had happened.

When she started to laugh, he couldn't have been more surprised.

"What do you find so entertaining?"

"Did you see her face? God that was rich. 'I'll be back!'" She mocked Grainna's words. "Hah! And I thought I watched too much TV."

"She may be back. We have no way of knowing she won't." Duncan's words sobered her slightly.

"We'll be ready if she does. Now we know what she's capable of, she won't be able to use the same tricks twice."

She sent her husband the most endearing look. "I've found my gift, Duncan." Tara rested her hand over her growing child. "Grainna had better learn not to mess with Mother Nature!"

To prove her point Tara lifted her hands, the woods they traveled through parted, clearing a path for easier travel and gave them a clear view of the meadow beyond.

Epilogue

Tara's hands wrestled with each other, neither of them won. Their squeezing and twisting wouldn't stop. If she had to wait much longer, her fingers would most certainly be raw.

Duncan, tried his best to calm her, but it was useless.

It was Christmas Eve and when everyone in the family was about to turn in for the evening, Amber and Lora heard and felt Myra's presence.

She had returned, and was even now on the back of a horse accompanied by Finlay, Cian and Ian bringing her home.

Lora stood beside Tara, with Amber poised and waiting.

Amber smiled in a wistful way, frequently looking up at Tara as if she had a big fat secret that was about to be revealed.

The unmistakable sound of horses' hooves clapping on the stones of the yard could be heard over the loud thumping of her heart.

One horse moved forward and into the torch light by the door where they stood.

Myra, dressed in a skirt, not long enough for this time, but appropriate for the century from which she had returned, jumped off her horse and ran to her mother's waiting arms.

Tears of joy sprang to Tara's eyes as she watched their reunion. The moment Myra glanced up and into Tara's waiting face, the joy she saw there, mixed with something else. A small cut of pain was laced in Myra's expression.

Tara answered her with a look of concern.

Myra gave a pensive smile and a little shake of

the head, as if to say, "Later, I will tell you."

The sound of the other two horses came slowly.

Tara had to squint to see why they moved at such a snail's pace.

Her heart beat a bit faster. She took a few steps down the stairs. Duncan held her hand so she wouldn't slip on the newly fallen snow.

Two other riders were being helped off the horses. When Fin helped his passenger, he looked down at the obvious female form and kept his hands on her waist a fraction too long.

The woman stared at him, nodded a quick thanks, and then looked at Tara.

Tara clenched Duncan's arm. Her breath came in small sharp clouds of forced air. "Lizzy?" she whispered in shock.

"Lizzy!" She chanted her name with every running step it took to get to her sister.

Everyone watched the women embrace, no one unaffected by the expression of love they saw between the two sisters.

Simon waited patiently for his turn, inspecting the faces of the strangers surrounding him, and then he took in the steep walls of the Keep.

Tara pulled him into a fierce hug and smothered his eleven-year-old face with embarrassing kisses.

"How? Why?" Tara asked.

Lizzy choked back a sob. Tears streamed down her face. "I made Myra promise to bring us. I had to see you safe with my own eyes." Lizzy peeked over Tara's shoulder to Fin. "It's only a visit, Tara. Only a short visit."

Fin lifted a brow, and then turned and walked away.

"You're here now. That's what matters."

They hugged again, Tara unbelieving, but ever so thankful for her family's presence. It was the best Christmas she would ever have.

"Merry Christmas, Lizzy."

###

SILENT VOWS

BOOK TWO

BY
CATHERINE BYBEE

Chapter One

My life is over.

Myra MacCoinnich sat astride her horse, marching toward death, death of her life as she knew it.

Why?

Why were the Ancients, the benevolent Druid spirits, dictating her destiny by sending her into the future now?

Beside her, her sister-in-law, Tara graced her with a wry smile, a grin holding enough doubt to leave Myra with a giant hole in her heart.

"'Tis far enough," her brother, Duncan, announced as he brought their horses to a stop.

Sliding from the back of the mount, Myra gave her mare a final pat.

"This isn't goodbye, Myra. You'll see her again," Tara lifted an arm to Myra's shoulders in support.

"Are we doing the right thing?"

"Have your mother's visions ever been wrong?"

"Nay." Her mother's clear vision had warned of Myra's death if she stayed in 1576.

"Say 'no', Myra. The twenty-first century will be hard enough without tripping on words from the sixteenth-century. If Lara's visions have never failed, then we must believe you aren't safe here. You're going to love my time." Tara sent her a much more convincing smile.

"'Tis time, lass," Duncan called.

"Remember, 'Lizzy' is short for Elizabeth. Elizabeth McAllister."

Myra nodded, understanding Tara searched

for any missing detail about her sister that would help Myra in the future, or so they hoped.

"If for any reason she won't listen, find Cassy. Cassandra Ross."

"You've told me all of this. I won't forget." Myra removed the heavy cloak covering the twenty-first century style pants and shirt. "Here, I won't be needing this." She couldn't believe she'd soon be walking in public with the clothes she wore.

Tara's eyes glistened with unshed tears.

Duncan's fierce hug filled Myra with warmth. She remembered the last words her younger sister Amber had uttered to her the night before. Tara was with child, yet neither of them knew it. Amber always knew such things. Much like their mother's visions, Amber was never wrong.

"Congratulations, brother."

"For what?" he asked, drawing away from her embrace to glance down at her.

"You'll see."

Duncan moved from her arms to spread the sacred stones in a perfect circle. He touched each one, lending them part of his Druid power to help them move Myra through time. Pulsating energy beat within the stones, waiting.

Myra placed one unsteady foot in front of the other, and found herself in the center of the stones. She repeated the chant in her head. Energy built.

"Godspeed," Duncan lifted a hand.

The wind started to turn, and heat, along with light, shimmered and burned from each stone reaching far above her head in a kaleidoscope of colors.

"Hey, Myra?" Tara yelled out in an obvious attempt at distracting her.

"What?"

"Have Lizzy take you to Magicland. The rides don't compare to this, but you'll love it."

Myra clenched her sack to her chest. Air within the circle thinned making breathing difficult. "Magicland, I'll remember."

She wanted to run, flee away from the stones, away from the power that started to surround her body; instead, Myra raised her voice and chanted. "Ancient stones, and Ancient power, take me safely to Lizzy this hour. Keep me safe and from harm's way, from prying eyes and the light of day. If the Ancients will it so, take me now and let me go."

The earth trembled beneath her feet. She stepped forward, fear slammed into her from all sides. Air filled her lungs before expelling in a near scream.

From the corner of her eye, she witnessed Duncan draw Tara tight to his chest.

The power within the circle, held steady by the stones entrusted only to her family, roared. She couldn't escape. This was her destiny. Dread slid up her spine and burst in her head, followed by an eerie sense of calm.

Myra squeezed her eyes shut. *Magicland, Elizabeth McAllister, oh, God.*

The earth fell from her feet and time swept her away.

~~~~

Amnesia. Who believes in that shit?

Some woman woke up on the Island of Atlantis, smack dab in the middle of Magicland before the first employee arrived, and Todd needed to take the report. It sounded like a case for an ambulance chaser.

Scammers came in all shapes and sizes. This one had scammer written all over her. Someone was always searching for a way to make a quick buck.

Officer Todd Blakely asked the elderly woman at the reception desk of Anaheim General Hospital where the ER had taken Jane Doe, then made his
~~~~

way to the elevators.

He walked past the nurse's desk and smiled at the blonde behind the counter who eyed him up one side and down the other.

Obviously, she liked what she saw.

He didn't know if it was him or the badge and uniform. The department called them Badge Bunnies. Women who went out of their way to gain the attention of anyone in a uniform, police or fire, they didn't care which. The men often took advantage of the women's attention, which explained the high divorce rate among the ranks.

Todd walked toward room number 840 to visit Jane Doe.

Behind the slightly open door, he heard a small laugh. The sound was a little happy for someone who woke without a memory.

He glanced through the doorway, and saw Miss Amnesia sitting up in bed. The flat screen television, held on to a platform by a C-arm, swiveled in front of her. Her hair, the darkest shade of brown fringing on black, traveled down past her shoulders all the way to her elbows. Her deep umber eyes sat atop beautifully shaped cheeks and plump lips that smiled about whatever she watched.

Todd felt the air leave his body. Jane Doe was drop-dead beautiful.

Impulsively, Todd straightened his shoulders and forced his jaw into a hard edge. He would have to watch his step. Women as stunning as the one in front of him had a way of disarming the strongest of cops.

The woman in the bed hid a smile behind her hand.

Todd's mouth ran dry. *Sweet Jesus!*

About the author

New York Times bestselling author Catherine Bybee was raised in Washington State, but after graduating high school, she moved to Southern California in hopes of becoming a movie star. After growing bored with waiting tables, she returned to school and became a registered nurse, spending most of her career in urban emergency rooms. She now writes full time and has penned the novels Wife by Wednesday, Married by Monday, and Not Quite Dating. Bybee lives with her husband and two teenage sons in Southern California.

Connect with Catherine Bybee Online:
Website: http://www.catherinebybee.com
My blog: http://catherinebybee.blogspot.com
Facebook:
https://www.facebook.com/pages/Catherine-Bybee-Romance-Author/128537653855577
Goodreads:
http://www.goodreads.com/author/show/2905789.Catherine_Bybee
Twitter: https://twitter.com/catherinebybee
Email: catherinebybee@yahoo.com

Discover other titles by Catherine Bybee

Contemporary Romance
Weekday Bride Series:
Wife by Wednesday
Married By Monday

Not Quite Series:
Not Quite Dating

Paranormal Romance
MacCoinnich Time Travel Series:
Binding Vows
Silent Vows
Redeeming Vows
Highland Shifter

Ritter Werewolves Series:
Before the Moon Rises
Embracing the Wolf

Novellas:
Possessive
Soul Mate

Erotic Titles:
Kiltworthy
Kilt-A-Licious